DEMON GATE

MORNINGSTAR

DEBBIE CASSIDY

Contents

.

ONE

ARTIMUS

I never once doubt that Nyx will complete Prince Merihem's challenge. The bastard turns her siblings into objects and hides them amongst hundreds of artifacts, then puts a timer on how long Nyx has to find them. He expects her to play his game and lose. A game for his insane entertainment. But she knows her siblings well enough to win. I'm sure of it. And when Tristeene, Gus, and Mallini reappear on the platform beside me, triumph roars in my chest.

Nyx has won.

But where is she?

I want to scream for Merihem to pull her out of the game, to return her to me, but I press my lips together, eyes burning as I stare at the room below and wait.

She appears a moment later.

Safe.

The contracts that sentence all Satan spawn to death

once the trials are complete will now be destroyed. We have what we came here for.

I can feel her victory as if it's my own. My thighs bunch and I clench my fists to stem the impulse to rush to her side. I can't show the princes how much she matters to me. No one can know. Not yet.

She stands and turns to face the princes.

"No!" Prince Merihem bellows. "I want another test."

"Enough!" Prince Ramiel says. "We had a deal, and we will honor it—"

A roar cuts off his words. My gaze whips to Dhuma as he lunges past Merihem. His dark eyes are filled with determination and fixed on Nyx.

Foreboding starbursts in my chest a moment before he slams into her. Her body jerks and a reedy cry explodes from her lips.

What...What is this?

Hrath lets out a bellow of rage, and a gust of air whips my hair back as he vanishes. But it's Veena's shrill scream that finally penetrates my shock and galvanizes me into action.

"Nyx!" I leap off the platform, and the demons and devils below part to let me through.

Chaos greets me.

Ramiel drags Dhuma back with a hand around the daimon's neck while the hulking daimon thrashes and bucks, spewing words I don't understand.

Veena screams again and again before dissolving into sobs.

Hrath is on the floor with Nyx in his arms. One hand is pressed to her chest where a dark crimson stain spreads. His eyes are wild as he looks up at me, as if he can't believe what he's doing, who he's holding. As if this whole episode is a nightmare.

I meet his gaze with horror, then drop it to Nyx.

Her eyes are closed. Her chest unmoving.

"She's dead," Veena sobs. "Oh earth, oh earth, she's dead."

No, no, no. It can't be. It can't. My chest grows tight, pulse racing, blood pounding in my head.

Someone starts to laugh, high-pitched and crazy.

Merihem.

Rage bubbles up inside me and detonates, turning my vision red. My hands are around his throat before I can stop myself, and I'm squeezing and squeezing, but he continues to laugh, the sound ricocheting inside my skull, louder and louder until it's all I hear.

Hands grab me, tugging and yanking. Voices order me to release the prince. But I squeeze harder, and this time his laughter cuts off for a moment.

My satisfaction is short-lived.

Pain explodes at the back of my skull and my vision goes dark. I lose my grip for a moment, but it's enough for the guards to slap cold metal onto my wrists and shove me to the ground.

I try to shake them off, but they hold me down easily.

The cuffs mute my power. "Fuck!"

"Stop it!" Mallini cries out. "Let him go!"

I raise my head, blinking back the dark spots resulting from the blow to my head, and focus on Nyx and Hrath. He holds her to his chest, rocking back and forth, his eyes dark pits of sorrow.

Any hope I have that we're wrong evaporates. I've failed Satan. I've failed Nyx. I've lost...Oh earth, it hurts.

Words fill the air, urgent and incomprehensible.

Dhuma.

He did this. He stabbed her. *Killed* her. I bellow and try to break free of the guards again, my gaze an inferno desperate to incinerate Dhuma.

Ramiel no longer has him pinned, but the daimon is on his knees, the collar at his throat glowing white to hold him in place.

I want his head.

I want him dead.

But I need to know something first. "Why? Why did you do it?"

He grits his teeth and shakes his head before speaking in daimonword again.

Merihem appears behind him. "You're a naughty boy, Dhuma. A very naughty boy. Use your demon tongue. I know you can."

Dhuma's chest heaves and he speaks in daimonword, this time focused on Hrath.

Hrath blinks sharply and looks up at him. "What? What do you mean?"

"What did he say?" I need to know.

"Tell us now!" Ramiel orders.

Hrath's lip curls. "If you'd deigned to learn their tongue, then you would know."

"How dare you speak to your prince like that?" Levistus says. "Do not forget your place."

"The place *you* put them in?" Mallini snaps. "You know, with the lies you told everyone."

The room falls into a hush.

"Everyone out," Levistus orders. "Now!"

The room clears of everyone, even the guards, and I'm suddenly free. I stand, hands still bound, power still muted, but no longer being held down.

Mallini faces off against Ramiel. Her crimson plumes are puffed up—a sign that she's in fight mode. Her hands fist at her sides, her chin comes up, emerald eyes flashing with rage. In that moment she looks every bit the Erinyes she is. Powerful. A true warrior. "Were you so arrogant that you never learned the language of the people that dominated the world you joined?" Her tone drips with derision.

Levistus mutters a curse, but Ramiel remains calm. The only sign he's affected by her words are his whiskey eyes that flare amber at the rims for a moment.

Mallini snorts dismissively and focuses on Hrath. "What is he saying?" Her tone softens for him. "Please, why did he do this?"

Hrath's dark eyes are filled with confusion. I've known the sylph for a long time. And like the Duke of Flame that he serves, Hrath is always composed and in control. But in this moment, he looks undone.

When he speaks, his deep baritone holds a tremor. "Dhuma says it is the only way. He says that it must be done." Hrath speaks to Dhuma in daimonword, his words stilted and fractured.

"What does it matter," Tristeene says, falling to her knees beside Hrath. "Nothing matters now." Tears slip down her pale cheeks. "Nyx...Oh, Nyx..."

"It matters," Mallini snaps. "It matters *why*." She turns on Dhuma. "Why?" she screams in his face.

The daimon doesn't take his eyes off Nyx, his gaze intent and almost...hopeful. As if he's waiting. When he speaks, his words are soft and hushed.

Hrath frowns, then his eyes snap wide.

My scalp prickles and I force myself to look at Nyx's still form. To look at the bloody patch on her chest covered by Hrath's hand. At her pale lips, parted where she exhaled her last.

"She's not gone," Hrath says. "He says..." He blinks slowly and carefully, then peels his huge hand from her chest. The dagger has torn the fabric of her tunic, but the skin beneath, although bloody, is smooth and unbroken.

The wound has healed.

Hrath exhales sharply.

"I don't understand," Tristeene says.

The air crackles and fizzes and a gust of warmth hits me in the face. I squint at the portal that's opened across from us.

What the—

Ignatius steps through. His eyes are filled with wild power and his golden hair is in disarray, as if he's walked through a storm to be here. His fiery gaze zeroes in on Nyx in Hrath's arms. His shoulders slump and a soft keening sound breaks from his lips.

His pain is loud in the silence.

"No..." He walks toward us. "No..."

Hrath speaks to him, his words quick and urgent, and Ignatius's expression morphs from devastation to shock, then to hope.

"What the fuck is happening?" I stare at Hrath. "What did he say?"

"Answer him!" Ramiel demands.

But it's Ignatius who answers. "She's not dead. She's on a journey of rebirth."

Thick silence follows his statement and then Veena breaks it with an incredulous sob, asking the question on all our minds. "What? What does that even mean?"

And suddenly I know what's happened. I know it with a clarity that steals my breath. One look into Ignatius's eyes confirms it.

"This can't be," Levistus says.

"What can't be?" Veena demands shrilly.

Tristeene answers, her tone almost reverent. "Nyx *is*

dead, but she'll be reborn, and only one breed of supernatural that we know of can do that."

Veena sucks in a sharp breath, her dark eyes going wide with shocked comprehension.

I finally find my voice. "Nyx has higher daimon blood."

Two

NYX

Black shadowy scavengers circled in the red sky overhead. My palm met dry earth and then skimmed prickly grass.

What was this? Where was I?

Memory returned like a sledgehammer to my chest.

My fucking chest! I grabbed at it, searching for the blade.

It was gone.

I was fine. No dagger wound. No blood.

But I'd been stabbed by Dhuma.

He stabbed me and said...What did he say?

I sat up, and above me the birds cawed louder.

"Fuck you!" I gave them the finger and pushed onto my feet.

I was in a circle of dry earth dotted with patches of green grass, surrounded by stone statues. The world beyond the stones was an expanse of arid, reddish earth that went as far as the eye could see, but this space...It was as if nature was valiantly attempting to keep things lush and failing.

Where was I? How could I get back?

The birds cawed louder, sounding pissed off now. They swooped closer. Fuck, they were huge! Curved, sharp beaks angling my way.

I ducked even though they were far from close enough to do damage, then shook my fist at them as they rose back into the air.

"Back off! I'm not dead yet, you bastards!"

Or was I? My nape pricked. I mean...I'd been stabbed. I hadn't imagined that part so...*was* I dead? Was this the afterlife? Tarrifel? No...No, if that was the case, Loke would be here, right?

He wouldn't leave me to flounder. Heck, was this my destiny?

Panic lit up my chest. "Hello!"

My voice sounded small in the vastness.

The birds overhead screeched and circled low again.

I needed to get out of here. I rushed away from the birds and between two stone statues but slammed into invisible resistance that forced me back into the circle.

What the heck?

I touched the air and ripples expanded outward from beneath my fingers. This was a shield. A ward. Something mystical, keeping me trapped.

Just what I needed.

I tried another route out of the circle and once again met resistance.

Yep, I was trapped for sure. Bloody fabulous.

Okay, focus, Nyx. There had to be a way out of here. Ignoring the urgent cawing above, I focused on my surroundings, on the five stone statues that created a perimeter I couldn't breach.

Maybe they were the key to getting out of here? There had to be some meaning to this place. To my being here.

Was this a test?

Urgh, I'd never been good at tests. But sod it, bring it.

The statues were humanoid. Male and females all in the same somber pose, all staring ahead, which in this case made it so they were all looking at me. Creepy much?

The nearest one had a slender build and was shorter than the rest, but he wore a robe like the other five. There was an emblem etched into the stone robe. A leaf? Yeah, it looked like a leaf in a circle. The female to his left had long wavy hair and her hood was pulled up. She also had an emblem of three squiggly lines on her robe. The next female along had a spiral on her robe. Statue four was a stocky male with a beard, a frown, and what looked like a flame on his robe. The final statue was a tall, broad-shouldered male, with hair that fell to his shoulders and a clean-shaven, aquiline profile. His symbol was difficult to decipher. It looked like a door or gate with a wheel in the center.

Okay, so they all had symbols, but what did they mean?

What was I supposed to do with them?

Was I *supposed* to do anything?

Urgh, this was a Gus problem. The thought of my brother made my chest ache. Were my siblings safe? They must have been so worried about me. I needed to get back to them.

I placed my palm on the statue with the gate and wheel emblem. I wasn't sure what I expected, but I couldn't say I was surprised when nothing happened.

I touched each one, just to be sure, and nothing happened.

This was starting to get old.

Maybe I needed to touch them in some kind of order?

Or maybe not.

Or maybe...Bloody hell. Those damned birds. I couldn't think straight. They were so loud now that they made my head ring. I slapped my palms over my ears.

What the heck was this? Were the powers that be trying to torture me?

The cawing became one loud buzz, a rage-filled vibration that put my teeth on edge. Then it stopped suddenly, leaving only blissful silence.

Either that or my eardrums had ruptured.

I slowly lowered my hands and warily peered up at the sky.

The birds were still there, circling. Silently now.

Wait, *had* I gone deaf?

Nope, there was the *whoosh* of a breeze and—

"Who wakes me from my slumber?" a male voice boomed.

My pulse spiked and I spun toward the voice. The statue with the flame on his robe glared at me, no longer a statue but a man. Brows hung low over his eyes, and his mouth was a thin line beneath his neatly trimmed mustache as he scowled at me accusingly.

"Well?" he demanded.

"My name's Nyx, and *I* didn't wake you. Those damned birds did."

I pointed at the sky.

"Oh, it feels good to stretch," a female voice said.

The statue with the squiggly lines was also alive. I backed up a step and glanced at the others. All alive, stretching and working out the kinks in their bodies.

Okay, now we were getting somewhere. "Who are you... people? Where am I?"

"We are the wardens," flame dude said. "And—"

"Lewin, look..." The female with the squiggly lines gripped his arm and pointed.

Lewin, the flame guy, broke eye contact with me to look past me to the arid landscape beyond. His mouth parted in shock. "No...it can't be..."

"I feel it," the male with the leaf on his robe said. "The sickness. It's here."

"How long have we been asleep?" the woman with the squiggles on her robe asked.

The male with the gate on his robe stepped forward, his chin tipped up as he studied the sky. "Too long. We have forsaken too many souls."

"But how?" the woman asked him. "Parlos, how many have we forsaken?"

The man closed his eyes as if listening. "I cannot count. They were not loud enough to wake us. They were not strong enough or pure enough, until now." He opened his eyes and fixed them on me.

"She survived the sickness?" Lewin raked me over as if he could hardly believe it.

I shot him a sharp glance. "I have no idea what you're talking about."

"It found its way here..." the woman with the squiggly lines said.

"It was bound to happen, Tiana," Lewin said. "We are all connected, and once the gate opened..."

Gate? "You mean the gate to the abyss?"

Lewin fixed his gaze on me. "The abyss? Pfft, the abyss is a sapling in comparison to Inferis."

Inferis...the pit? I was so confused. "Why am I here?"

"To take the path." Tiana beamed at me.

"She must choose her guide," the guy with the gate on his robe said.

"Yes, Parlos, you're right," Tiana said. "We must do this properly despite..."

"Choose," Lewin demanded, cutting her off. "Choose who will guide you."

I was so confused right now. "Guide me to what?"

"Back to life," Tiana said softly.

Back to...shit. I *was* dead. Oh, crap.

Dhuma's words filled my mind. *Find the power and be reborn.*

How was this possible? "I don't understand this. Is this Tarrifel?"

Parlos approached me and peered down at me intensely. "No. But this is not your first death."

"Wait, what?"

"How is that possible?" the woman with the swirl on her robe asked. "All higher daimons come to the circle upon death."

Higher daimons? What the fuck? Wait...Wait a second. Something niggled at the back of my mind, something about higher daimons having three lives. But I was a Nephilim, and I'd never died before. "Look, there's been a mistake. I'm not any kind of daimon, and I've never died before."

"Yes, you are, and yes, you have. Although you may not recall it," Parlos said. "You are higher daimon, and you are... more. You belong here and you belong elsewhere also."

I was so confused right now.

Lewin's eyes went wide. "No. That is not possible. All daimon souls are ours."

"Not this one." Parlos's eyes narrowed. "This one is... something new." He reached out to touch my cheek, his expression almost pitying. "There are many paths open to you, child."

I pulled away from his touch and narrowed my eyes. "Isn't that a good thing?"

"Only to those who are confident in their choices. For some, the freedom can be crippling."

"I'm not the kind of woman to shy away from making a decision." I had so many questions, but I wanted to get out of this place more. I needed to get back to my siblings. "What do I have to decide? What are my choices?"

Parlos stepped away from me and the wardens fell back into their circle.

"First you must pick a warden to guide you," Lewin said.

"Um...Okay... Guide me through what?"

"That will depend on the warden you choose," Tiana said with a smile.

Okay, so the path, whatever, was dependent on the warden. "I'm assuming some paths are harder than others?"

"A valid assumption," Lewin said coolly.

"So, it's luck of the draw."

"No," Lewin said. "Not if you choose correctly."

"What the hell is that supposed to mean?"

No one responded. They watched me silently. Waiting.

It looked like the ball was in my court. Fine, I was good with that. I'd always lived life with my gut as a guide. Listening to my inner voice had kept me alive, kept me safe. In this situation, with no clue how to proceed, there was no choice but to fall back on intuition and instinct.

I cleared my mind and let my gut guide me, scanning the wardens' faces one by one. Lewin, so stern and forbidding; Tiana, sweet and warm; and Parlos, so intense and insightful. The other two seemed to fade into the background. Maybe because they hadn't spoken much to me, or maybe the reason they hadn't spoken much to me was because of a lack of connection.

But these three...

I grinned. "I've made a decision."

"Speak," Lewin ordered.

"I'll take you." I pointed at him, and his eyes flared bright in triumph, but I wasn't done yet. "And you." I pointed to Tiana, and she blinked sharply and looked to Lewin as if for guidance. "And you." I ended on Parlos. The corners of his mouth dimpled in a suppressed smile.

"You must pick one," Lewin said.

I arched a brow. "Oh, is that a rule?"

Lewin frowned. "I..."

"It isn't," Parlos said. "There is no rule to state a soul can only pick one warden. However, every soul has always assumed it to be the case."

"Oh..." Tiana's hand went to her mouth. "This will mean..."

"Yes," Parlos said. "It will."

I placed a hand on my hip and tipped my head to the side. "Enough of the cryptic crap. You guys are meant to guide me, so guide. What does this mean, and how do I get out of here?"

Tiana, Lewin, and Parlos stepped forward to surround me. My skin prickled, and my nape tightened. "What are you doing?"

"Creating a path," Parlos said. "A new path, just for you."

THREE

SEV

"**N**yx!" I jolt into wakefulness with a weight on my chest.

Chase peers down at me, his paw on my shoulder, his warm brown eyes filled with shadows. He whines softly, and the awful foreboding in the pit of my stomach intensifies.

Something is wrong.

I place my hand on my chest, at the spot that's felt different ever since Nyx claimed her blood debt. It feels... hollow. As if she's far away, which she is, but she was far before, and it didn't feel this way.

Chase whines again.

He feels it too.

"Something is wrong, isn't it?" I meet his gaze. "She's in trouble, isn't she?"

He leaps off the bed and pads to the door to the Court of Ivory, then to the door to the Court of Flame.

"Yes...we need to check up on her. One of the dukes might be able to. Good idea."

I push back the sheets, trying to ignore the dark pit opening in my belly. "She's fine. She's with Artimus and Hrath. Keelan is there. She's safe."

But I need to be sure.

I may not be able to get to the demon realm, but one of the dukes might. All I need to do is send a message to each one.

I head out of the room in search of the creature who keeps the spawn fed and watered. The female who's adopted me as a son.

Zinichi will know what to do.

TRISTEENE

Nyx has daimon blood? How is that possible? According to what Ignatius told Nyx about our history, the daimons were either killed or trapped in the abyss. Sealed off by powerful allure.

If Nyx has enough daimon blood for her to be reborn, it means that Satan lay with a daimon. But how, when there are none to lay with? The only known daimon on this side of the abyss is Dhuma.

Dhuma must be wrong. "How can he be sure? *Hmmm*?" I look from Ignatius to Dhuma, then back again. "How can he know she has daimon blood."

Dhuma speaks, his voice gruff and low.

Hrath translates. "He says that he can feel it. That he can...see it." Dhuma continues to speak and Hrath translates. "He says that it is his gift to know the truth of things." He frowns slightly, his gaze flicking up to Prince Merihem.

Dhuma speaks urgently now, his words almost rushed.

Ignatius tenses and I catch a look pass between him and Hrath. My scalp tightens.

Something isn't right here, and my gut tells me it's got nothing to do with Nyx.

"This is impossible," Prince Levistus says. "We know it's impossible." He looks to Ramiel for support, but the Prince of Pride has his chin tucked in, his expression thoughtful. "Ramiel?" Levistus prompts, his tone irritated.

"Satan and a daimon sitting in a tree..." Merihem sing-songs.

Ignatius takes Hrath's place by Nyx and carefully, reverently scoops her into his arms. "I have you, *Qalbi*..."

I have no idea what that word means, but there's a softness to it that tells me it's an endearment. It seems Nyx has captured another heart, and how could she not? My brave, shining sister.

I want Dhuma to be right. I want her to wake so badly it's a twisted knot in my belly.

"Beelzebub always had a soft spot for daimons," Ramiel says finally. "It would not surprise me if he had a daimon mistress that he managed to save from the Chaos, but this..." He looks troubled.

"But why keep her a secret?" Mallini asks. "He was Satan. He could do whatever he pleased."

Artimus should know. As the Seneschal, the closest person to Satan in this room, he'd surely have been aware. He was raised by him, for earth's sake. He would know if Satan had a daimon mistress. But the look of raw betrayal and shock on his face tells me this was a secret kept even from him. Yet, he's protected Nyx. Mentored her.

Did Satan ask him to?

I need to speak to him, but not here. Not now.

"Dhuma must be wrong," Levistus says confidently. "This is impossible."

I don't understand the vehemence. How can he think that it's completely impossible for Satan to have a child with a daimon?

"We must hope that he is wrong," Ramiel says. "We must hope that she does not wake."

"What? You want her to stay dead?" Artimus stares at him, incredulous.

Ramiel slow-blinks and focuses on the Seneschal. "Yes. Because if she wakes, then we may be forced to kill her."

ARTIMUS GROWLS, a lethal sound that has my hackles rising. A sound that says *touch her and die.*

Ramiel's eyes narrow to warning slits. "Watch your tone, incubus."

I expect Artimus to snap back, but it's the Duke of Flame who responds.

"No one will touch her," Ignatius says. "She is Satan spawn and under both *my* protection *and* the protection of the ascension contracts." His grip on her tightens and Hrath moves closer to him, a stance that is both protective and a warning.

"Oh, none of that counts if she is what *he* says she is." Merihem jerks his thumb toward Dhuma, a twinkle in his eye. "Nothing will save her then."

He sounds too gleeful about the prospect.

"Why?" Veena asks the question on all our minds. "Why would you want to kill her?"

Ramiel looks down at Veena, and his expression softens a little. Veena has that effect on people. "If your sibling is indeed the offspring of a fallen and a daimon, then she should not exist. Our species are incompatible for breeding. She is an impossibility."

"An abomination," Prince Merihem sing-songs.

I want to punch him in the face.

"Fallen and daimon could never produce offspring," Ignatius explains. "It was found that they were not biologically compatible." He looks down at Nyx in his arms. "Yet here she is."

He says it as if he believes. As if he...knows?

Mallini joins Ignatius and Hrath. "No one touches her. No one hurts her."

Veena takes my hand, and we join Mallini beside Ignatius so that we're now standing in a small group facing off against the princes.

Us against them.

Us against three original fallen.

Our odds are slim, but it doesn't matter. We'll fight nonetheless.

Something passes across Levistus's face, a shadow, a darkness that dulls his eyes and turns his mouth down. Sympathy? I can't read him. He looks to Ramiel, the designated spokesperson in this situation, it seems.

Ramiel lifts his chin and looks down his nose at us. "Your unity is commendable. I admire it. But we cannot risk the balance of our world being disrupted. The fact remains that Nyx should not exist, and if Dhuma is right and she is what he claims her to be, then we, the princes, will form a council to decide what is to be done with her."

"The law is clear," Levistus says. "When faced with an event or situation that could upset the balance of our world, a conclave will be called to decide the way forward."

And is execution one of the actions? But wait... "If you

kill her, won't she come back stronger?" Daimons have three lives, after all.

His eye twitches, so imperceptibly that I almost miss it. "We are prepared."

They're afraid. Afraid of what kind of power she'll wake with. Afraid of what she'll become, or what she might already be.

"And if she does not wake"—Ramiel looks at Dhuma— "then you will pay for the attack on a Satan spawn. You will pay with your life."

"You forget where you are," Merihem says. "You forget who the daimon belongs to."

"Enough!" Levistus throws up his arms. "Enough..." he says again, but his tone is weary now. "Summon seven conji and prepare a room. We must be ready."

"Ready for what?" Veena asks.

"For if she wakes."

Four

NYX

A gray, angry sea rushed over wet sand, fingers of salty water reaching for my boots before being dragged away by the tide.

I took a deep breath and looked up at the dark, stormy sky, then across the churning expanse of water to the dark smudge of land beyond. "Where are we?"

"On the first step of your path," Parlos said.

He stood beside me, sandy hair whipping about his shoulders in the wind, aquiline profile pointed out to sea.

Tiana stood hugging herself, her gray eyes dark with an emotion I couldn't define.

Lewin tugged his cloak around his stocky frame and sniffed.

"The sea is angry," Tiana said finally. "Wild and lost."

Lewin sniffed again. "The sickness affects everything. Our role is to ensure the soul in our charge finds her way back, and quickly."

I groaned. "Please don't tell me we're on a timer."

"You must return to your body soon or be locked out of it," Parlos explained. "That has always been the way."

Fabulous. "Fine, so we're here, now what?"

"You must follow the path," Lewin said.

"What path? I can't see..." A shimmery line appeared in front of me, leading across the ocean and straight toward the smudge on the horizon. "Are you serious? How am I meant to get across the sea?" I peered up and down the beach. "There are no boats."

"But you have your guides," Parlos said. "And it is up to you to use us."

Use them...I stared at them, then down at the emblems on their robes. What had Tiana said? The sea was angry, as if she had an affinity for it. The squiggly lines were water. Of course. And Lewin's flame had to represent fire. They both represented elements, but what about Parlos's gate and wheel? What was that?

I pointed at Tiana. "You're the water guide, right?"

She beamed at me. "Yes."

"Can you get me across the sea?"

She gnawed on her lip. "Yes, I would usually just calm the waves and lure them to carry us but...the sickness..."

Great. "So what now? Any ideas, team?"

"I can open a door," Parlos said. "But I can only open one on this journey. If we use it now, then I will not be able to assist you later."

"A door, you mean...like a portal?"

"Yes, to the land mass beyond."

"Is it wise to use it now?" Lewin asked. "Tiana, is there nothing you can do?"

She glared at him. "Don't you think I'd do something if I could?"

I exhaled heavily. "Use the portal."

All three wardens looked at me.

I raised my eyebrows. "Just do it. We need it now, and we can figure out the rest later."

Parlos stepped forward. "As you wish."

He raised his hands, and the air grew charged, the particles singing against my skin. A door appeared in the air —unremarkable brown wood standing upright with no frame to hold it.

I shoved it open to find darkness beyond. "Is it meant to look like that?"

"We enter to find out what's on the other side," Parlos said.

"Fine." I took a breath and stepped through.

A cold, crisp smell, almost sharp in its intensity, hit me. The chilly downpour assaulted me next. Sheets of rain fell from the night sky, and the rumble of thunder was followed by flashes of lightning. Something moved in front of us. A pale, eerie mass.

"What is that?" Tiana said in a hushed tone.

Another flash of lightning, brighter and prolonged, answered her question.

The land before us was filled with lumbering bodies. They faced away from us, toward the towering, shadowy shape of a hedgerow.

"A labyrinth," Lewin said. "Your gate must be inside it."

"Look!" Tiana pointed upward. "Do you see it?"

The lightning flashed, the world went dark, and I caught sight of a golden beam of light shooting up from somewhere within the labyrinth.

"We have to get you there," Tiana said.

"We have to get past...them." Parlos's gaze was fixed on the people.

"Who are they?"

"Lost souls," Parlos said.

"No..." Tiana took a step closer to me. "This can't be."

"It is," Lewin said. "We slumbered deeply, and they went unheard because of the sickness."

What was this sickness? Could it be the same sickness Ignatius had told me about? The mystical virus that had come out of the pit along with the monsters and infected the daimons during the Chaos War?

It had to be.

And this place was some kind of in-between that the higher daimons went when they died. Three lives. This, according to them, was my second death, and if that was the case, everything I thought I knew about my origins was a lie.

But now wasn't the time to worry about that. I'd figure it out once I was out of here.

Once I was alive again.

Bloody hell, what a thought to have. "Okay, so we just walk past them, right?"

"We can't do that," Lewin said. "They hunger for a way out, for the power inside the labyrinth. But this is not their path, and they cannot get through. They will, however, tear you to shreds if you attempt to pass."

"They aren't tearing at each other."

"Because they are kindred. Lost souls. You are not lost, and they'll sense that."

"Then what?" I patted my hip and checked my thigh for my dagger. "I have no weapons."

"You have us," Lewin said.

"Flame and water? Burn them to death or drown them? Look, I don't want to hurt them. This isn't their fault. There's got to be another way..."

"Fire doesn't have to burn," Lewin said. "It can light the way like a beacon or act as a warning to ward off danger."

My gaze whipped up to meet his. "Can you do that? Can you make a fiery path to get us through the mass?"

Lewin nodded curtly. "That I can." He held out his arms

and the ground a few feet from us lit up on either side, creating a passage.

"Walk behind me," Lewin said.

He set off, trailing fire either side of him, and I followed with Tiana and Parlos in tow.

The mass ahead of us shuddered as they felt the heat. Then, one by one, they began to turn toward us. I caught the gleam of dark, mournful eyes and yawning mouths set in slack jaws. But as their gazes fell on me, their expressions lit up with hunger. Their mouths widened, curling up to become manic grins filled with needle-sharp teeth.

"Oh...oh my." Tiana gripped my hand. "Lewin..."

The flames rose, turning purple, and the masses shrieked and pulled away from us, opening a path to the labyrinth gates.

"They won't come close," he said.

He was right. They backed up, growling and snapping, eager eyes fixed on me. Drool dripping from their lips.

My stomach trembled. It took a shitload to freak me out, but these fuckers did the trick.

Lost souls indeed. Piranha in human skin more like.

We kept moving, closer and closer to the labyrinth. I kept my eyes on the mass as it closed in on us, out of reach of the flames but still too close for comfort.

The flames flickered and dropped for a moment, and they rushed in, pushing heat toward my skin. Tiana cried out and Lewin cursed.

The flames roared up again, allowing us to go another meter or so before they dipped once more. The lost souls surged toward us again. Tiana screamed. Parlos bellowed. Lewin roared with frustration.

The flames *whooshed* to life.

"What's happening?" Tiana asked. "Lewin, what's wrong."

"I'm not sure," Lewin said. "But the flames are fighting me."

We'd stopped completely now and were surrounded by lost souls as our shield of flames sputtered and then rose.

Lewin met my gaze, his eyes wide with horror. "I can't hold it much longer."

My heart sank. "Then we make a dash for it. It's not far. We can make it."

"You won't." Parlos's tone was calm and even. "Not without intervention." He turned me to face him, his expression filled with urgency. "I thought we may have a little more time, but I was wrong. My journey must end here, but you have far to go. Do not falter. Do not stumble. If you fall, you must rise and continue."

"What?" I locked gazes with him, drawn in by his dark eyes filled with...regret? "What do you mean?"

He cupped the back of my head and brought his mouth down on mine. Not a kiss but an imprint, a warm brand that seeped into my skin. He released me abruptly.

"I hope it will be of some use to you."

"Parlos, what are you doing?" Tiana made a grab for him as he backed toward the sputtering flame.

"What needs to be done," Parlos said. "She must live. Make sure she does."

The flames dipped, and Parlos stepped through. The masses descended on him, and he opened his arms as if to embrace them. A silvery light burst from his chest and washed over the lost souls. They froze, mouths going slack once more, eyes going blank.

"What is he doing?" I looked from Lewin to Tiana, but Lewin was too focused on keeping the flames up and Tiana's face was a crumpled mess, tears streaming down her cheeks.

Whatever it was, it was bad.

Parlos looked toward us, his face lit by the silvery glow

he was creating. He smiled, then tipped his head back. The lost souls screamed in unison as they were whipped off their feet and straight into the light.

Into Parlos.

A stream of souls.

Too many souls for one body to host. Parlos shuddered and jerked, his head falling back, his mouth yawning wide on a moan.

The flames dropped.

"Run!" Lewin yelled.

Tiana grabbed my hand and hauled me away from Parlos and toward the silver gates of the labyrinth.

The last thing I saw before the gates closed behind us was Parlos's body exploding in a burst of starlight and shadow.

FIVE

ARTIMUS

The chamber they lock us in has a vaulted ceiling and no windows. Sconces fixed to the walls light up the space. Seven conji occupy the balcony high above us. They don't speak. They merely stand in their hooded robes, faces cast in shadow.

They've lain Nyx inside a circle ringed in arcane symbols —runes saturated in conji allure, no doubt. They mean nothing to me.

There is only one exit from the room and those doors are now barred.

The princes urged us to leave the chamber, but we opted to stay.

So they locked us in.

The prickle of allure is hot against my skin. The conji are prepared for when Nyx wakes. Because she will. I believe it with every fiber of my being.

I believe that she's what Dhuma says she is. It makes sense to me. It explains why Satan asked me to watch over her. Why he asked me to be her guardian. He would have told me the truth eventually. He must have planned to, but then he was killed.

Does his killer know the truth?

Does the killer know what Nyx is?

What *is* she, though?

The spawn huddle beneath the balcony whispering. Ignatius and Hrath stand a little way from them, heads together, speaking in quiet tones while Ignatius keeps one eye on Nyx.

I don't like how he looks at her. How he held her. I don't like it, but I understand it because it's how I want to look at her. And how I want to hold her. There's something between them, and although it needles at me, I understand it.

This is Nyx.

This female...I have no words to describe my awe and admiration of her.

I won't let them snuff her out.

Ignatius beckons me, his expression somber. I join him.

"We need to talk," he says.

The calculated gleam in his eyes is encouraging. "You have a plan?"

"Not yet, but I think we may be able to curry some favor with the princes. Maybe convince them to be lenient on Nyx when she..." He looks across at her unconscious form. "When she wakes."

His words ease the tangle of emotions in my chest. "You believe she will, don't you?"

"Yes. I do. Dhuma would not have hurt her if he wasn't sure of what she was."

The memory of Dhuma pushing a blade into Nyx, of her shocked gasp, tears through me. I grit my teeth against a wave of rage. Where had he gotten that dagger? How? "You know him. Trust him. Why?"

"Knew him, yes. A long time ago. Trust him? How can I not? The male is a warrior. An honorable general and one of the daimon queen's mates."

"And he knew what Nyx was. I get that, but why kill her? I mean, daimons have three lives but they don't *have* to use them."

Hrath and Ignatius exchange a look.

They're hiding something.

"Why? Ignatius, tell me."

"Dhuma said he was releasing her." He sighs. "He believes she's some kind of...reincarnation of Soreena."

I'm momentarily thrown. "Who?"

"Soreena. The daimon queen," Hrath says. "He says she has Soreena's aura."

That's...preposterous. "You believe that?"

He shakes his head. "I don't know what I believe. But Dhuma believes he's bringing his lover back."

I stare at him blankly. "Like hell."

Ignatius's jaw ticks. "We'll know soon enough."

"It's still impossible," Hrath says. "It doesn't change the fact that fallen and daimons can't procreate."

Ignatius glances at Nyx again, his gaze lingering. "It makes no sense, and yet it makes every sense. All we can do is focus on saving her from a second death."

I have no idea what he's talking about, but if there's a way to save Nyx, then I'm in. "What did you have in mind?"

He moves closer and lowers his tone. "We solve a problem for them. Save one of them."

"Oh?"

"Prince Merihem."

I scan his face. "You know what's wrong with him."

"Yes. Dhuma told me. The prince is in the grip of an outside power. He can sense it. And this castle is filled with hidden creatures that mean harm. Creatures from my old world."

His old world? "The djinn realm?"

"There is much I need to share with you."

Ignatius and I have never been close. We've barely interacted in the past. The only thing that's brought us together is Nyx's arrival. Nyx is the tie that binds us all. "Why would you trust me?" Why the fuck am I asking him that?

"I see the way you look at her. You would die for her."

I don't bother to deny it.

His smile is mirthless. "Yes, she commands that kind of loyalty without asking for it. It's what makes her who she is."

The way he says it, as if there's more...something he's not sharing. "What aren't you telling me?"

His expression shutters. "Do you wish to save her life?"

"Of course."

"Then let us focus on that. On saving Merihem and gaining the princes' favor."

I hate to let it go, but he's right, we have to focus on the task at hand. "Fine. What's your plan?"

HRATH CALLS the Satan spawn to join us. This involves them as much as it involves us. Nyx is their sibling and I have no doubt how much they care for her.

It turns out they've all noticed something strange about the fortress. A sense of being watched. A sense of eerie foreboding.

"This shiqq thing makes sense," Tristeene says. "Why didn't we make the connection sooner?"

Ignatius replies in a hushed tone. "Because a shiqq possession that leaves the host intact must be consensual.

Why would we ever consider that a fallen would agree to such a thing? If a host is taken by force, it drives them completely insane and kills them."

"Maybe he didn't agree," Gus says. "You saw him. He's not exactly sane. Maybe a fallen's mind and body are strong enough to withstand a takeover."

"But it would take a powerful shiqq to claim one," Hrath points out.

"So we've got to be careful." Gus tugs at his bottom lip. "We can't let him know we're on to him. Not yet. We'll have to lure him into a trap."

"A location where he can be bound and then forced out of the prince's body," Hrath says.

"We'll need Levistus to summon our most powerful conji," Ignatius says. "Just as he summoned me."

So that's how he got here so quickly. "Why *did* he summon you?"

"I wished to speak with him about this very thing. About the fawda."

"But now we're locked in this chamber until Nyx wakes." I glance at the door. "How are we going to speak to Levistus."

"*We* won't," Hrath says. "*I* will." He smirks. "A sylph cannot be bound by allure. Something which we like to keep to ourselves." There's a warning in his dark eyes. But I doubt anyone in our circle of trust will break it, and he must know it too or else he wouldn't be revealing this tidbit of information. "I'll slip out and find Levistus."

"But then what?" Tristeene asks. "How do we trap the thing inside Merihem?"

"The circle won't hold Nyx for long," Gus says. All eyes are on the imp, and his ochre cheeks flush slightly under our collective scrutiny. His throat bobs and he continues. "The runes aren't that strong. They must plan on using it to hold her while they bind her some other way. But... but then the circle will be free to be used by another." His bright blue eyes settle on me.

I catch on to what he's thinking. "By Merihem, you mean?"

"Yes." Gus grins, showcasing tiny white teeth. His small wings flutter in excitement. "We can use the element of surprise to push him into the circle when the time is right."

"We have a plan," Ignatius says. "Be wary, Hrath, there are lower-level elementals everywhere. Watching and listening."

Hrath nods curtly. "I will."

What the fuck? "But it's safe to speak in here?"

"Yes," Hrath says. "The allure the conji are creating acts as a ward to anything outside this room. I've scanned the chamber. There are no entities in here but us."

"Go." Ignatius squeezes Hrath's shoulder. "May stealth be with you."

Hrath backs up. His form shimmers and disintegrates before vanishing through the wall.

"Now what?" Mallini asks.

Ignatius looks past me at the circle in the center of the room. At Nyx. "Now we wait."

Six

NYX

Tiana sobbed softly. Parlos was gone and he'd somehow taken a bunch of lost souls with him. But not all of them.

Those that remained lumbered toward the gates with blank expressions and unseeing eyes, their bodies acting on desperate instinct, drawn to the power hidden in this labyrinth.

"What did he do?" I turned to Lewin. "What was that?"

"Parlos is a gatekeeper. His element is spirit. He has... had the ability to connect to souls and to find hidden doorways. He was the best of us."

Tiana wiped at her cheeks. "We must keep moving."

"Yes," Lewin said. "Time is running short."

I pulled away from the gate and into the labyrinth proper. The silvery path guiding me shimmered, stretching ahead and then curving right at the intersection. "This way."

We set off, following the light. The labyrinth walls rose

high either side of us, the path easily wide enough for us to walk side by side.

We walked in silence for a minute as I followed the ethereal silver trail. "Who are you? Higher daimons?"

"We were once, yes. But we were chosen to be guides for our people. This is...was our afterlife. A vast place with many layers, a place for souls to pass through and for some to stay. But now..."

"I can't bear it," Tiana said. "I can't bear what we've done."

"What *you've* done?"

"She refers to our people," Lewin said. "Hubris is the root of many downfalls. As it was for the daimon race and our old world."

My mind worked, making connections. The daimon city, the abyss, had been a technologically advanced place, but it hadn't been their original world. They'd come here from a place called Inferis, led here by a messiah who'd then sealed up Inferis. The gateway to Inferis was named the pit. They'd run away from something. Something maybe they'd created?

Oh, shit. "Did the daimons create the sickness?"

Lewin's mouth tipped in a wry smile. "You could say that. They had technology but they wanted more mystical power. The higher daimon race was spawned from that desire—daimons with inherent mystical abilities. And as that race grew and flourished, a new ambition developed. They wanted to open doors to other worlds and explore the cosmos. And they did. They found a way to create bridges into other worlds, and that was the beginning of the end."

I followed the path left, then hard right.

"We let death into our world," Tiana said.

I wanted to know more, to ask more, but we'd come to

the end of the silvery light. "What is it?" Lewin asked. "Why have you stopped?"

"The path is gone." I looked both ways at the intersection. "I don't know which way to go."

Tiana and Lewin exchanged a worried glance.

My stomach hollowed. "What does that mean?"

"It means time's running out," Lewin said. "If we don't get to the gate in the next few minutes, then..."

Crap. "I need that path. Without it we could end up going in circles." I peered up at the top of the hedgerow. "I need to get up there."

But the hedge didn't want to be climbed. The leaves slipped from my fingers and the surface became smooth and unyielding, resisting any attempt to scale it.

"Shit!"

There had to be something we could do. Something to get me to the top of that hedge. Wait... I looked at Tiana. "Can you summon water? From the atmosphere? Or the ground?"

She blinked rapidly and then nodded. "Yes. Yes, I can. I see what you want. A geyser of water to raise you up?"

I nodded. "That would work."

She shooed me away from her. "Step back."

I backed up, giving her space to work. Lewin joined me, watching her intently as she crouched and placed her hands to the earth. She closed her eyes and began to hum.

"Ah, there you are...Yes, come to me. That's it." Her brow pinched in a frown. "No. Wait...not so much. Wait..." She squealed as the earth exploded outward, flinging her backward. A jet of water burst into the air.

But this was no small geyser, this was a dam bursting. Water flooded the path in seconds and began to rise.

"How is this possible?" Tiana yelled. "The labyrinth is huge. It should spread out."

"The laws of physics do not always apply here," Lewin yelled back.

The water rose fast and was at my chest before the idea hit me. "Swim!"

I began to paddle, rising with the water.

Tiana and Lewin splashed alongside me as the top of the hedge got closer and closer. Yes! I was going to make it.

The water surged, pushing me up, then began to drop.

"No!"

"I have you," Tiana said.

I felt a shove at my back, then I was riding a jet of water, shooting up to the top of the hedge.

I grabbed hold of the ledge and scrambled on. "I did it! I can see the golden beam where the gate must be." I waved at Tiana and Lewin in the water below.

"Keep going!" Tiana said. "You need to keep going. Head for the beam."

A rumble, like thunder but deeper, shook the air. I dropped to my knees on the hedge, sinking my fingers into the foliage to hold tight as the earth shook. A gust of wind blew my hair forward. I looked back the way we'd come, and my heart leapt into my throat at the sight of the wave headed toward us. It towered higher than the hedge, powerful and lethal.

My words came out as a screech. "Watch out!"

I caught the horror on Tiana's face and the resignation on Lewin's, and then the wave hit and the maze was underwater. I held onto the hedge, my anchor against the violent pull of the wave. For a moment there was nothing but the pounding of blood in my head and the heat of breath trapped in my lungs, and in the next moment I was free, gasping cold air, soaked to the skin, but free of the weight of water.

I peeled myself off the hedge and peered over the side.

Water lapped at the hedge a few feet below me. There was no sign of Tiana or Lewin.

Shit, shit, shit.

My chest grew tight. No. Nyx. No, you can't lose it now. Where was the beam? There! Not too far, but it looked duller.

Panic bloomed in my stomach. I had to get to it fast.

The top of the hedge was sturdy, making it easy to run along it. The gaps were wide, but not too wide, so I risked swimming to bridge the distance between ledges and get closer to my target.

In less than a minute I was at the center of the labyrinth. The whole area was flooded. The beam flickered and dulled.

I was running out of time. The gate was somewhere below the surface.

There was only one thing for it.

I took a deep breath, then dove. Darkness surrounded me, and the panic simmering in my belly threatened to explode. I stemmed it and focused on the light, swimming toward it. A stone plinth was planted on the ground and the light shot up from that.

This had to be the gate.

I kicked out and swam for it.

I was almost there when something bumped my thigh. I spun in the water and almost screamed at the sight of Tiana's sightless eyes. Her neck was at an odd angle. Broken.

She was dead. Oh, earth and stars.

My chest ached with the need for air.

I kicked toward the plinth, fighting the darkness edging at my vision. I was dead but not dead, and if I didn't make it to that plinth I'd stay dead or worse. This place was corrupted. Tiana and Parlos were wardens and they were gone, able to die even in this afterlife.

If I failed, there was no hope for me.

But the plinth seemed to be getting farther away. My limbs were getting heavier.

Oh, earth. I wasn't going to make it.

A shadow slid up beside me and a hand gripped mine and tugged.

The plinth hurtled forward, or maybe I was hurtling toward it. The fog in my brain made it difficult to think, but I caught sight of Lewin's bearded face, his dark, determined eyes.

He was alive.

He was with me.

Helping me.

He nodded, his hair floating about his head, then raised my hand and pressed it to the plinth.

I wanted to say thank you, to mourn the loss of the other wardens, but the light was too bright.

Much too bright to do anything but float away.

SEVEN

HRATH

The fortress is silent but that does not mean it is empty. Elementals are wily djinn, especially the lower air elementals. In hindsight I should have sensed their presence, but I'd been distracted by the attack, by my almost failure at keeping Nyx safe.

The moment when Dhuma plunged a dagger in her heart runs through my mind.

My pulse spikes.

I push away the memory and focus on the task at hand —a stealth journey to Levistus.

The route has been clear so far, which is favorable as I cannot afford to be seen or heard. Prince Merihem must not learn of what we plan to do.

I slip down the corridor that leads to Levistus's quarters and am almost at the door when my scalp tightens in awareness.

I'm being watched.

I don't freeze or pause; I don't give any indication that

I'm aware of the spy. Instead I swerve, smooth and swift, to shoot back up the corridor toward him.

I catch sight of a pair of glowing eyes before the elemental vanishes through a wall.

I follow.

He's fast, but I'm a sylph. I'm faster. I catch up to him in a storeroom and wrap my hand around his neck, forcing him to materialize.

He spits and bares his teeth at me, cursing in the old tongue.

I respond in kind. "What is the name of your master?"

He replies in the ancient tongue. "Leave me, swine. You are nothing, and I will tell you nothing."

I allow my lips to curl, cruel and filled with lethal intent. "Then you shall die."

I tighten my grip and his eyes bulge. He claws at my hand, but his efforts are ineffectual. His mouth moves as he tries to speak. I relax my grip a little, allowing him to take in air.

"Please," he gasps. "If I tell you, he will tear me to shreds."

I tighten my grip to remind him of his imminent demise. "Tell me his name and you may live long enough to run from him."

He makes a strangled sound and I loosen my grip again.

"Velarin." He says the word as if it should mean something to me. "He has the prince. He is powerful. One of the most powerful generals in the fawda."

A general? "Shiqq were never generals for anything or anyone."

Fear saturates his features. "He is no shiqq."

My stomach tightens into knots. "What is he?" I ask the question even though I know the answer. A sick sensation fills my gut. I hope that I'm wrong. "Answer me."

"A marid."

Fuck. Marids are one of the most powerful of the jinn. They are the reason we won the battle against Shaitan, but they're also the reason he gained the upper hand in the first place. Too many joined his cause. Too many turned their back on peace.

"Please, let me go. I must run. I must hide," he pleads.

I snap his neck.

His body slumps to the ground and I lift him and throw him over my shoulder. Proof for Levistus, should he doubt my word.

I make my way to the prince's quarters, urgency lava in my veins, because if what the little spy tells me is true, then freeing Merihem may not be as simple as we hoped.

TRISTEENE

"She's been gone for too long," Gus says.

"You don't know that for sure," Mallini snaps. "There's nothing about higher daimon rebirth in the textbooks, only that they have three lives."

"I know but...I feel it." Gus's lip trembles. "I'm scared."

Veena hugs him. "It will be all right. Nyx is strong. She'll find a way back. She won't leave us."

I cross the room and crouch by the circle beside Ignatius. He's been like this for the past fifteen minutes. Watching her silently. Artimus stands on the other side, his hands shoved in the pockets of his slacks, his expression unreadable.

"How long has she been gone now?"

Ignatius shakes his head slightly. "She'll wake." He rubs his breastbone with his knuckles. "She's not gone."

He sounds sure.

Artimus makes a ragged sound and turns away. "She's been dead for almost an hour, Ignatius. An hour. What can come back from that?"

"She can." Ignatius unfurls his imposing frame to stand across from Artimus. "I would know if she was gone completely."

"And how would you know that?" Artimus's eyes narrow to slits and he makes his way around the circle to face off with Ignatius. "What's between you two? What aren't you telling me, efreet."

He says it like it's a dirty thing. He says it to provoke, and I understand what he's trying to do. He wants to fight. To vent his frustration.

"Stop it!" I put myself between the two males. "This won't help. Nyx needs all of us to work together." I look from Ignatius to Artimus. "We have to be a team."

Artimus's jaw ticks and then he exhales through his nose and drops his gaze. "I can't stand this. I can't stand her being gone."

"Are you talking about me?"

Nyx pulls herself into a sitting position in the circle and my heart leaps.

Chanting breaks out above as the conji start whatever allure they've prepared to hold Nyx captive.

She frowns up at the balcony. "Why are they singing?"

"Nyx." Artimus drops to his knees outside the circle. "Thank the stars."

She shoots him a smile. "Did you miss me?"

"You died," Artimus says gruffly. "You fucking died." It sounds like an accusation.

"Yeah." She stands and rubs the back of her neck. "Dying is bloody exhausting."

The chanting gets louder, and Nyx shoots the conji an

annoyed glare. "First the birds and now this. I think I'm cursed."

"It's okay," Artimus says. "They just need to keep you contained for a little while. To make sure you're not a threat."

Her eyebrows flick up. "Because they think I'm a higher daimon."

"You are," Ignatius says. "You have high daimon blood. Dhuma saw it, which is why he—"

"Stabbed me? Nice way to greet someone."

"No," Artimus says. "He stabbed you because he thinks you're the daimon queen reincarnated and he wanted to free you."

She stares at him as if he's offered to put on a ballgown and dance for her. "And I thought people thinking I was higher daimon was far-fetched." A look of exasperation crosses her beautiful face. "I'm me. Still me. Not dangerous, just cranky, tired, and super hungry." She pats her stomach. "I need food."

And then despite the conji's chanting and the crackle of allure saturating the room, she steps out of the circle.

Just like that.

The conji let out a unified bellow.

Nyx places her hands on her hips and tips her head back to glare at them. "Will you *please* shut the fuck up."

Mallini snorts with laughter. "Containment spell indeed."

But no one else laughs because we all recognize the saturation of power in the room, the amount of effort the conji have put into the allure to keep Nyx bound.

But Nyx has walked through it as if it's nothing. As if it doesn't exist.

She says she's the same, but she isn't, and with that

realization, any hopes of convincing the princes to go easy on her fly out the window.

Nyx is a higher daimon.

Nyx is powerful.

And because of that, she's now in danger.

EIGHT

NYX

The way that everyone was staring at me, then at the circle, then back at me, gave me goosebumps. "I wasn't supposed to step out of it, was I?"

"No," Artimus said. "You weren't."

The balcony was now empty. The conji had vanished, probably to get reinforcements.

This was real.

I somehow had high daimon blood and enough power to break through a conji-constructed ward without even feeling it.

"Nyx, this is bad," Gus said. "The princes want to execute you."

"That isn't strictly true," Ignatius said. "There'll be a conclave to discuss—"

"Puh-lease!" Mallini rolled her eyes. "That's bullshit and you know it." She looked to Tristeene. "I get it. I shouldn't have laughed. I get it now. Nyx, we need to get you out of here."

"There's nowhere to run," Artimus said. "Not from the demon realm. We need to play this smart. Get back to Morningstar and convince the princes that you aren't a threat. If we get the votes, then—"

"She just walked through a conji ward," Gus pointed out. "Do you think they'll let that slide?"

Silence reigned and the tension in the room was palpable. "Look, it's been a long day and night. I don't know how this happened, how I could be a high daimon. But I didn't ask for it, and I deserve the opportunity to understand it. I'm not running from this. If they want to kill me, then they'll have a fight on their hands."

Artimus groaned. "Nyx, you cannot go up against the princes. They're original fallen angels. Their power is incomparable."

"In which case, they have nothing to worry about when it comes to me or whatever power I might have."

"It's not your power they're afraid of," Ignatius said. "It's your existence."

"What?"

"You're an anomaly. An impossibility," he continued. "Fallen and daimons cannot produce offspring. They're biologically and mystically incompatible. You have Satan blood in your veins, there is no doubt about that, and now that it's come to light you also share high daimon blood, you're an unknown factor. Which makes you a threat to the balance of things."

My chest heated. "So because they don't understand what I am, because they can't pigeonhole me, they get to decide whether I live or die?" I shook my head. "No. I'm not going to stand for that. I've fought too hard to just sit back and let someone else decide my fate."

Ignatius's eyes lit up. "You have my support, Nyx, and my protection."

Artimus made a sound of exasperation. "And you'll protect her, how?" His lip curled. "You're Levistus's bitch just as I'm Morningstar's. Neither of us have the power to protect her. Only the princes can do that."

"Then we convince them," Tristeene said. "We save Prince Merihem and we put them in our debt. We force them to be lenient."

I wanted to hug her for her optimism, but I could see the doubt in Artimus's eyes. This guy grew up in the world of demon and fallen politics. He knew how it worked and he wasn't confident of a positive outcome. But I wasn't running away, not if there was a chance that I could fight this. Not if there was a chance that I could keep my place here with my family.

"I'm not going anywhere. Not until I've exhausted all other avenues."

Tristeene's eyes gleamed with understanding. Mallini lifted her chin, her eyes flashing with determination on my behalf, and Gus's jaw tensed but he nodded once.

Veena approached me and took my hand. "Promise me you'll run if it starts to look bad."

Running away always grated, but I'd done it to survive once or twice. I wasn't a fool, and as much as it would hurt to leave them behind, I would do what needed to be done to live another day, because if there was life, there was hope.

"I promise." I squeezed her hand. "Now tell me, what's all this about saving Merihem?"

Veena opened her mouth to speak but a loud crackling sound cut her off. The air fizzed against my skin and an invisible fist punched me in the chest, sending me flying backward.

I landed smack bang in the center of the circle, winded and more than a little pissed.

"Nyx!" Artimus and Ignatius cried out in unison.

But my attention was on Veena as she ran toward me. Toward the circle around which the air sparked and fizzed.

A shield. A ward. Shit. "Veena, no!"

Too late.

She hit the ward.

The air sparked, and she flew across the room. Her cry of shock cut off with a sickening thud as she hit the wall.

"Veena!" I rushed the barrier, not caring what it might do to me. Contact slammed me back onto the ground. I rolled and sat up. "Veena!"

Mallini and Gus were already beside her, helping her up.

"She's fine. She's alive. Just a broken arm," Gus babbled. "It's healing."

Rage burned a path up my throat as I slowly raised my head to look up at the balcony. I expected to see the conji had returned, but I was mistaken.

In place of the robed figures stood Ramiel.

His dark hair was swept off his forehead, giving his earlier boyish look a hard edge, reminding me who and what he was. He peered down his nose at me with whiskey eyes rimmed in bright gold.

He did this?

Knocked me down and hurt Veena.

He did this alone?

I stood, hating the way my knees wobbled.

"Stay down," Artimus hissed. "Nyx, don't challenge him."

But rage was an inferno in my chest, bubbling and rising. It pressed against my skin, wanting out.

"Don't," Ramiel said. "Don't make me hurt you, Nyx."

"There is no need for violence." Ignatius's voice washed over me like a soothing balm.

I locked gazes with him, and a sense of calm fell over

me. The conviction that everything would be okay. That he had my back.

He inclined his head slightly. "Nyx does not intend to fight you, Prince Ramiel. She was merely stunned by your attack, and her sister's injury upset her."

Ramiel kept his attention on me. "You will show good faith and put on the shackles."

A conji appeared outside the circle holding a set of gold bracelets in his hand.

"Is there really a need for that?" Artimus asked Ramiel.

I eyed the bracelets. Shackles, he'd called them. "What are they?"

"Power muters," Ignatius said. "You won't have access to your higher daimon powers, or any power, while you wear them. They will render you essentially human."

I gave Ramiel a wry smile. "I've lived as a human all my life. I came here as a human, entered the trials, and survived as one. I don't need powers to kick anyone's ass if I decide to do so."

Was it my imagination or did the corner of the prince's mouth lift in an almost smile? "Then we have an understanding."

I held out my wrists but the conji merely threw the cuffs into the circle. They passed through the shield with a fizz.

I picked them up and shot Ramiel an impressed glance. "Neat trick with the shield."

A slender shadow moved behind him, and a woman appeared at his side. She had sharp, pale features and spots of color rode high on her cheeks. The only soft thing about her was her mouth. Full and pouty, but her cold, hard eyes negated the softness.

Even her voice was cold, like icicles. "The shield is no trick. It's power. My power. You won't be getting past me."

Ramiel's jaw ticked. "Thank you, Odette. Your allure is appreciated."

I arched a brow. "And here I was thinking you were doing this all by yourself."

Odette's eyes narrowed. "Do not doubt the prince or his abilities. I may have created the cage, but he was the one to put you in it." She looked up at him, a sidelong sly glance that reminded me of a cat that had stolen the catch of the day. "The prince and I make a fine team."

Ramiel's expression didn't change. In fact, I could be wrong, but I thought I caught the hint of annoyance in his whiskey eyes.

I slipped on the bangles and they tightened to fit my wrists, snug against my skin. I held up my arms. "All done. Happy?"

"You can drop the shield now, Odette," Ramiel said.

"Or we could end this now," Odette replied. "Save the conclave the trouble."

The air around my neck tightened, squeezing and cutting off my breath. I grabbed at my throat.

"What is it?" Artimus demanded.

"She can't breathe!" Tristeene said.

"Stop this!" Ignatius bellowed. "Stop it now!"

"Odette, cease," Ramiel ordered.

But the constriction got worse and dark spots danced at the edge of my vision. I looked up at Odette, and the evil bitch grinned at me.

"Odette!" Ramiel snapped. "Enough!"

A loud pop assaulted my ears followed by a whoosh of air as a body appeared in the circle with me. Huge dark wings blocked my view of the room, the feathered tips flared as if in anger.

My eyes watered, mouth parted, desperate for air as I stared at the back of Zepar's head.

"Stop!" Zepar bellowed.

The constriction stopped.

I gasped, sucking lungfuls of air.

Zepar's wings vanished so they were merely an incorporeal shimmer in the air. He turned to me and cupped my elbows to steady me, scanning me for injury. "Nyx, are you all right?"

"I'm okay." Crap, my voice was all croaky.

"You dare to come here without a summons?" Ramiel's voice trembled with rage.

Shit, how *had* he come here without a summons?

Zepar tensed and a muscle in his jaw ticked. He exhaled through his nose, then slowly turned to look up at the prince, one hand still bracing me.

"On this occasion I felt it necessary to come uninvited." He lifted his chin. "I feared for my custodia's safety and, as is my right as sponsor, I made the decision to check on her." He flicked a glance my way, down to the cuffs on my wrists and then back up again. "I see my concern was not unwarranted. You may be a prince but you are not above Morningstar law, which clearly states that a sponsor may go to all reasonable lengths to protect his custodia."

My throat pinched as I stared up at him. Damn, he was formidable.

"Zepar, darling, I'm so sorry, I didn't know the spawn belonged to you," Odette said.

Darling?

"Why would you, Mother," Zepar replied. "We haven't spoken in over a decade."

Mother? Oh, shit.

She pouted. "That was not my choice." She slid a glance Ramiel's way. "I refuse to take sides between you and your father."

Ramiel's eye twitched.

Whoa...hold the fucking phone. Was she saying what I think she was saying?

"I have no father," Zepar said. "Only a prince."

Ramiel sighed and briefly closed his eyes. "Zepar, now is not the time."

Oh my God. Ramiel was Zepar's dad! Now that I knew, I could see the resemblance. No wonder Ramiel seemed familiar to me.

"What is this?" Zepar pointed to the circle, then the cuffs on my wrists. "What is her crime?"

"The crime of being an aberration," Odette said. "She has higher daimon blood."

Zepar's eyes widened a fraction, but he recovered quickly. "I see we have much to discuss." He put his arm around me. "Which we will do once my custodia is back in her quarters in Morningstar."

Ramiel inclined his head. "Very well. The cuffs have disabled her power. There is no reason to hold her here." He looked to Odette, who nodded. I felt the shield on the circle drop. "You may take her."

"No one is going anywhere." Merihem sauntered through the door. He looked like he'd just rolled out of bed: hair in disarray, shirt open to reveal his slender, muscled torso, pants low on his hips. His gaze fell on me, and his lips curved in a wicked smile. "This daimon belongs to me."

NINE

Ignatius and Artimus moved to stand between me and Merihem.

The prince chuckled. "Oh, how sweet. The alpha males jumping to the defense of a damsel, except for the fact that she is no damsel." His mouth thinned in a hard line. "She's a higher daimon."

"Merihem, there is no need for this," Ramiel said. "We have her power muted and we will call a conclave to discuss what to do with her."

"Yes, yes." He waved a dismissive hand. "But in the meantime, she will remain a guest of Libidine."

"No," Ignatius said. "She belongs at Morningstar. She is Satan spawn first and foremost, and you do *not* have the monopoly on Satan spawn. She is *my* custodia."

"And mine," Zepar added.

I couldn't recall the last time I'd had so many people stand up for me, protect me, and although I'd never asked, never needed it, there no denying the comfort it brought.

I glanced up, sensing movement on the balcony, and

caught a glimpse of Levistus's golden head, but he quickly stepped out of sight, taking Ramiel with him.

"You can't keep any of us here," Artimus said. "The conclave is over. The ball is over, and we have committed no crime to be held against our will. Free passage to and from Libidine is woven into an invitation to the conclave."

"For you, maybe," Merihem said. "*You* were invited, but you decided to bring the spawn with you. Using the portal sent for you to transport *uninvited* guests. Therefore, free passage is mine to give or take away. And as for a crime..." He pointed an accusatory finger at me. "Her existence is a crime in itself."

"Enough," Levistus said from above us.

Merihem's head whipped up and then his face broke into a smile. "Ah, brother, good of you to join us."

Levistus smiled tightly. "I apologize for the delay, but it seems as if Ramiel has everything under control."

Merihem snorted. "If this looks like he has things under control, then I dread to think what chaos looks like."

"Zepar, vacate the circle," Ramiel ordered.

Zepar's grip on me tightened. "And what about my charge?"

"We are in Prince Merihem's domain and therefore she will go with the prince." Zepar looked like he was about to argue, but Ramiel cut him off. "I am your prince, and you will do as you are bid."

"She will not be harmed," Levistus said. "Cannot be harmed by law until the judgment of the conclave."

"He's right," Ignatius said.

I looked over at him, noting the tension in his shoulders and the almost deliberately flat look in his eyes. I didn't know him well enough to read his body language, but I sensed something...an expectant air.

My pulse sped up a little.

"You're safe now," Zepar said to me.

I nodded.

He released me and stepped out of the circle.

"There you go, Merihem," Levistus said. "She's all yours. Put her where you will and then we can talk."

"No!" Veena tried to move toward me, but Mallini held her back.

"It's okay." I smiled at Veena and my siblings. "I'm fine."

Merihem smirked and ambled toward me. He stopped just outside the circle and held out his hand.

My gaze flicked to Ignatius, and it was as if he was holding his breath.

My gut told me to stay put. To not leave the circle and make him come to me. It made no sense, but it felt like the right thing to do.

I crossed my arms and arched a cocky brow. "You want me, then you'll have to drag me out of this circle kicking and screaming."

My sentence must have conjured up an enticing image because his smirk broke into a grin.

"With pleasure." He stepped into the circle and a blur hit me from the side, plucking me off my feet and carrying me out of the circle.

A sharp elemental aroma stung my nostrils.

Hrath.

The sylph had me.

The air popped and a loud cracking sound left my ears ringing. A golden light shot up around the circle. A new ward. Several conji ran into the room and began to chant.

Merihem turned this way and that, staring at the robed figures, then finally tipped his chin up to glare at Ramiel and Levistus. Odette was no longer on the balcony. She swept through the doors a moment later, hands out in front of her, throwing allure at the circle.

"What is this?" Merihem demanded. "What game is this?"

Hrath materialized with his arms still around me. "Not a game. An intervention."

"We know what you are. Who you are," Levistus said from above.

Merihem snorted. "If this is some kind of ploy to wrest control of my domain, then you're in for a nasty surprise." His gaze flicked to the door. "I am not defenseless."

Hrath released me. "Are you waiting for your minions, Velarin?"

Merihem stilled.

"Yes, I know your name. I know what you are. A marid hiding inside a fallen."

Ignatius sucked in a sharp breath.

"Your minions are...indisposed," Hrath said. "And by that, I mean I killed most of them. The rest ran away."

Merihem tucked in his chin.

"Show yourself," Ramiel demanded.

Merihem looked up. All the humor had been wiped from his features. His expression was hard and stern, and his eyes burned with an inner fire. "You cannot force me out. This skin belongs to me now. This power..." He held up his hand and glowing tendrils of power snaked between his fingers. "Belongs to me!" He shot out his hand and a stream of white light hit the barrier of the circle.

The conji chanted louder and Odette laughed. "Your power is no match for mine. Or that of the princes."

Ramiel's eyes were narrowed and focused as he looked down at the circle.

Merihem began to shake. His hand trembled and he slowly lowered it to his side. He growled low in his throat. "You may be able to hold me here, but you cannot force me out of this vessel."

"That is no vessel," Levistus ground out. "That is my brother."

He raised both hands and Merihem's back curved, his head fell back, and a bellow of pain tore from his throat, but as soon as Levistus let up, the bellow morphed into laughter.

This time when Merihem spoke his voice was deep and gruff. Nothing like the dulcet tones of the prince. "You fool. All you do is hurt your brother. You cannot touch me."

Ignatius stepped forward, a cool smile on his perfect lips. "Maybe *they* cannot because they are not of our world and their allure cannot affect us as it does others. But *I* am not of this world, and I bring with me the knowledge of our ancestors."

The thing inside Merihem, the marid, Velarin, stilled. "You know nothing."

Ignatius slow-blinked. "I know that your kind are weak, which is why you hide inside a powerful vessel."

Velarin balked. "I am not weak."

Ignatius rolled his eyes. "So weak that you must have taken this vessel when it was vulnerable. Maybe you took him in his sleep after long nights of whispers and chipping away at his defenses."

"I did no such thing. I took him decisively, with power." He thumped his chest with his fist.

"You're so weak that you hide inside him even now because you know that once you reveal yourself there is no escape. No fighting your way out of here. You, Velarin, are a coward."

"You have no grasp of my power," Velarin said. "But you will see. You will witness the true magnitude of what I am."

Merihem's body convulsed and then a form began to push out from it. Ethereal and bulky, it tore from the fallen's body, discarding it on the ground like a used napkin.

Velarin was so huge he almost filled the circle. His skin had a turquoise hue, and his head was bald. His eyes were slanted with white irises and pinprick pupils.

"What do you say now, efreet?" Velarin demanded.

Ignatius looked to Hrath. "Do it."

Hrath grinned and pulled a bottle from his pocket.

Velarin's eyes widened at the sight of the object. "No." He dove for Merihem's unconscious form, but the fallen prince's body was yanked out of the circle by invisible forces.

Hrath pulled the stopper out of the bottle, and it lit up with strange markings.

Velarin let out a rage-filled bellow. "You'll die. You will all—"

His body contorted into a stream of ethereal essence and shot out of the circle into the bottle. Hrath pushed the stopper in, and the glowing symbols died.

Silence reigned for achingly long seconds and then a familiar yet confused voice broke it.

"Where am I?" Merihem stood inside the circle, a dark frown on his face. "And why am I dressed like this?"

TEN

W e'd moved from the containment chamber to Prince Ramiel's plush private quarters, large enough to house a family of six.

Merihem sat on a low-back armchair, his eyes dark in his pale face. He was understandably shaken, with no memory of what he'd done over the past few months. As far as he was aware, he'd fallen asleep a few months ago and only just woken up.

The marid had been in full control with access to Merihem's body and memories.

It was trapped now. Hrath had its new vessel strapped to his belt—a small golden bottle with a stopper. Was it enough to hold the creature?

Hrath and Ignatius obviously thought it was.

Apparently Levistus had allowed Hrath to take a portal back to the Court of Flame to fetch the artifact. One of the only ways to trap a marid.

The princes agreed that the Court of Flame was the best place to keep the creature, safe in Ignatius's charge, until they found a way to safely release and question it about the fawda.

Prince Ramiel and Levistus stood by the window, speaking in hushed voices. Odette stood with Zepar across the room. He had his head bowed slightly as he spoke to her.

To his mother.

My gaze flicked to Ramiel again. Zepar's dad.

Ramiel chose that moment to look my way. Our gazes snagged and a strange zing shot through me. I looked away, suddenly uncomfortable, and absently rubbed at my wrists where the cuffs hugged them. They weren't tight or uncomfortable, but they were there and that was enough to bug me.

Artimus gently gripped my wrist to stop me from twisting the bangle. "You'll chafe your skin," he said softly. "You could get an infection."

I opened my mouth to say I'd heal, then snapped it closed again. I *wouldn't* heal because my ability to heal was muted.

He smiled dryly, then looked across the room at Ramiel. "In light of what you now know, are the cuffs necessary? Nyx has proven her loyalty to her siblings and to the demon realm by helping to thwart the fawda plans."

I glanced at Veena, who was pressed up against Tristeene, her expression wary and fearful. To demonstrate the full scope of the fawda's reach, Hrath had been forced to tell Levistus about Veena's possession by a shiqq. It had been the only way to impress how much of a threat they were. That information, coupled with a dead air elemental, had convinced the prince that his brother was under the influence of outer forces.

But the whole truth, the fact that the shiqq had used

Veena to murder our other siblings, was still a secret that only a handful shared.

I planned for it to stay that way, because I had no clue what kind of contract or law the princes would pull out of their asses if they found out my sister was a spawn killer. The fact that she'd been possessed might not be enough to protect her.

I couldn't risk it.

I gave her a small smile of reassurance and she seemed to relax.

Ignatius's baritone dragged me from my thoughts.

"As Nyx's custodia I will take responsibility for her actions," he said to Ramiel.

"And so will I," Zepar added.

"We have no doubt that your intentions are honorable," Ramiel replied. "However, the law in such matters is clear. The spawn's power must be bound until the conclave reaches a decision as to what to do with her."

"You should let her continue the trials," Zepar said. "She's risked her life more than once to protect our people. She is Satan spawn and that must count for something."

"And we will abolish the execution contracts as requested, but we can't ignore the fact that she should not exist. We can't ignore the fact that we have no idea *how* she exists."

A shiver passed over me. "You think I'm an abomination, don't you?"

He pressed his lips together. "I think you could pose a threat and that cannot be ignored."

"A threat can become an asset," Merihem said softly. "If the threat is aimed elsewhere." He looked at me for the first time, his expression haunted. "You coming to Libidine saved my people. It saved me from the clutches of a monster and

63

revealed to us that we are not as infallible as we believe ourselves to be. There is a bigger threat rising, silent and stealthy, and now, because of you, we are aware of it. Trust that I will bear all this in mind when I cast my vote at the conclave."

I exhaled and nodded. "Thank you."

At least we had Merihem kind of on board, but the other two...It could go either way with them.

Merihem dragged a hand down his face. "Where is Dhuma? Why is it taking so long for him to answer my summons?"

He'd summoned the daimon?

Ramiel cleared his throat. "Brother, you had Dhuma incarcerated for murdering your mistress."

He blinked sharply. "I would do no such..." He closed his eyes and sighed heavily. "But I didn't, did I?"

"No. It seems the marid was in control," Levistus said.

Merihem's eyes flashed with anger. "I do not believe Dhuma would do such a thing. The marid must be responsible." His jaw went slack as a thought occurred to him. "Does that mean... I killed her?"

"We don't know that for certain," Levistus said.

There was a knock at the door.

"Enter," Ramiel called out.

The door opened and a guard stepped in followed by Dhuma. The daimon had to duck to get through the door. The collar around his neck glowed softly, muting his power, but my attention went to the side of his face, covered in dry blood. There was a deep gash across his cheekbone. It had to be painful. But if he was hurt, he didn't show it. There was pride in the way he held himself. The aura of a warrior.

He'd stabbed me and set a chain of events into motion that might result in some seriously bad shit for me, but I couldn't bring myself to be pissed at him.

The truth was always better than a lie.

At least in my book.

Dhuma scanned the room, then zeroed in on me. He searched my face for long seconds, then his shoulders slumped as if in defeat.

"She isn't Soreena," Ignatius said. "But she does have higher daimon blood."

Dhuma nodded and flicked another glance my way. "I had to know for sure. I'm sorry for taking one of her lives. But she has Soreena's aura. I see it clearly. She has her blood."

Ignatius tensed. I glanced around the room but no one else seemed shocked.

"What do you mean?" Ignatius asked him. "She has her blood?"

"Soreena's bloodline," Dhuma said. "There is no doubt about it now."

"You think I'm related to the daimon queen?" I stared at Dhuma. "I'm Satan blood. Fallen can't produce offspring with daimons."

Artimus let out a shocked exclamation and Ignatius stared at me in surprise, but Dhuma merely smiled, the action lighting up his weathered, brutal face.

"What?" I shook my head. "Why is everyone staring at me?"

Because they were. They were all looking at me as if I'd started speaking in tongues...

Wait a second.

I pointed to Dhuma. "Did you just speak in daimonword?"

"Yes."

"*You're* speaking it now," Ignatius said to me. "Perfectly."

I squeezed my eyes shut. "How do I stop."

"Stop what?" Artimus asked.

I turned to him. "You understand me?"

"You're speaking mortal tongue."

I threw up my hands. "I'm going insane."

"No, you're not," Gus said. "You're switching tongues based on who you speak to and what tongue they speak to you in. You're doing it without realizing it." His eyes were bright with excitement.

"Your brain is working on instinct," Ignatius said. "You'll learn to differentiate with time." His gaze dropped to the cuffs. "Those shackles may be muting your mystical abilities but not your nature."

"They might also be interfering with your ability to differentiate between languages," Gus added.

So I was multilingual now and somehow blood-related to the daimon queen. I glanced at Ramiel and Levistus, who were watching the exchange in silent confusion. I doubted any of this would go down in my favor.

"Dhuma?" Merihem stood slowly. "I'm so sorry."

I leaned in toward Artimus. "Is he speaking daimonword?"

"No, demon tongue. Dhuma understands the language, and Merihem must be able to understand daimonword." His brows shot up. "Wait a moment, did you understand what Merihem said? Do you understand demon tongue?"

I winced and nodded.

"You were not yourself," Dhuma said to Merihem.

"I punished you for a crime you did not commit."

"No," Dhuma said. "I *did* commit the crime."

Merihem blinked sharply. "You killed Rosetta?"

"I killed the creature pretending to be her. I don't know what became of the true Rosetta. The one I killed was working with the monster inside you. I believe that she may have been weakening you somehow to prepare you for possession."

"A ghul," Ignatius said. "They can take the form of the

creature they devour."

So Rosetta was dead then, just not at Dhuma's hand.

Merihem pressed his fingers to his temple. "The lemon tea. Every night. It would help me sleep. Deeply..." He walked up to Dhuma. "I am in your debt, friend. Again." He reached up and grasped the collar around Dhuma's neck.

It fell to the ground with a thud.

Dhuma inclined his head. "I have never considered there to be a debt between us, but I would ask two boons of you now."

"Ask me anything."

"Spare the female. Do not leave me as the last of my kind."

Merihem's shoulders rose and fell. "I cannot promise you my vote, but I can vow to keep an open mind." He turned to look at me. "Whether it will be enough, I cannot say."

"Very well," Dhuma said.

"What is the second boon?" Merihem asked.

"Release me from your service."

Merihem sucked in a breath. "Dhuma...You were never bound to me by force."

"Merely by obligation."

"We are both obligated to each other."

"Then you will release me?" Dhuma asked again.

"Of course," Merihem said. "You are free to come and go as you please. As you have always been."

Dhuma fixed his attention on me. "Then I will join your party, if you will have me."

I wasn't sure why he wanted to join us, but there was so much I wanted to know about the daimon realm, and Dhuma was the perfect person to educate me. "I'd be honored to have you."

Merihem looked between us, his expression conflicted.

"You cannot protect her. If the conclave decides—"

"I will not challenge the conclave's decision," Dhuma said. "You have my word."

Merihem nodded thoughtfully. "Then so be it."

"What?" Ramiel asked. "So be what?"

"Dhuma will be leaving with the Satan spawn," Merihem said.

"I don't think that's wise," Levistus said.

"He's given me his word not to interfere with the conclave's decision," Merihem snapped. "And that's enough for me."

A thought occurred to me. "Will you be able to withstand the atmosphere?"

Dhuma smiled, and once again I was struck by how it transformed his face. "Daimon blood is hardy. It is the reason that some abyssbloods can enter Morningstar and others cannot."

So it was the saturation of *daimon* blood, not *demon* blood that allowed them to do so? It made sense because pure demons struggled in the atmosphere. Nephalem and abyssbloods seemed to, on the whole, be okay with it.

And then there was me.

A new breed.

"Now what?" Mallini asked. "What do we do now? Can we leave?"

"The conclave will be called in three days," Ramiel said. "It will be held at Morningstar." He looked to the guard who was standing silently by the door. "Inform the conji to prepare a portal to Morningstar. Duke Zepar, Duke Ignatius, you will be responsible for your custodia." He dropped his gaze to me. "You and your siblings will leave within the hour."

Thank the earth. I was so ready to get the fuck out of here.

ELEVEN

"Who's setting up the portal?" Tristeene asked Prince Ramiel.

"I'll see to it myself. You won't be put in danger again. I give you my word."

The portal we'd taken here had spat us out in the old forest, and Keelan and I had nearly been killed. At first, we concluded that someone wanted Artimus dead, but then we'd realized Merihem was insane, and the only entity that could take control of Libidine away from him was Satan. One of us. Once we realized this, realized he'd known about us being here, we'd assumed that he'd been responsible for the carriage diversion. But he wasn't insane. He'd been possessed. So, the question was, would all our deaths have benefited the fawda?

No.

They wanted the seat, and for that they *needed* one of us. Killing us all would have been pointless. Something else occurred to me, and my gaze flew to Veena. The marid had set her aside when he'd posed the terms of his game.

He'd put all our lives on the line except Veena's.

Once again, she was somehow a focal point.

Now wasn't the time to voice this revelation, though. If the princes thought Veena was of interest to the fawda, they might keep her here. Lock her up. Who knew. No. I needed to deal with this. Me and my siblings, once we were out of here.

"We need to check on Keelan," Tristeene said, dragging me from my thoughts.

"Your sibling is safe," Levistus said. "I have some of my personal guards watching him."

Merihem tugged at the cuffs of his shirt. "I need to change. And wash." He grimaced.

"Stay here," Ramiel said to us. "We'll inform you once the portal is ready."

The princes headed out of the room, closing the doors behind them. The air felt lighter without them in the room, as if a load of tension had been removed.

But it wasn't tension they'd taken with them, but the palpable power they'd been exuding.

Odette broke away from Zepar and sashayed over to the window seat, parking her butt so she could take in the view while keeping an eye on the room.

Zepar joined me on the chaise longue, adjusting his body until the shimmer at his back settled. He was making sure his wings weren't squashed. So that's why all the seating in the room was low-backed.

"Why do you hide them?"

He arched a brow. "Hide what?"

"Your wings."

"They can be cumbersome at times. The glamour makes them...smaller. It's...easier this way."

His muscled thigh brushed mine and heat spread outward from the contact.

I nudged him with my knee. "How did you know I was in trouble?"

"Your nightmare sent me a message."

Sev... He must have felt something was wrong through our bond. Earth and stars, he was probably freaking out. "Can we get a message to him to let him know I'm all right?"

He frowned slightly. "You really care for him, don't you?"

"Yeah, I do. I care a lot."

"And what has he done to earn your devotion?"

What had he done? I wasn't even sure. I mean, he'd saved my life, but that wasn't it. It was so much more, a tangle of thoughts and feelings impossible to put into words that someone outside of the two of us would understand.

"Sev is just...Sev, and that's enough. It's more than enough."

He seemed to consider this. "And does my coming to find you mean anything?"

I met his tawny gaze. He had beautiful eyes, fringed in thick, dark lashes any woman would be proud to have.

"Yes. It does."

His gaze was heated as it skimmed across my face. "I won't allow any harm to come to you, Nyx."

His tone was low and intimate, and my mouth went dry.

"That's good to hear, but I doubt you'll have a choice if the conclave decides to, you know, *do* harm."

His jaw ticked and his warm eyes hardened to topaz chips of determination. "There is something you should know about me, Nyx. I always find a way to get what I want." His pupils dilated, darkening his eyes. "Always."

And it was obvious from the way he was looking at me that in this case, the thing he wanted was me, and the heat in his eyes told me it wasn't for political purposes.

I was no stranger to men wanting my body. I was no shrinking violet, afraid of taking what they had to offer.

Pleasure was nothing to run from. But the way the males of Morningstar looked at me was all-consuming. It was fire and coals. The need to own and possess. They wouldn't be satisfied with just my body. They wouldn't be satisfied until they'd claimed my very soul.

I smiled at Zepar to cover my fluster. "Noted. But word of advice, make sure you can handle the things that you think you want." I winked at him. "You wouldn't want to bite off more than you can chew."

His mouth twitched as he held back a smile. "You'd be surprised what I'm able to handle."

Oh boy.

"Zepar, sweet boy," Odette crooned from across the room. "I need to speak with you."

Zepar's expression flattened to a long-suffering one. "Excuse me. Duty calls."

"I wouldn't have pegged you for a momma's boy."

"You'd be right." He crossed the room to join Odette, and Ignatius took his place beside me. He looked troubled.

I nudged him with my shoulder. "What is it?"

He dropped his gaze to mine. "Nothing for you to be concerned about."

"Oh good, because I think I have enough to worry about."

I jerked my chin toward Odette. "Who is she? Aside from Ramiel's lover and Zepar's mother."

"A powerful conji and second-generation fallen," Ignatius said. "Although I wasn't aware of her relationship to the Duke of Ivory."

"Did you know Ramiel was Zepar's father?"

"Not for certain, although there have been rumors."

Odette broke off talking to Zepar to slide a glance my way, the corner of her mouth tipping up slyly.

I repressed a shudder. "She gives me bad vibes."

"You're not the only one." Artimus joined us. "Odette is the Erinea of Superbia, but five times as powerful and cunning."

Superbia? That was Ramiel's realm.

"Nephalem—the product of fallen and demon matings —are common," Artimus continued. "They tend to have some fallen characteristics. Maybe wings, or strong allure. They usually have celestial physical features, but it's rare for the offspring of a fallen and a demon to be born as a conji. Odette is one of a kind."

"She had fallen and demon parents?"

"Yes. Which makes her a nephalem. But there must have been a powerful conji in the demon side of her bloodline. Zepar should be third-generation fallen, but his fallen aspect is as strong as second-generation."

"How?"

"The consensus is that his mother's powerful conji nature allowed the fallen aspect to dominate."

So Artimus had known who Zepar's mother was.

"Wait, so second-generation fallen usually only come from two fallen mating?"

"Yes. But there aren't many female fallen so the second-generation fallen are rare."

"Did you know Ramiel was Zepar's father?"

"I suspected."

Odette stroked her son's arm and then slipped from the room. Zepar's shoulders slumped a little, and for some reason my heart went out to him. I'd been desperate for a mother all my life, but that didn't mean having a mother was always a good thing.

From the look on Zepar's face, he would have happily done without interacting with his.

"What happened to you?" Ignatius asked me.

"What? When?"

"When you...died." His throat bobbed. "What happened?"

"It's a long story, and kinda fantastical."

"As fantastical as dying and coming back to life?" Artimus said dryly.

I smiled wryly. "Point taken."

"You'll stay with me at the Court of Flame when we return," Ignatius said. "You can tell me everything then."

I glanced at Artimus, thinking he might argue with that plan, but even though his expression was stiff, he didn't say anything.

"The Seneschal knows you'll be safe with me," Ignatius said, reading my thoughts.

"Do I have something to worry about if I stay in my quarters?" I looked between them.

"Despite our best efforts, I have no doubt news about your...change will get out," Artimus said. "Not everyone will abide by the law and wait for the conclave to come to a decision about your fate. You're safer away from the keep until the conclave begins."

"You'll be safe at the Court of Flame," Ignatius said.

"And the Court of Ivory," Zepar added.

Ignatius looked like he was about to argue, but Artimus cut in.

"One night at the Court of Flame, one at Ivory, and the final night before the conclave you will be in my care. I will deliver you to the meeting once we are summoned."

The dukes agreed.

I looked across the room at my siblings. "I'll go to the Court of Flame and to the Court of Ivory, but not without my family. They're the only ones I trust completely to have my back."

"Very well," Ignatius said. "So be it."

Zepar looked over his shoulder at my brother and sisters, and I caught the slight downturn of his mouth.

"Problem?" My tone was hard. The spawn and I were a package deal, and if he had a problem with that, then I had a problem with him.

He shook his head. "That is not why I'm concerned. Your imp sibling and the zuni are sponsored by other courts. The Duke of Shadows and the Lady of Lunar may not be amenable to them attending our courts."

Crap, I didn't even think of that. Regardless, "I'm not leaving them. What if someone tries to use them to get to me? I can't risk them being hurt because of what I am."

"They will be safe," Dhuma said, joining us. "I will make sure of it."

He'd been silent and still for so long that I'd forgotten he was there, no small feat for such a large, imposing male. There was a cool conviction in his gaze, and I had no doubt he'd keep his word.

We were kindred.

The last of our kind on this side of the gates to the abyss.

I nodded. "Thank you."

The door opened and Ramiel appeared. "The portal to Morningstar is ready."

It was time to go home.

TWELVE

We made it to Morningstar a handful of hours before dawn. The portal Ramiel created opened directly into the courtyard of the keep, and Artimus ushered us across the cobbles, through the arch, up the wide stone stairs, and into the building.

Dhuma walked beside the Seneschal, his bulky form dwarfing Artimus's leaner, muscular frame.

The daimon was huge.

Had all the daimons been this big?

He glanced over his shoulder at me as if he could sense my thoughts, and I lifted my chin in acknowledgement. I had questions for him, but they'd have to wait till tomorrow. I wasn't sure whether it was the after-effects of dying and battling forces on the mystical death plane, or the fact that my abilities were shackled, but my body screamed for sleep.

The keep, silent and moonlit, smelled like home. My muscles unwound the deeper we went. It was safe here, and as if sensing it, my exhaustion grew. The urge to lean against one of the two males walking either side of me was almost too much to resist.

Ignatius and Zepar made me feel like the filling in an alpha-roll. Bad thoughts scrolled through my tired mind but vanished when Keelan cried out in pain from behind us.

"Keelan?" I spun, searching for him.

Hrath had his arm around my brother's waist to brace him on the trek. But they'd come to a standstill. Keelan stood, chin tucked in, hand curled into a fist. He was hurting.

"Let me carry you," Hrath said.

"No," Keelan bit out. "I can do this."

"And undo all the healing?" Tristeene pointed out. "Stop being a stubborn ass and take the help."

He snorted mist from his nostrils, clearly agitated.

"Please." Veena took his hand and peered up at him with her huge dark eyes. "Keelan, I want you to get better."

He snorted again but this time in resignation. He was no fool. He knew he wasn't in good shape. "I will accept your help, Hrath."

Hrath swung Keelan into a fireman's lift and set off after Artimus.

We reached the chamber that housed the portals to the other courts and Ignatius and Zepar slowed their pace.

This was their stop. I gravitated toward Ignatius instinctively, not wanting him to leave.

The corner of his mouth lifted, and his ember gaze settled on me like a warm caress. "We won't be separated for long." For some reason it felt like more than a promise. It felt like an inevitable outcome. "I'll send Flint for you at midday."

Midday...the hottest time at the Court of Flame. My gaze dropped to the cuffs on my wrists. "Will I be able to stand the heat?"

"The cuffs mute your abilities, not your full nature," Zepar said, answering for him.

I glanced across at the fallen. "Good to know."

"Sleep well, *Qalbi*." Ignatius made to step away, but I grabbed his hand, curling my fingers around his and giving in to that overwhelming need to be close to him.

I scanned the golden planes of his face. "What does that mean?"

The corners of his mouth dimpled, and he leaned in and brushed his lips across my forehead in a tender gesture that made my chest constrict. Fuck, I didn't want him to go. What was this feeling deep in my chest? This tug? This need to be close to him.

I breathed him in, biting back a whimper as he pulled away. He tore his gaze from mine. "I will meet you back at court, Hrath." And with a final lingering look my way, he stepped through the portal into the Court of Flame.

I turned away and caught the look of longing on Zepar's face, but it was gone in a blink, replaced by a cool, impassive mask. "I will send for you in a day's time."

He strode away without a backward glance and vanished through the Court of Ivory portal.

"Someone's jealous," Mallini whispered.

Zepar was a contradiction I wasn't sure I had the energy to figure out. "Let's go. I'm fucking knackered."

"You spent three hours dead," Mallini pointed out. "How tired can you be?"

"You have no idea."

"Can we please move now," Keelan said from his position slung over Hrath's shoulder.

"I don't think Keelan's enjoying the view," Gus chuckled as we got moving again.

"I know someone who would," Mallini said, shooting Tristeene a sly look that the succubus deliberately ignored.

I guess I wasn't the only one who'd noticed the dynamic between the sylph and my sister.

Nugen greeted us at the spawn quarters. He ushered Hrath and Keelan inside, but when his attention zeroed in on Dhuma, his eyes grew round.

"This is Dhuma," Artimus said. "He'll be staying with us."

"Not here he won't." Nugen crossed his arms, recovering his composure. "No room."

"I will stay close to Nyx," Dhuma said firmly.

Nugen glared at him, then at Artimus. "What is this? Who is this male?"

It was Dhuma who answered. "I'm a daimon and I choose to provide protection to Nyx, Blood of Knightwood."

Knightwood. Was that the name of Soreena's bloodline?

"And who the feck is that?" Nugen demanded.

Wait, he could understand Dhuma? Of course he could. We were in Morningstar now. Although most inhabitants of Morningstar spoke and understood both mortal tongue and demon tongue, this place was also saturated in an enchantment that allowed the inhabitants to understand each other no matter what language they spoke.

While here, Dhuma would be able to communicate freely with everyone.

"I am Dhuma, consort to the daimon queen Soreena Knightwood, sworn to protect her bloodline." He glanced at me. "Which is now you."

Nugen paled. "Daimon queen..." His gaze flicked to me and grew wide again.

"Long story. Not for tonight."

"You'll prepare a room for him," Artimus said. It wasn't a request. "And then you and I will speak."

Nugen dragged a hand down his weary face. "Fine, but I need ta know everything. These spawn are in my charge until the trials are over. If something's changed"—his gaze flicked to me again—"then I need ta know."

He ushered the rest of us into the hallway and everyone trailed off toward their rooms.

"You, follow me," Nugen said to Dhuma.

Dhuma ignored him and focused his attention on me. "You have questions, and I will answer them when you are ready."

"Thank you."

He inclined his head and finally followed Nugen down the hall to the room at the far end.

"Are you all right?" Artimus asked.

"I'm alive and that'll have to do for now."

"You'll be safe with the dukes, and I'm sure Dhuma will be sleeping with one eye open."

"And you? What will you do? Someone tried to kill you, Arty. I doubt it was Velarin. What would he have to gain from your death? And he couldn't have known we were *all* coming. I think he only found out once we got to the fortress."

"His spies..."

"Yes. We thought he wanted us all dead so there'd be no Satan to curb his mad rule but that doesn't fit any longer."

"I know."

"So the fact remains that Velarin expected you to come alone, and he had no reason to kill you. Nothing to gain."

"The only person who knew the real deal was Erinea," Artimus said. "And she tried to prevent you all from coming with me." He looked thoughtful.

"You think *she* wanted you dead?" I gave him a skeptical look. "Makes no sense. Besides, she didn't have control over the portal, did she?"

"No." He sighed and reached forward to pluck at a tendril of hair brushing my cheek, rubbing it between his fingers before releasing it reluctantly. It was such an intimate gesture, done almost absently, but it left me with a twisted longing in my chest.

He smiled wryly, as if he could read my thoughts. "Leave this to me, Nyx. You need to get some rest."

So did he. There were dark smudges beneath his eyes, and his hair was tousled as if he'd been raking his fingers through it. The top buttons of his shirt were undone and there were spots of blood on the collar. My blood?

"I'm all right," he said softly.

I swallowed past the lump in my throat. "What will you do?"

"What I do best." His smile was thin and cunning. "Root out the truth from the lies."

THIRTEEN

My room was silent and empty when I entered. No sign of Sev or Chase. I stripped and stepped under the shower, ignoring the hollow of disappointment in my chest.

What had I hoped? That they'd be waiting for me with bated breath, desperate to know that I was all right? That Chase would bound up to me and headbutt my side in the way he does to reassure himself I'm okay? Or that Sev would lift me off my feet in a squeezy hug, then take me to bed and fuck away the horror of the past few hours?

Yep. That's exactly what I'd hoped for.

After all, Sev had alerted Zepar that something was wrong with me. I expected him to be here to greet me. If I didn't feel like I was about to pass out, I'd go looking for him. But Sev could take care of himself. He'd fed recently. He'd be okay, and he probably had Chase with him. Those two had developed a bond of their own. I had no doubt they'd look out for each other.

The bed called to me, promising blessed oblivion. I crawled naked under the sheets and closed my eyes.

A weight settled over me. Exhaustion pushing me down into the mattress.

Perfect.

A FIELD OF FLOWERS SWAYED, large yellow heads bobbing on the breeze as if saying hello. Spires and gleaming buildings peeked out from gaps in the mist on the horizon. Fresh, sweet air filled my lungs with the first bloom of spring and a promise of wonders to come.

This was a dream, but it wasn't my dream. I was certain of that fact the same way I knew I had five fingers on each hand. I was here because I'd been invited. So, I waited.

I didn't have to wait long.

"It's beautiful, isn't it?" Parlos joined me.

"This is your dream."

He smiled down at me. "It is. But you are very welcome here."

"You died..." My chest grew tight as the memory of his death filled my mind. "You saved us, and you died."

He sighed. "I died a long time ago, Nyx. And then I died again and again. Then I was offered a boon. A chance at a final life, one that would guide souls, and I took it. I served, and now...Now I can dream."

But he wasn't the only warden I'd lost. "What about Tiana?"

A nostalgic smile lifted the corners of his mouth. "I sense her from time to time. And sometimes our dreams cross paths and merge, but it has been a long time since we met."

Part of me understood and accepted what he was saying, but the other part, the small part that was tethered in my conscious world, was confused. "You died a few hours ago."

"Did I?"

"Yes. You died like...five or six hours ago."

"I die tomorrow, or maybe it was yesterday, or it could be a hundred years from now or a thousand years ago. Time isn't linear, Nyx. It's how we know things sometimes. How we feel that an event or action is wrong or right."

I studied his face, so open and free now. He looked...happy. "You knew...You knew as soon as I woke you that you'd die."

He shrugged. "I know many things. Too many things. It's been my curse forever. The curse of understanding that everything is relative. That what you call today is someone else's tomorrow and all your yesterdays are someone else's future."

His words made sense. They struck a chord inside me, resonating with truth. "You know what'll happen to me. You know what the conclave will decide."

His expression sobered. "I can see the outcomes. Several paths that lead to the same fate and a singular destiny."

Destiny... "My fate? My destiny?"

His smile fell. "If you *choose* to follow it."

"It's not good, is it?"

He shook his head.

"But I can choose? You just said all paths lead to the same fate."

He smiled enigmatically. "I did, didn't I?"

"So what the heck am I supposed to do?"

He smiled. "Forge your own path, Nyx. Forge your own."

A gust of wind blew my hair back and he looked up sharply. "It's time to go now."

Panic seized me. "No, wait. How the heck will I know if I'm forging my own path. Hey! How will I know?"

"When it hurts." The wind howled, trying to drown out his words. "When it feels like the powers that be are fighting against you." The world grew darker. "When it seems like it's all too hard. Then you'll know. You'll know..."

The dream slipped away, and I fell into another.

One of my own.

Remember what he said.

Remember it. Don't forget.

But memory was a fickle thing, and what was that? A fairground? I love fairgrounds.

Fourteen

SEV

The beautiful thing about being a nightmare is the ability to blend into the shadows. I use that ability now as I navigate the keep with Chase. The hound is huge but somehow manages to squeeze into the shadows with me, moving just as silently as I am despite his size and bulk.

Zinichi confirmed my message was delivered to Zepar, but the winged bastard hasn't replied. I have no way of knowing if he went to investigate, no way of knowing if Nyx is safe. But the turmoil in my chest is gone and I can only hope that means Nyx is all right.

Still, Chase and I couldn't bear sitting around and doing nothing. Impotence claws at my insides even at the thought.

I should be with her.

Protecting her.

But we can't do either of those things, so here we are. Spying. Creeping about the keep in the hope of finding information that might tell us what's happened to the woman who has my insides in knots. The woman who makes me want to live to be...more than I am.

I slip down corridors and up steps, using the night as a cloak. The scent in the air changes.

Erinyes.

I'm in their domain now.

Good, if anyone knows what's happened to the spawn, it will be the bitch Erinea.

There's a room up ahead and the door is ajar, spilling warm light onto the tiles in the hallway. Voices drift out to greet my ears.

I sidle closer, ears straining.

"What will you do?" This voice is male. Familiar.

"Whatever needs to be done," Erinea says.

Who is the bitch speaking to?

"Surely you have an idea," the male says. "Some idea how the conclave might vote."

"If I didn't know better, Loke, I would say you were overstepping your bounds."

Loke? The male from Tarrifel. Nyx knows him. She hasn't said so, but I've smelled him on her and seen the shift in her eyes when his name is mentioned.

There is history between them, but she doesn't want others to know.

"My bounds?" Loke's tone hardens. "And what would you know about my bounds, Erinea. I am the source's eyes and ears. I am her voice, and you will report to me just as Satan will."

Erinea's tone softens. "I meant no disrespect. I'm not sure what the conclave will decide."

Conclave? They're talking politics. This isn't about Nyx. I sigh and begin backing up.

"Nyx is Satan spawn," Loke says. "That must weigh heavily into your decision."

Glass clinks and liquid is poured.

"She's a higher daimon," Erinea says. "An abomination. Who knows how or why Satan sired her. For all we know she could be a ticking time bomb of mystical energy. It would explain why he sent her away. Why she grew up in the mortal realm. He must have believed she was a danger to us, but his death brought her back and now...Now we must deal with her."

For a moment the blood rushing in my head eclipses all sound. Higher daimon...Nyx? How can this be?

"You've woven a fine tale," Loke says dryly. "Some might be fooled into thinking you believe it."

"I do." Her tone hardens.

"No, you don't. You've been threatened by Nyx ever since she came here, haven't you?"

"Excuse me?" There's warning in her tone, but Loke ignores it.

I like this male.

"I have my eyes and ears too, Erinea," he says smoothly. "I know what you've done. I know what you've said."

"She is nothing to me."

Her tone reeks of lies.

"But she might be," Loke points out. "She might be your Satan and that frightens you, because although you may be able to manipulate the other spawn into allowing your continued rule, you know Nyx won't be so easily swayed. And now that she has the love of her siblings...now that they're unified, you feel your grasp on the reins slipping altogether."

Silence reigns for long seconds before Erinea speaks, her words tight and succinct.

"My duty is to the throne. To Morningstar and its citizens. I will serve whoever takes the seat. But I will not stand by and allow a threat to claim Satan's power."

There's another lengthy silence. A third voice breaks it, and my hackles rise.

"I see your point, Erinea," Umbrane says. "There is an abundance of power in Satan's seat, and we cannot allow it to go to a higher daimon."

That bastard. Of course he wants Nyx gone. She shamed him by freeing me. Umbrane does not like to lose.

"There is nothing in the contracts that discriminate against higher daimon blood," Loke says.

"Because there was no need to add anything," Umbrane says. "Fallen should not be able to procreate with daimons. There was no need to think one would ever be vying for Satan's seat. She should not exist, which is another reason to get rid of her."

"I see," Loke says. "Well, you may air your thoughts at the conclave." The scrape of a chair. "I must report to the source."

"Yes, please do," Umbrane says. "But may I remind you that the source's influence extends only to the fair execution of the contracts. Which, from what I've been informed, have now been whittled down from three to one. The source can ensure that the triumphant spawn takes the seat, but she has no jurisdiction over the matter of whether an abomination be permitted to live."

There's a beat of silence. "I'll be sure to point that out to her, and to inform her exactly who the reminder came from."

Bootfalls approach the door and I slip away, deeper into the shadows.

A figure emerges, tall with dark cropped hair and angry eyes. He strides down the corridor but slows as he passes my pocket of shadow.

I tense. He can't see me. He can't possibly sense me.

But his next words tell me I'm wrong. "If you want to help her, then follow me, but stay out of sight."

He continues past me and Chase chuffs softly.

I look down at him, unsure.

He meets my gaze steadily, then turns and pads after the source's lackey.

I follow quickly, lending Chase my shadows. If the hound trusts this male, then so will I.

Fifteen

ORINA

The air smells odd here. Spicy and edible, but it pricks against my skin, leaving an almost uncomfortable sensation.

I never thought I'd take the shooting star to Morningstar territory. My kind steer clear of this place, but that note Nyx sent...

It doesn't smell like her.

It's her writing, but for all I know she may have written it under duress. Not to mention it tells me zero about why she's here.

Don't worry about me, I'll be back as soon as I can.

That's it.

Nyx can take care of herself, but that note leaves a lot to be desired. It raises way too many questions, and with the situation in Morningstar at present, I can't help but wonder if my bestie has gotten herself involved in something she shouldn't.

I need to find her and speak to her in person, and there's only one person who might know where she is.

Sin.

I've never met the demon, but Nyx trusts him, and that's enough for me. Problem is, I have no clue where his workshop is.

Demons skirt me, watching with wary eyes and ignoring me when I attempt to speak to them to ask for directions. I know they can understand. Part of the Accords are dedicated to the language here being universal. Something mystical in the air that allows all residents to understand each other.

But no one stops to speak to me. It's almost as if they're afraid of me.

Fuck it. I'll have to find the place myself. Nyx said it was close to the station. A workshop.

I scan the awnings, the stalls, the small, tightly packed buildings, looking for a sign that screams workshop.

And there it is.

Bingo. I head under the blue awning and shove at the door, but it doesn't budge. Locked.

Shit.

"Looking for someone?"

I spin to find thin air.

"Down here."

The imp stares up at me with curious hazel eyes. "You're not one of his regulars."

"You know where Sin is?"

"Nope. But he asked me to keep an eye on his place while he's gone."

"Fuck."

The imp crosses his arms and tips his head to the side. "Sin's not the only one with connections. Maybe I can help?"

"I doubt it."

"Try me."

"I'm looking for a woman."

"Aren't we all." His gaze is a little too leary for my liking.

I arch a brow. "Not interested."

"*Pfft*, you don't know what you're missing, but whatever, you're not my type anyway. Too tall."

I bite back a smile because I'm far from tall, but in comparison to him I'm a giant. "My friend's a demon blood. Her name's Nyx, and it's been almost two weeks since she came here."

His brows shoot up. "The demon blood who isn't a demon blood."

"What?"

"Dark hair, kinda scary, has a beast with her?"

"Yeah, that's her. You know where she is?"

He snorts. "You say you two are friends?"

I don't like his smug tone. "Best friends."

His eyes narrow. "And you didn't know she was a Nephilim?"

"What?" I stare at him, dumbfounded. "Bullshit."

"Oh, no. It's true."

"And how the fuck would you know?"

"Because I was here when the mark found her."

"What mark?"

"The Satan spawn mark."

Ice fills my veins. "Satan spawn... Nyx is Satan spawn?"

"That she is, and from what I've heard she's caused quite a stir at the keep. After the trials that killed the Erinyes male and—"

"Trials? What trials?"

He smirks. "Oh no. It doesn't work that way. You want to know more, you're gonna have to pay."

My scalp tightens as his gaze sweeps over me, then zeroes in on my silver locks.

"What do you want?"

He grins. "Your hair. I want your hair."

Nyx is in trouble. My gut was right. They're pitting the spawn against each other in insane live-or-die trials, and my friend, despite the fact that she's Nephilim, doesn't have the power that her siblings have.

I take a seat on the shooting star and move to flip my hair over my shoulder but skim the shorn edges of a blunt shoulder-length bob.

My throat tightens.

It's just hair, for fucksake.

But damn, I loved my hair.

That fucking imp.

The train begins to move, and soon the world outside is whizzing by as we cross the bridge back to the mortal side. I'm leaving, but I'll be back.

I've got to get into the keep and see Nyx. I've got to make sure she's safe, unhurt. Alive. But there's no way I can go alone. There are protocols that come with the Accords. You can't just walk into the keep. There are barriers. Creatures keeping the uninvited out. I've heard about the Eyes that man the perimeter of Satan's domain. Lethal demonic entities that can kill with a glance.

If I'm going to get in, then I'll need an official invitation. Luckily for me, working with the Order means I have access to the authorities that may be able to obtain one for me.

Now all I need to do is convince them to do so.

Sixteen

NYX

I woke to Sev's scent and his warm breath on my nape. Chase stared at me from the side of my bed, his hazel eyes gleaming in the predawn light. He chuffed softly and nudged my hand with his nose.

"Hey..." I lifted my hand to invite him closer and he dropped his chin on the mattress so I could rub his head. "Did you miss me." I turned my head slightly to include Sev in the question.

"What happened to you?" Sev asked, his tone gruff.

"I died."

He sucked in a breath and held me tighter. "You've changed, haven't you? You're higher daimon."

"Wow, news travels fast."

"I can feel power but it's far away."

I stopped stroking Chase and held up my wrist. "Power blockers."

"Tell me everything."

I rolled onto my back and settled against the pillows

before filling them both in on everything that had happened since we left for Libidine.

Sev listened without interruption but Chase chuffed a few times, the timbre indicating either distress, anger, or acting as a prompt to continue.

Sev was silent once I was done, his expression thoughtful and tense.

"Well? Say something." I reached up to tuck a tendril of his silver hair behind his ear.

His silver eyes darkened. "You're in danger."

"Tell me something I don't know."

"No. This is serious, Nyx. Erinea wants you dead and Umbrane's on board. That's two votes for your demise already."

"But I'll have three in favor of keeping me alive with Merihem, Ignatius, and Zepar."

"Your sponsors won't get a vote and neither will Artimus. They'll be bringing on board neutral voters. Lady Minera is one, and a couple of lords who've been angling for favor. The princes get the final say, but they're obligated to take all votes into account."

So not so neutral, then. "How do you know all this?"

"Loke told me."

"You spoke to Loke?"

"Yes." He studied me for several beats. "He told me he knows you, that he wants to help you, but his hands are tied, so I've offered to be his eyes and ears leading up to the conclave. To find out which way the conclave members will vote."

Merihem may have agreed to keep an open mind but that meant listening to Erinea too. What if the princes were swayed to Erinea's way of thinking? And who knew what the lords would do. And Lady Minera was a stranger to me. If too many of them sided with Erinea, then the princes would be under pressure. Merihem's open mind would be made up against me.

"You have to leave," Sev said. "The odds aren't in your favor. Leave now while you still can. Once you're in the mortal realm, they can't touch you."

But he was forgetting one thing. Something everyone had forgotten when we'd discussed my escape earlier. Something I'd deliberately neglected to remind them because I didn't want to take away their hope. "I can't leave Morningstar. None of the spawn can. Not until the trials are over and a Satan is chosen. The mark they put on us may have vanished, but whatever it did to us makes it impossible for us to leave Morningstar."

Sev propped himself up on his elbow and looked down at me. "I know. But that's no longer the case for you. You died, and when you died, so did that enchantment."

I could leave? I stared up at him, hope blooming in my chest. But I locked it down. Running wasn't an option. "I won't do it, Sev."

In the short time I'd known Sev, I'd seen him face torture and almost death. I'd seen into his heart, into the wounds that Umbrane had inflicted, but I'd never seen him cower, I'd never seen him afraid.

But he was afraid now. Not for himself but for me.

A vise gripped my lungs. "I can't run, Sev. I won't. Not until there's no other choice."

He made a ragged sound of exasperation. "It might be too late then."

I reached up to stroke his cheek. "This is bigger than me. There are forces out there that want to control my siblings, that want my father's power. I can't run away from that, not if there's a chance that I can fight it. I'm staying, and I'll fight as long as I can."

He gripped my hand tight, his silver eyes blazing against

his Aegean skin. "If they take you from me, I'll burn everything down. Everything and everyone. There won't be *anyone* left to save, do you understand?"

I understood him all right. I believed him too. But I couldn't let him become that person. I needed him to be more.

I curled my fingers around his. "No."

His jaw ticked. "You don't get to decide that. You won't be here to stop me. If you die, then they all die. Period."

"If I die, they're all that's left of me. They're a part of me. My blood. My family. If anything happens to me, I need you to watch over them. Because while you have them, you have me." He growled and tried to pull away from me, but I held on. "Promise me."

"Damn you, Nyx."

I cupped his face and pulled him down to press my lips to his, speaking against them. "Please." My voice trembled because despite my bravado, despite everything I'd said back in Libidine while trapped in that circle, beneath my cocky comebacks and confidence was real fear that this time I might not make it. Because if I left it too late, if I miscalculated and they chose to put me down, they'd do it in a way that would be irreversible. "Please, Sev. I need this from you."

His sigh warmed my lips. "I'll do what you ask if you promise me something."

"What?"

He spoke rapidly against my mouth, his breath sweet, his tone intense. "If I find out the vote won't be in your favor, you'll run. You'll leave your family in my care, and you'll run."

Chase whined softly, urging me to agree.

I swallowed the lump in my throat. "I promise."

He swallowed my exhale, then pressed his forehead to mine, breaking lip contact. "Then I promise too."

THE TEMPTATION TO hide in bed with Sev till it was time to go to the Court of Flame was a weight pushing me into the mattress. I made to get up, but Sev pulled me back against his taut body.

Chase padded to the door and flipped the handle to let himself out. It closed with a thud behind him. Did these two have some kind of unspoken understanding?

Sev kissed my neck, then dragged his lip down to my collarbones, leaving a delicious ache in their wake.

I groaned softly and sank my fingers into his silken silver hair. "I don't have time."

"You need this," he said. "I need this."

I couldn't argue with that. Didn't want to.

I gave in. Surrendering to heated kisses and caresses, reveling in the friction of his calloused hands roaming over my sensitized skin and the slide and dip of his thick tail as it entered me.

I pushed my hips up, opening my legs wide to give him full access to my hot, greedy core.

He knelt over me, braced above me, his mouth parted, eyes dark with arousal as he watched his tail push in and out of me.

I looked down between us, moaning at the sight. Fuck, this was hot. He cupped my throat, holding me down before claiming my nipple with his mouth.

My mind shut down, sensation taking over as I bucked and moaned beneath him, the tide of arousal rising until it was choking me. He released my nipple with a pop and pressed his mouth to my jugular.

"Yes."

The pain was sharp but quickly overshadowed by the tight, sweet ache of the building orgasm between my thighs.

He drank deep and my head reeled. "Your cock...Sev, fuck me."

His tail withdrew and his hands found my thighs, bracing before he entered me, thick, hard, but wet with slick.

He swallowed my cry with his coppery mouth. We kissed, angry, hungry, desperate, our tongues wrestling for dominance as our bodies moved together until we were riding the wave of a powerful orgasm, mouths sealed together, ragged breath locked in our throats.

We lay, limbs tangled, bodies slick with sweat, breathing hard and heavy, and a feeling swelled inside me. Three words I'd been holding back teased my lips, desperate to be spoken.

Sev took my hand and laced his fingers through mine. "I know what that feeling is now...That pain in my chest."

My breathing grew shallower. "What?"

"Look at me."

I turned my head and locked gazes with him, seeing the words in that look, seeing my feelings echoed there.

"I've fallen in love with you," he said. "I'm not telling you because I expect anything in return, I just need you to know that I—"

I kissed him hard on the mouth, lingering, savoring, absorbing his words and allowing mine to bubble to the surface. "I love you too, Sev. I fucking do."

And that was the truth of it. My cold, impregnable heart had been thawed, and now...Now there was no turning back.

Seventeen

ARTIMUS

Erinea pours herbal tea into her cup and peers up at me from beneath her eyelashes. It's a coquettish look and I'd usually play along, but I'm not in the mood to pander to her this morning.

This morning I want answers, and the only way to get those is to demand them. To show her my indignant rage and remind her why Satan chose me as his right-hand man.

When I don't offer a compliment or ask her how her night was, she lowers her cup, a slight frown pinching her brow before she quickly smooths it away.

"Is something wrong?" she asks, her tone light and airy as if she doesn't really care but is merely being polite.

I sit back in my seat and tip my head to the side. "You're no fool, Erinea, you know exactly what's wrong. You went against my express wishes and attempted to keep the spawn away from the trip to Libidine."

"And don't you wish I'd succeeded now?" She sips her

tea, then purses her lips. "Your precious Nephilim spawn's true identity would have remained a secret."

"And I'd be dead."

She stares at me blankly. "What?"

Her confusion is genuine. I sigh. She isn't the culprit, then. "The portal was tampered with, and we were all thrown into the old forest. We almost died."

She drops her cup into her saucer with a rattle. "Oh earth. *All* the spawn...We would have been left without an heir."

"Yes. Satan's seat and the power would have been lost to us."

"But how? The portals are set on the other side, and nobody there knew you were coming with the spawn." Her eyes widen. "Oh..."

Yes, she's come to the same conclusion as Nyx and me. "I believe someone wants *me* dead."

Her eyes harden. "That won't do. That won't do at all."

Fucking hell, she puts on a good show about caring. But then, right now, she sees me as her property. Her male. And an attack on me is an attack on her.

I pick imaginary lint off my cuff. "I'll root out the bastard responsible, don't worry."

"You're safe at Morningstar. No one would dare attack you here. But it seems that despite my efforts we have spies here at Morningstar." She says the word *spies* as if she's referring to rats. "I'll inform the Erinyes guard to be watchful of any suspicious activity. We have our eyes and ears too. If this spy is still among us, then I assure you will find him...or her." She arches a brow. "Speaking of which, how is the daimon blood taking the news of her new status?"

It takes a moment for me to realize she's referring to

Nyx. "She's shocked, as is to be expected. Dying and coming back to life can't be easy."

She sits forward in her seat. "Did she tell you what it was like?"

"Death?" I shrug. "We haven't spoken about it, but then there hasn't been an opportunity to do so."

"Yes, I heard the princes were quick to mute her abilities." She refills her cup. "It's a shame," she says archly. "She was a promising candidate."

Like she gives a fuck about that. "She still is. Her fate hasn't been decided yet."

She rolls her eyes. "Oh, come now, Artimus, it's obvious what the conclave will decide. She's an abomination. We allowed her to live once when we thought she was Nephilim, when we sensed no power in her, but now that death has released her true nature we cannot be so forgiving."

It takes everything I have not to curl my lip or draw my hands into fists. It takes every ounce of self-control to remain relaxed and flippant. "I suppose you have a point. But execution could simply activate more power. As a high daimon she has three lives."

The princes intimated that they might have a way to prevent this from happening, but I need to know more. I've learned enough in my time fucking Erinea that the bitch likes to brag.

Sure enough, her lips curve in a sly smile. "I forget how little you know of the time before."

I'm momentarily thrown. What has the time before got to do with a weapon to kill a daimon? But I recover quickly and throw back a mini bomb of my own. "You mean the truth behind the lies the princes fed us about the Chaos War?"

Her face blanches. "What?"

Ah, the satisfaction. "You forget I was Satan's confidant." Let her think he told me the truth. She doesn't have to know how I came about the knowledge. "And I'm not the only one who knows the truth. The spawn have come to learn of it also."

She sucks in a sharp breath. "Do the princes know this?"

"Yes."

She drains her cup and refills it, as if the herbal concoction will soothe her nerves. "This cannot become common knowledge."

"Why? Because it makes the fallen look like assholes?"

"This isn't about appearances. This is about possible consequences."

My scalp pricks. "What do you mean?"

Her eyes narrow. "What do you know about...the truth."

I relay what Nyx has told me and she listens intently.

"And you still don't understand?" She shakes her head with a wry smile. "Opening the pit resulted in chaos that almost lost us our new home. Do you think Lucifer would have gone against the daimons' advice and opened the doorway if he didn't believe that it was worth the potential risk?"

I'm intrigued. The information Ignatius gave Nyx didn't cover this part, only that Lucifer believed, in his hubris, that he could control whatever horror lay beyond. But what Erinea is implying makes more sense—a tangible reason to take the risk.

"What did he expect to find?"

"The high daimon called it the prism. An artifact that could open doorways into other realities. They used it to get to this world, but it was left behind when they ran from the beasts they unwittingly let into their world."

The beasts and the virus. "Why would Lucifer want it?"

She sits back in her seat. "I wonder sometimes how close you really were to Satan."

"And I wonder how you know all this."

"I have my sources." She toys with her cup handle, and for a moment I think she won't answer my previous question, but she surprises me.

"The fallen were forced out of their home. Locked out. I don't know why. It's something that isn't even whispered about, but the prism could take them home."

"Wait...they didn't change the narrative just to trick the demons, they changed it to hide the truth from the second-generation fallen? They don't want anyone else going after it."

"Yes. The prism is a powerful relic, and the lure of that power could turn the head of someone who didn't witness the horror of the Chaos War first-hand. They couldn't risk anyone else trying to open the pit, so they rewrote history. Lucifer became a savior and the abyss a place filled with monsters. The existence of the pit was wiped from history and the daimons were painted as villains. Dangerous, lethal monsters." She sips her tea and gives me a close-lipped smile. "All this is why I know how the princes will vote on your little aberrant Satan spawn."

My hackles rise but I keep my tone neutral, ignoring her jibe about Nyx being mine. "Oh?"

"The kind of power she has, the kind she *could* have if she takes the seat, could be used against us. Against the world we've built here. A new, safe world for the fallen to thrive in. A world they've literally rewritten history to keep safe."

Panic blooms in my chest, hot and urgent, but I paint a smile on my lips. "The princes will make the right choice, I'm sure. But none of this explains how they intend to stop her from coming back to life if they decide to execute."

She side-eyes me and refills her cup. "Firstly, not all high daimons seem to come back after death."

"What do you mean?"

"Some just...don't. And in other cases, if a body is broken thoroughly enough, there is nothing to come back to. It's the tactic that was employed in the Chaos War against the infected. The daimons were not only killed but torn to shreds. The fallen had been working on a weapon but it wasn't ready when the pit opened."

"They were working on a weapon *before* the infection hit?"

She snorts delicately. "Do you think for one moment the fallen would have accepted living in a world where they didn't hold the most power?"

"No...I suppose not."

"It was completed *after* the Chaos War, and tested..." She looks away and I catch a hint of distaste on her face.

"What do you mean tested?"

"Not all daimons died in the abyss. Not all remained trapped."

Oh earth. "They experimented on daimons?"

She presses her lips together. "They did what they needed to do to prepare."

"For what?"

She leans forward. "The daimons in the abyss are sick. Infected. If those wards ever fall..."

Then we'd have infected daimons who'd grow more powerful with each death on our hands. "I see."

I reach for a cup and take some tea, although it'll take more than herbs to settle my nerves now.

Nyx is in even more danger than I anticipated.

It's time to set up an exit strategy.

Eighteen

NYX

Sev's red-rimmed eyes spoke of way too many hours without sleep. He'd spent the past day worrying about me. He needed his rest. I kissed him and told him to sleep, that I'd wake him when I returned tomorrow morning.

His evening would be spent scouting, no doubt.

I had four hours until I went to the Court of Flame, and I'd commandeered Keelan's room for a meeting. He was still healing, so moving him around wasn't a good idea.

I sat on the bed beside him, my back propped against the headboard, legs stretched out in front of me. Veena sat cross-legged at the foot of the bed with Gus beside her. Tristeene and Mallini had pulled the chaise by the window closer to the bed. Dhuma stood by the door, arms crossed, as if guarding the entrance.

I'd invited him because I had questions. Best to get them answered with everyone here so that I didn't have to spend time relaying the information to my siblings later.

But first, I needed to fill them in on my death experience. They listened without interruption. It was strange talking about the wardens, about the in-between place that death had taken me to. A place ravaged by the effects of the sickness.

"Two of them died to save you," Dhuma said. "That matters."

Died...something about that concept. Something important...The thought skated the edge of my consciousness but slipped away before I could grasp it.

I blinked and focused on Dhuma. "You've been there, haven't you?"

He nodded. "Twice. There was no sickness back then."

"Which warden did you choose?"

"Dorian," he said.

That had to be the third guy. "Leaf dude?"

He made a sound of affirmation.

"Why him?"

"It felt right. Just as it felt right for you to pick three wardens," Dhuma said.

"Bit greedy, if you ask me," Mallini drawled, but the smile on her face told me she was teasing.

I winked at her.

"But why?" Gus said. "Why does it matter who you choose?"

"It does not always matter," Dhuma replied.

I waited for him to elaborate but he was silent.

I arched a brow. "That's it?"

The corner of his mouth dimpled in a suppressed smile. "For now."

"Fine, but I have other questions. You said I shared Soreena's blood. How can you be so sure about that?"

"I can read auras. Demon and fallen and everything in between, but a daimon aura is different. Bloodlines share characteristics, and yours shares Knightwood characteristics."

"Like a mystical familial fingerprint?" Gus asked.

Dhuma inclined his head.

"You thought she was Soreena reborn," Veena said softly. "It must have been painful when you realized she wasn't."

His throat bobbed. "She is not my mate, but she is a connection to her, and I will die to preserve that."

"What was she like?" The question fell from my lips before I could think. "Shit, I'm sorry, I don't mean to pry."

"Don't be sorry." He gave me half a smile. "It's been too long since someone asked about her. Since I spoke of her. Soreena was fierce. Unflinching in the face of adversity and protective of her loved ones and her people." He sighed. "When she loved, she did so with every fiber of her being. She died protecting us all."

"How?" Mallini asked.

"Mallini!" Tristeene chided.

"No. It's all right," Dhuma said. "I want people to know what she did. I want them to understand that she was a hero."

"Tell us," Veena said.

He smiled but his eyes were sad. "The battle against the infected waged for days. We were thin on the ground. The marasguard were all but wiped out."

"Marasguard?" Keelan asked.

"Nightmares." I shot him a quick smile. "The nightmares used to be called maras. They're a breed of morpheses and the queen's personal guard. They worked for Dhuma."

Dhuma frowned. "How could you know this?"

"I have a maras in my bed right now. Sev is my... He's mine."

"Umbrane keeps them," Veena said. "He has them locked in stables and he treats them badly."

Dhuma's jaw clenched. "Umbrane...The weasel."

Keelan snorted. "I like that. Weasel. It suits him."

"Maras should not be treated thus." Dhuma's nostrils flared. "They are noble blood. This is wrong."

"Tell that to Umbrane," Mallini said. Her eyes lit up. "Yes, you should totally pay him a visit. I bet he'd shit himself."

Gus and Keelan chuckled and Tristeene smiled, but Veena was silent and pensive.

"Veena?" I nudged her knee with my foot.

"Don't go to see him," she said to Dhuma. "You might be large, but he has...creatures." Her eyes were haunted with shadows of pain.

My chest tightened. "He won't hurt you ever again, Veena."

She gave me a small, watery smile. "He's my sponsor."

"Only if you allow him to be. The contracts putting us in danger are gone. As long as we look out for each other, we can all get through this. No one can touch you. We won't let them."

"He hurt you?" Dhuma's tone was deceptively calm.

Veena tucked in her chin so that her hair fell over her shoulders to shield her face.

Dhuma's jaw ticked. "He is a coward and one day soon he will receive a coward's death."

Silence reigned for long minutes and then Veena broke it. "You were saying how the daimon queen died..."

Dhuma made a soft huffing sound and then crossed the room to look out the window. "I was not there. I was the last of her mates. The others...The others perished. She left me behind and slipped out into the night. I would have sensed it. Gone after her had she not drugged me deeply. She was protecting me, I understand this. She knew I was living my final life. But I should have been with her when Lucifer sealed the gate. I should have been by her side, lending my power to the allure that helped to place a seal in the tear in the fabric of reality."

"Wait...Soreena was there?" Mallini asked.

"Yes. Beelzebub relayed what happened to me. Lucifer knew he would be sacrificing his light to seal the pit. He knew it would end him, but he could not do it alone. He needed Soreena's power."

"Why her?"

"Her ancestor was the one to close the gate in the first place. Her power was unique. Beelzebub and his battalion fought to clear the way so that Lucifer and Soreena could close the gate to the pit. He told me that she stood behind Lucifer, her hands on his shoulders, when his light exploded from him." He looked toward us. "It obliterated her and most of Beelzebub's battalion."

"And they left her out of the story," Keelan said gruffly. "Lucifer took the glory."

"He didn't take it," Gus said bitterly. "It was given to him by the princes."

"All to save face," Mallini sneered.

Dhuma grunted. "No. Not to save face. To protect this world."

"What do you mean?" Gus asked.

"The Chaos War began because of a powerful relic trapped in the pit. It's what Lucifer wanted, and it almost resulted in the destruction of this world. It's why those of us who survived vowed not to reveal the truth. To allow history to be rewritten. We cannot risk the relic being found, and the fewer creatures that know about it, the less chance there is of some fool attempting to reopen the pit."

"Is that even possible?" Mallini asked. "To reopen it?"

I snort-laughed. "Where there's a will, there's a way."

"I don't care about any of that," Veena said. "All I care

about is Nyx." She crawled across the bed and into my lap. "I just want this conclave to be over and these to come off." She tugged on my shackles. "I want to get on with the last two trials and be done with all of this."

I hugged her and propped my chin on her head. "Me too. Me too."

There was a knock at the door and Zinichi popped her head in. "Nyx, this message came for you." She hurried over and handed me an envelope with my name on it.

I ripped it open, aware of all eyes on me, and unfolded the slip of paper inside.

There were only three words on it.

The mirror awaits.

Loke wanted to see me.

NINETEEN

L oke greeted me on the other side of the mirror. "You got my message."

I gave him a cocky smile. "Bit risky, don't you think?"

"Worth the risk." He bridged the distance between us and pulled me into a hug. "Fucking hell, when I heard what happened..."

I nestled against him, wrapping my arms around him and allowing him to hold me, just hold me. "I'm fine." And being here, like this, in his arms, made everything seem better. I rubbed my cheek against his cotton shirt, reveling in the heat of his body seeping through it. "I'm okay."

"Of course you are," he said softly. "Nothing surprises me when it comes to you. You died and came back. No big deal," he said dryly.

I pulled away, putting just enough distance between us so that I could look up at him and try not to focus on how tantalizingly close his mouth was to mine. "Did the source know what I was?"

His words came out on a sigh. "I don't know. I tried to

contact her, but she hasn't responded yet. I would assume she did, though."

Anger tightened my chest. "I don't like being a pawn, Loke, and that's how this is beginning to feel. Like your source is playing some game, with me as a centerpiece. I'm not up for this shit."

His jaw flexed. "I know. I wish I could do more." He broke away from me with an exasperated sigh. "I hate feeling useless. I hate not being able to help when you're in danger."

A frisson of fear skated up my spine. "I can handle myself."

"Erinea is out for your blood. She has Umbrane on her side already."

"No surprise there."

"You're in danger if you stay here."

"You want me to run?" I arched a brow. "After everything I've been through, everything I've found here, you want me to turn tail and run?"

He exhaled heavily. "I want you to live."

His words jogged something in the back of my mind. Something one of the wardens had said to me. "I died once before…"

Loke's head whipped up and his gaze locked with mine. "What?"

"The wardens told me this was my second death."

He dropped his gaze. "Interesting."

Something about the way he said that had alarm bells going off in my head. "I think I'd remember if I'd died before, right?"

"Possibly."

"Loke, why won't you look at me?"

His jaw ticked and an awful possibility bloomed in my mind. "The wardens were confused how I could have died before, but Parlos said...He said I was a shared soul, which means...The first time I must have gone to Tarrifel."

"Nyx—"

"You know, don't you? You know I died because you were there. You're *from* Tarrifel."

"I can't talk about this," he said tightly.

"Fuck you and all your restrictions." I glared at him, eyes burning with indignation as I recalled the case we worked on together all those months ago. "It was that night, wasn't it? The night I saved Jenny from Charon. I can't remember what happened after he stabbed me. I woke up in the hospital, but I must have died." Fuck. "Did I meet the source?"

He gritted his teeth.

"Talk to me, dammit!"

He shook his head stiffly, as if it was an effort to do so. "My fault. Intervening in your life made it...caused..." He made a sound of exasperation. "Was too soon."

"What was too soon? My death? My death was too soon?"

He just stared at me, his eyes screaming yes.

My mind whirred. "I wasn't meant to die that first time."

"I don't know for sure."

But it made sense. "I didn't get any powers the first time I died, but something changed. Something that allowed Dhuma to see me for what I was."

"There are many paths, Nyx," Loke said.

His words nudged a memory in my mind. I desperately tried to latch on to it, but it slipped away again.

Dammit.

"But all paths lead to the same fate and destiny," Loke continued.

His words felt hollow. Like a lie. "I don't believe that. I

don't believe that we're puppets in some kind of fucked-up show."

"Nyx—"

"No. I'm no one's pawn or plaything. *I* get to decide my fate. *I* get to decide my destiny, and if all paths lead to a shitty fate, then I'll make a new path." Indignant rage was a vise around my chest, and the unfurling possibilities of what I'd just said swelled against the restriction.

The air between us crackled with tension and my chest heaved. He matched my breaths and our gazes locked with a snick that reverberated through me.

"Nyx..." His tone was a ragged thing, and I knew what was coming.

I should stop it. Walk away now. But my body was in control, making the decision for me.

We collided in a kiss that knocked the sense from me. Every atom of my being focused on his mouth. On the firm pressure of his lips, his summer-day scent, and the calloused pads of his fingers where they gripped my jaw. I opened for him, taking the length of his tongue and stroking it with my own. This was hunger. This was gratification, and the only oxygen in the room was trapped between our lips. It lasted seconds, it lasted minutes. It went on forever and not long enough. But it was over too soon.

He tore his mouth from mine and shoved me away.

My heart thudded painfully and each breath hurt. I blinked back tears. "Fuck you, Loke. That was out of order."

He devoured me with a ravenous gaze that made me want to throw caution to the wind and risk a broken heart.

No. I wasn't going there with him. Couldn't open myself up to anything more with someone who couldn't be open with me. "Stop fucking looking at me like that."

He dropped his gaze. "I'm sorry. You should go. Ignatius will be waiting for you." He looked up and his gaze was composed, the fire hidden. "Sev and I will keep tabs on what happens here while you're gone, and I'm sure Artimus is preparing an exit strategy for you."

"I'm not running, Loke. Not until all hope is gone."

"I know," Loke said. He offered me a small smile that was probably meant to be reassuring, but the shadows in his eyes told me he didn't think it would be too long before hope left the building.

TWENTY

I entered the spawn quarters to the sound of hearty sobbing. The door to Veena's room was ajar. The crying was coming from there.

My heart shot into my throat. "Veena!" I rushed into her room to find her crouched on the floor with her arms around a small female with short dark hair and the black and silver tunic of the Morningstar staff.

Another zuni.

Veena looked up at me. "This is Yimi. We used to work together in the kitchens."

Yimi sniffed and peered up at me with red-rimmed eyes. "Oh...Oh, I should go. I should leave." She pulled away from Veena.

"No." Veena drew her back into a hug. "You need to stay and calm down."

Tristeene entered the room behind me carrying a tray laden with tea things. "This will help your nerves." She set the tray on the rug beside Veena and then joined them on the floor.

I felt like an idiot standing over them, so I lowered

myself onto the ground too. "What's happened? Why are you crying? Did someone hurt you?" I was so sick of the power play in this place. Of the little guy getting fucked over. "You tell us who and we'll sort it out."

She sniffed again and gave me a watery smile. "It cannot be fixed. It is now my fate."

Fate. I hated that word. "Only if you allow it to be?"

"No, Nyx, Yimi is right," Veena said. "This isn't something we can intervene in. It's ancient zuni law and exists outside of Morningstar rule."

"Okay, what is it?"

"Yimi's hand in marriage has been set," Veena said. "But she is in love with another. Her mother will not concede, and so Yimi will marry the zuni male chosen for her as is the way with our people."

"Wait...an arranged marriage?"

"It's more than that," Tristeene said. "Zuni are a matriarchal society. The head female in each household makes the decisions including who joins the family. Zuni are not permitted to form romantic attachments prior to them being mated."

"And the head matriarch chooses the mates?"

"Yes," Veena said. "It's always been the way and there is no escaping it."

"You could just say no."

"It's more than that," Tristeene said. "Once the promise has been given, only the matriarch may break it. If Yimi refuses to go through with the mating, then she will wither and die."

What the fuck? Had I just heard right? "So you're telling me that if Yimi refuses to marry the guy her mother's chosen, then *Yimi* will die?"

"Not straight away," Veena said. "But yes. She'll grow weak and sick and then she'll die."

"And her mother would allow that to happen?"

"She'd be considered a rotten branch in the family tree," Veena said softly. "Best to cut it off to allow the rest of the tree to flourish."

I shook my head. "I thought zuni were meant to be the nonviolent race. I guess you guys just get your kicks killing off your own."

Yimi made a keening sound and doubled over sobbing again.

Veena shot me a stern look that on her sweet face was too adorable not to make me smile, but I bit it back. "I'm sorry, Yimi. Maybe we could speak to your mother—"

"No!" She stared up at me in horror. "It would bring shame to my family."

I honestly didn't get it. "What can we do to help?"

"Nothing," Veena said. "Yimi just needed to vent."

"Drink this." Tristeene offered Yimi a cup of herbal tea.

Yimi sipped and sniffed and sipped some more.

"Well, it looks like you guys have this under control." I pushed to my feet. "I best get going. I need to pack an overnight bag."

"Say hi to Ignatius for me," Tristeene said with a sly smile.

I rolled my eyes. "It's not like that...yet." I dropped her a wink, and her soft laughter followed me out of the room.

CHASE LAY SPRAWLED across the floor beside my bed closest to Sev. Their snores filled the room. Looked like my hound had adjusted his sleeping patterns to match my nightmare.

A tender feeling filled my chest. These two...I wish I had a camera so I could take a picture of them, but a mental image would have to do.

I packed a bag with underwear, sleep tee, shorts, my toothbrush, and some deodorant. I didn't have any clothes suitable for the heat, but I was sure Ignatius would find me something to wear.

It was almost midday. Flint would be here to collect me any moment now. I climbed onto the bed, careful not to jog it too much, and tenderly brushed Sev's tousled silver hair off his forehead to drop a kiss on his temple.

"I love you. Sleep well."

I rounded the bed and knelt by Chase and kissed the top of his head. "Love you too. Look after Sev for me."

Chase's chest rumbled and he opened one eye to look at me, as if to say, *you got it, Nyx.*

The Court of Flame portal lit up. Flint appeared by the door and blinked to adjust his eyes to the gloom.

I held my finger to my lips, warning him not to make noise, then hurried over to him, grabbing my bag on the way.

The blue flames on his head dimmed and he held his hand out to me. I took it and together we stepped into the portal.

Excitement bubbled in my belly along with the indescribable sense that I was going home.

TWENTY-ONE

T he last time I stepped through this portal I'd had Keelan in tow and we'd come out in a short corridor leading to Ignatius's chambers. This time we materialized in an impressively large, high-ceilinged room that smelled of musk and jasmine.

Floor-to-ceiling windows lined one wall, allowing in enough sunlight to illuminate the space, but despite the sunshine the room remained pleasantly cool.

Flint stayed close by my side, and when I tried to let go of his hand, he held on for a moment as if reluctant to let go. I glanced down at him to find him staring at me with a strangely enraptured expression.

I arched a brow. "Can I have my hand back?"

His gaze dropped to our joined hands. "Oh." He released me quickly.

Male grunts and the clang of metal on metal filled the room as djinn and Minorax sparred on mats, some hand-to-hand, others using scimitar-type weapons. Huge humanoid figures made of stone and clay stood to one side of the room, glowing eyes fixed on the djinn on the mats. The golems, no doubt.

But the magnificent golems faded into the background as I caught sight of Ignatius. He was bare-chested, his golden torso glistening in the sunlight streaming in from the windows. His hair was damp with sweat, clinging to his cheekbones as he slashed, stabbed, whirled, and jabbed at his opponent—none other than Hrath. The two sparred like it was life and death. Like they meant it. Their blades flashing dangerously close to skin.

"Are those scimitars real?"

"Why yes," Flint said. "There is no sense in using fake weaponry."

Was he serious?

Yep, the earnest look on his face said he was. "It is if you don't want to get hurt sparring."

He frowned up at me in confusion. "If there is no risk of injury, then where would the incentive to do well come from?"

Damn, the sprite had a point. But it was hard to watch, hard to breathe, as the two males went head-to-head as if their lives depended on it. Hrath lunged, slicing the air with his scimitar. Ignatius evaded by throwing his body backwards out of the blade's path. A wild grin spread across his face, and Hrath matched it.

They looked manic as they fought. One moment Hrath was the aggressor and the next it was Ignatius, and on and on until my lungs ached, and my heart felt too large from watching this beautiful lethal dance.

It was impossible to say who had the upper hand, but then Hrath stole the edge. He moved so fast he was impossible to track, and the next moment he was behind Ignatius, his blade pressed to the efreet's neck.

Ignatius froze, his jaw tight.

"I win," Hrath said, matter-of-fact.

"You cheat," Ignatius drawled. "As usual."

"I use the abilities available to me."

Ignatius's eyes lit up like flame. "Is that so?"

Hrath let out a curse and dropped his blade, releasing Ignatius in the process. The duke spun and pressed his blade to the sylph's chest. "I win."

Hrath shook his head, tutting softly as he looked down at his blade. The metal was tinged red from where Ignatius had heated it using his ability.

"Who's cheating now?" Hrath asked.

"Simply using the abilities available to me," Ignatius threw back.

"Touché, brother, touché."

They stepped away from each other, chuckling amiably, and only then did Ignatius turn his golden gaze to meet mine. There was no surprise in its ember depths. He'd known I was here all along, and for some reason that made me all warm and gooey inside. A wholly new sensation.

I couldn't help but smile. "Epic skills, guys."

Ignatius and Hrath approached, bringing the sweet scent of the fight with them. Up close, the duke's presence was a questing aura pushing up against mine, both comforting and exhilarating.

I locked my knees to stop myself from getting closer and sniffing him. "So, did you have Flint bring me here so you could show off your skills?"

The corner of Hrath's mouth lifted. "Yes, Ignatius, why did you have the sprite bring Nyx here?"

Ignatius slow-blinked. "I didn't want to have to wait to see her, and I hoped she wouldn't want to wait to see me either?"

My pulse quickened at the candid answer, delivered so simply but with the hint of a question at the end, showing me that despite his confidence about our attraction, there was a vulnerable uncertainty there too.

"You're right." I did step closer then, tipping my chin up to skim my gaze over his delicious features, and inhaled deeply. "I wouldn't have wanted to miss that display of battle prowess for the world."

Ignatius grinned down at me, and my heart thudded hard against my ribs. He was beautiful. Even more so like this, all sweaty and hot from a fight. What would his skin taste like now? What would it feel like to press my naked body up against his hot, slick one? To join him in the shower and run my hands over the sculpted planes of his body and—

A nearby djinn cried out, yanking me from my thoughts.

I tore my gaze from his, but not before I caught the gleam in his eye that made me wonder if he knew exactly what I'd been thinking.

Across the room, a djinn lay on a training mat staring up at the Minorax who'd bested him. The Minorax raised his muscular arms in triumph, mist pluming from his nostrils in heavy puffs of excitement. One of the golems approached, its feet thumping on the ground ominously before it hit the training mat, but neither the djinn nor the Minorax seemed bothered.

"You spar with me now," the golem said to the Minorax.

The djinn rolled to his feet and exited the mat quickly, leaving the golem and the Minorax facing each other.

Hardly seemed fair. The golem was huge, his body impregnable. But I guess that was the point of the exercise.

The Minorax rolled his head on his neck and glared at the golem, but the golem stood impassive and unaffected by the stare.

The Minorax attacked, and the golem reacted by

stepping to the side and slamming a fist into the Minorax's back to send him sprawling.

"Shit, he's fast."

"They all are," Ignatius said. "Golems are a force to be reckoned with."

"But they can't be used in battle? Why's that?" Seemed like a waste to me.

"It would take too much conji power to keep them under control."

I glanced about the room. "I don't see any conji here."

"There is no need for conji when the golems are in training mode," Hrath said. "They have been activated and given instructions as to the parameters of their use. But in battle, those parameters need to be adjusted, and the golems must be given more autonomy to allow them to fight an unknown enemy."

"Hence the need for conji to hold the reins," Ignatius said.

Interesting. "What happens if the conji can't keep control?"

"Chaos," Hrath said.

"It's happened before?"

"Not here, but in our world."

Wait a second. "Are you saying the golems are a djinn construct?"

Ignatius shrugged a powerful shoulder. "There were no golems when we came to this world and there were no conji either."

"Whoa...Conji aren't demons?"

"They weren't originally," Ignatius said. "But generations of breeding with demons has diluted the bloodlines. There are only two pure bloodlines of conji now, and both are affiliated to the Court of Flame."

"To Libidine?"

"No, to me."

Behind us, the Minorax was getting his ass handed to him by the golem who continued to bark instructions while kicking the demon's butt and informing him where he was slipping up and where he could do better.

"Have you eaten?" Ignatius asked. I shook my head, and he gently took my hand. "Then we shall eat."

I waved bye to Hrath and Flint as Ignatius led me from the room.

"What are you hungry for?" he asked once we were in the cool sandstone corridor beyond.

His tone was lower than before, almost suggestive. My gaze flew up to meet his, noting how dark his pupils were. Nasty, dirty thoughts made a kaleidoscope in my mind.

I looked away, hating the sting in my cheeks.

How the heck did he do this to me?

He chuckled low and sexy. "Something meaty, I think."

Dirty fucker. Meaty indeed.

We turned down a corridor and slipped through a door into a room containing three portals. The middle one glowed a soft yellow compared to the two white ones. Ignatius guided me to it.

"Why the color difference?"

"The yellow portals are attuned to me." We passed through into a cream hallway I recognized.

We were outside his personal quarters. Sure enough, the next set of double doors opened into his chambers.

"Make yourself comfortable," he said. "I need to shower. Then we can eat. I won't be long."

He headed to the washroom and slipped inside.

He didn't close the door fully.

The urge to sneak up and peek was a visceral clawing inside me.

The sound of running water made it worse.

Nope. I would not be a creeper.

I parked my ass on the bed, sighing as the mattress dipped beneath me. I hadn't slept nearly enough last night what with all the sex and the early rising and more sex. Exhaustion hit me suddenly and I flopped backward onto the bed. Ignatius's bed. And boy did it smell good. All sweet and spicy like him. I rolled onto my side and fisted the material, bringing it to my nose.

This was creepy, yeah, but much less creepy than spying on his sexy naked ass in the shower, right?

There was something wrong with me. Depraved and hungry, but fuck it, I didn't have the energy to fight it. I closed my eyes and allowed the sound of running water and Ignatius's scent to carry me away.

Unconsciousness enveloped me just as a thought occurred to me. Ignatius had said the portal was attuned to him, so how had I gotten through?

TWENTY-TWO

"N yx?" A feather-light touch skated across my cheekbone. "It's time to eat."

I surfaced from sleep and stared blearily up at Ignatius, who was sitting on the mattress by my hip. I sat up too quickly and my head spun.

"Easy." Warm hands grasped my shoulders. "You obviously needed that."

I blinked to clear my head. "Sorry. It's been a tough few days."

"And you probably haven't fueled up as much as you need to." He glanced at the cuffs on my wrists. "Those cuffs may mute your abilities, but they don't change the fact that your body has changed. A daimon metabolism is higher. You'll need to eat more to sustain it."

"Then it's a good thing I like food."

He reached out to brush my hair back from my face, thumb lingering on my cheek for a moment before falling away to leave a warm, tingling imprint against my skin. "Would you like to shower and change before we eat?"

"I didn't bring any spare clothes." Funny how my voice

sounded so normal considering my pulse was racing at his touch. "I don't have anything suitable for the climate here."

"I can have something brought to us for later, but for now..." He crossed the room to an ornately carved wooden dresser and pulled out a long-sleeve tunic top. On him it would fall below his hips, but on me it would hit my knees. "This should suffice." He passed it to me, and our fingers touched, the light graze sending a shiver through me.

"Thanks."

"The food will be here by the time you're done."

I could have climbed off the bed on the other side, away from him and closer to the washroom, but my body had a mind of its own, drawing me closer to him until I was standing with the backs of my knees pressed to the mattress, almost chest to chest with him.

His gaze on me was warm and intense. His scent filled me, calling to me. His skin was smooth and warm beneath my fingertips. Yep, I was touching him. I should stop. I didn't want to.

He'd gone still. Was he holding his breath? A frisson of excitement laced with the heady euphoria of power raced through me. I was doing this to him.

My presence.

My touch.

I traced the golden lines of the patterns dancing beneath his skin, tracking them as they moved and bloomed beneath my touch. His chest heaved on a breath, then another. I pressed one palm to his chest, reveling in the quickening of his heart, and used the other to track the patterns to the dip between his collarbones and up his powerful neck.

A low rumble vibrated his throat. A purr of approval that had me swaying closer to him.

This was wholly inappropriate. This touching. This closeness. But I needed it. I wanted it, and his heavy lids and parted lips told me he felt the same. Still, he didn't touch me, didn't make a move to take the same liberties with my body that I was taking with his.

Was I being a creepo? Yep. Yes, I was.

I dropped my hands and made to step away from him and the bed. But his hands landed on my hips, holding me in place.

I scanned his face, pulse kicking up at the intent in his eyes.

"My turn," he said.

I gasped as his grip on my hips tightened, fingers digging in, thumbs sweeping back and forth over my pelvic bone, sending pulses of liquid heat down to the juncture of my thighs. I was small and fragile in his grasp. At his mercy. He dragged one hand up my side, then round to trail up my spine. He grasped my nape, and I bit back a second gasp, then a moan, as he forced my head back, forced me to look into his ember eyes, dark with desire and want that echoed mine. My breasts swelled and my nipples tightened painfully, hard and aching as they pushed against the fabric of my shirt.

My soft, quick pants kissed the air between us, and the word *please* teased my lips. His chest heaved as he brought his mouth mere inches from mine. I wanted him to kiss me so bad it was a pulsing throb deep inside me.

Instead, he dipped his chin and brushed the tip of his nose against mine with a sigh before releasing me.

The backs of my eyes stung, and I blinked rapidly, disappointment a fist in my chest. "What is this?"

His ember eyes flared, flames dancing in them, but in the next moment they winked out. "It's what hunger can do to your mind and body. Go shower and I'll get the food."

THE SHOWER COOLED my heated skin and overheated libido, so by the time I rejoined Ignatius in the bedroom, I had my shit together. My stomach did an appreciative growl at the aroma of food.

Ignatius was already seated on the cushions. I joined him, taking a spot opposite him. Enough distance to prevent me from getting handsy with him. But damn, his golden skin looked lickable.

Focus, Nyx. Food. Focus on the damned food, not on the way his sun-spun hair falls across his forehead or the way his golden gaze heats when he locks onto you. Do not look at his mouth. Too late. What would it taste like? Last time had been too brief, just the impression of his lips on mine along with the searing heat of promise.

Ignatius shifted slightly. "You look at me as if you'd like *me* to be on the menu."

I bit back a smile. Subtlety was never my forte. "Would that be such a bad thing?"

His eyebrows flicked up. "I thought you didn't mix business with pleasure."

But this was far beyond business. This was something more. An understanding, a connection that I couldn't put into words. Our relationship had gone beyond sponsor and custodia, beyond skirting trust and into safe waters. Confidant waters.

I trusted him.

Trusted him with my life.

But putting all that into words was beyond me. It would be like peeling back my shell and exposing my vulnerable center, and I wasn't ready to do that with him.

Not yet.

Yet. Fuck.

I plucked a grape off a silver plate and popped it into my mouth, reveling in the sweet juices that flooded my tongue.

"I could be dead in three days." I shrugged. "I'm willing to break the rules."

His eyes flared. "No. I won't allow it."

"My rule breaking?" I injected a tease into my tone, expecting him to crack a smile.

But he remained stony-faced, his eyes flickering with flame. "I will not let any harm come to you, Nyx."

My stomach flipped and my next words came out breathless. "I doubt you'll have much choice."

He leaned in slightly. "I always have a choice. I make sure of it." He broke off a piece of fragrant bread and held it to my lips. "Now eat."

I took the bread, lips grazing his fingers, eyes locked with his. His pupils dilated, drinking me in.

I licked my lips. "More." The word was a husky demand.

His jaw tightened but he obliged, this time holding up a sweet treat covered in syrup. I devoured it and licked my lips clean, but as he made to draw away, I gripped his wrist, brought his fingers to my mouth, and licked them clean too.

He made that soft sound again, the growly purr that shot straight to the juncture of my thighs. I locked gazes with him, breath coming fast and shallow as we balanced on the edge of the precipice, knowing we were about to take the leap.

"Your Grace." Flint's voice cut through the building tension, shattering the moment.

I let go of Ignatius's hand and he dropped it to his lap, his jaw ticking. "This better be important, Flint."

I glanced at the door where the sprite stood, hopping from foot to foot. "You instructed me to inform you when your...contact arrived."

Ignatius's annoyance evaporated and he sat up straighter. "Make him comfortable in the atrium. I'll be there momentarily."

"Yes, Your Grace."

I arched an inquiring brow. "Contact?"

"Business." Was that regret in his eyes? "Eat. I'll be back soon." He unfurled his powerful frame and stood. "Tipta will be by in a while to help you dress for our evening out."

"Where are we going?"

"Somewhere...fun."

He said the word as if it was alien. As if he hadn't experienced it in a while, and something inside me melted. "I'm looking forward to it."

"Good." He glanced at the meal, and once again that look of regret crossed his face, but before I could question him about it, he was gone.

I sighed and studied the feast on offer. It would be an awful shame for it to go to waste. But where to start...

Make the most of it. This could be one of your last meals.

Yeah, I wasn't going to listen to that voice.

I was stubborn, but I wasn't stupid, and no fallen was going to take me down. Not if I could help it.

Twenty-Three

There couldn't have been that much food on the trays, right? I mean, there was no way I'd eaten as much as I thought I had. But by the time Tipta appeared, most of the silver platters were empty.

Usually if I ate too much, I felt it. But not today. The lack of bloating was a marvel.

This daimon metabolism thing was real.

Tipta, the female sprite who'd done my hair the last time I was here, handed me a pile of clothes. "You pick from these." She spoke in mortal tongue, staring at me expectantly with wide jade eyes. The purple flame on her hair flickered and dipped a little before brightening.

Why was she looking at me so intensely? I cleared my throat. "Okay, let's see what we have." I laid out the outfits. "It would help if I knew where we were going."

"His Grace wants it to be a surprise. But you will love it."

"Is it outdoors?"

She pressed her lips together, her eyes sparkling with secrets.

"Fine. Don't tell me."

All the outfits were flowy with some beading and delicate embroidery. All gorgeous, but in the end, I picked out a cream ankle-length dress with a gold and emerald embroidered hem. The bell sleeves cinched at the wrist, and the cuffs were beaded. There was a wide gold belt to go with it that clipped at the front, and soft ankle boots to match.

I dressed, then turned to face the sprite.

She made a soft sound of awe and clasped her hands to her chest. "Mistress looks beautiful."

"My name is Nyx, remember." I gave her a stern look. "None of this 'mistress' crap."

She bobbed her head. "Yes, Mist—I mean Nyx." She grinned up at me, showcasing tiny kitten teeth. "Now I do your hair?"

I'd washed it earlier and the hot air had dried it, but it sat heavy against my neck. "Can you put it up for me? Just something simple. Nothing fancy. Just to get it off my neck."

"Of course."

I sat at the dresser and Tipta started to brush my hair. Had all these items been here before? The silver-handled hairbrush. The perfume. The face creams and pots of eyeliner and rouge. Bloody hell, this dresser was kitted out for a woman.

Oh...shit...

How had I been so stupid?

Of course Ignatius would have a lover. A hunky specimen like him would probably have several females swooning and spreading their thighs. And why did that image make me so mad? I exhaled and glared at the dresser. His lover's dresser. She stayed here, in this room with him. Where was she now?

Had he made her leave because he was hosting me? Wait, did she even know I was here?

Of course she did. Ignatius wasn't the kind of male to

hide something like this. He didn't need to. He was all alpha and in control and fuck anyone who didn't like it. But he hadn't told me.

Why?

I wasn't into playing with another woman's man. Nope. Totally not okay. It didn't matter if he was cool with it.

I didn't share.

Ironic, because I wanted Ignatius when I already had Sev, and...wait...Wait a fucking minute...Could this be my daimon aspect taking control?

"What you think?" Tipta asked.

"That being a daimon means I'm gonna get greedy and want loads of men."

She stared at my reflection in confusion, then down at my updo.

Crap, she was referring to my hair, which she'd expertly pinned up into a messy but chic bun, leaving tendrils free to frame my face.

I beamed at her. "I love it!"

She moved to stand by the dresser, facing me. "I offer me to you."

"Huh?"

"Me." She touched her chest. "To you...Your..." She said something in demon tongue, then tutted in irritation, searching for the word in mortal tongue. "Service." She smiled hopefully.

"You want to work for me?" I didn't need a maid. "Look, I don't need—"

"Tipta work hard. Tipta take care of mistress and—"

I held up my hands. "Whoa! Calm down."

She gnawed on her bottom lip for a moment, probably formulating her response. It pissed me off that I couldn't understand demon tongue and that she had to make all the effort. Wait a second. I could understand it.

"Just tell me in demon tongue. I can understand."

She nodded eagerly. "I need to serve you. I feel it in my heart."

Okay, I still didn't understand why.

Tipta stepped away from me quickly, dropping her gaze. Ignatius appeared in the mirror behind me.

"Tipta, you may leave," he said coolly.

The sprite cast one final lingering glance my way, then winked out.

I turned in my seat to face Ignatius. "What was that about?"

"She feels the draw to you. I should have anticipated it."

"Explain."

Maybe I was a little short with him. Maybe I was pissed off about the stuff on the dresser and his other women, and maybe that grated because I had no right to be.

No right to him.

If he noticed my tone, he didn't let on. "Sprites were created by the union of an efreet and a daimon."

"Like...offspring?"

"No, like a gift. The stories say that the first efreet to mate with a Knightwood offered the then-queen a gift. An ember from his heart, to which she added her royal breath, and the sprite was born."

"The union created a whole species?"

"The allure was powerful back then. The Ibris flame was close, and that, coupled with the high daimons' abilities..." Ignatius smiled wearily. "Tipta is drawn to you because her kind were created from your royal breath."

"I'm not royal."

"You have royal genes," Ignatius said. "It is what it is. But it's up to you if you want her to be yours."

I balked at his words. "She's not a thing to be owned."

Ignatius sighed. "I understand your reservation. But

sprites are content only when they are being of service. It is their nature to bond to a master, but since the daimons were infected and sealed behind the abyss gates their species has become...lost. They're drawn to this court because of their connection to the djinn." He smiled. "You'd be making her happy if you accepted her offer."

It explained why Flint had been so clingy earlier too. "If I get through the conclave alive, then I'll think about it."

He gave me a stern look. "No more talk of death." He held out his hand to me. "Let me look at you."

I wanted to forget that he had another woman. That he couldn't be mine. But I'd never been one to bury my head in the sand.

I didn't take his hand and stood unassisted with a polite smile. "How does your lover feel about me being here? In your rooms?"

He frowned, and damn if he didn't look genuinely confused.

I indicated the dresser. "These are her things. Unless this stuff belongs to you." I arched a brow.

His frown cleared and a smile tugged at his lips. "Why, Nyx, are you jealous?"

"Jealous? Me? *Pfft.*" I rolled my eyes. "I don't give a fuc—"

My body collided with his, all hard planes and silken skin. "I think you're jealous, Nyx. But there is no need to be. There is no one else. Only you."

My mouth went dry. "But the stuff..."

"I ordered it for you. For when you're here, home, with me."

Home...My eyes pricked with an emotion that made no sense, and my throat pinched. "Ignatius..." I reached up to touch his cheek, skimming my fingers down his jaw. "Why does that sound so good? So right."

139

He brought his mouth close to mine, his breath dancing with mine. "If I tell you, then I'll have to keep you...forever."

Our lips were so close I could feel the imprint of his mouth, ached for contact, for the cinnamon and sugar taste of him, for the connection that thrummed between us.

My stomach dipped and rose. "Then keep me..."

His eyes burned bright, then his lips brushed mine.

"Your Grace," Flint called out from somewhere behind us. "The carriage awaits."

Ignatius growled and dipped his head. "Flint, if you weren't so indispensable..."

I bit back a smile and broke away from him. "So we're headed out, then?" I arched a brow. "Where?"

Ignatius drew himself to his full height and offered me the crook of his arm. "You'll see."

Twenty-Four

The last time I'd been in a carriage it had been big enough to hold the two of us with a little leg room and required two karrak to pull it across the dunes. This time the carriage was twice the size and pulled by four karrak. The windows were covered in a fine mesh and hung with shutters. The seating was upholstered in soft, plush fabric and the floor was carpeted in thick pile.

The sun was setting when we climbed inside, and although the temperature had dropped it was still hot for me. Luckily the interior of the carriage was pleasantly cool.

Ignatius took the bench opposite mine so that he was riding backwards once we set off. There was plenty of floor space in the carriage, but it wasn't enough to allow Ignatius to fully stretch his legs. He looked like a god, thick, powerful thighs straining against the fabric of his linen pants. His short-sleeve cream shirt was open at the neck, leaving a tantalizing V exposed, and I couldn't help but ogle. Now that I knew what his skin felt like, all I needed to know was how it tasted.

"Are you thinking wicked thoughts, Nyx?" Ignatius asked.

I dragged my gaze up to meet his. "How can you tell?"

"You get a look about you." His ember eyes narrowed. "An intense look, as if you're getting ready to pounce."

"You make me sound like a cat."

"A beautiful, graceful feline." His gaze roved over my face and settled on my mouth. "Beautiful..."

My cheeks heated and I ducked my head. "I don't know how you do it."

"Do what?"

"Make me blush. I'm not the blushing type."

"I like that your body reacts in a unique way to me."

I hadn't thought of it that way, but he was right. I felt different around him. Strong but fragile, like I wanted to shelter with him. Beside him. Beneath him. Like I'd happily surrender control because I could trust him to never take advantage. To never hurt me.

These feelings, these emotions, this connection made no sense. We barely knew one another but it felt like I'd always known him.

I sat back with a sigh. "What *is* this, Ignatius?" I'd never asked a male that before because I'd always known the answer.

Desire. Sex. Always just sex.

But since coming to Morningstar, everything had changed. I wanted, needed, and *felt*...things. My senses were heightened, and since falling in love with Sev, my heart was open too.

There was longing for Arty. A deep connection to Loke. A draw to Sin that defied explanation, and an intriguing and poignant attraction to Zepar that, if I was completely honest, I wanted to explore. But Ignatius? My draw to him was different, almost...metaphysical. Like if I could blink and look beyond the veil at the ties that bound us all, I'd find glowing connections floating between us, holding us together.

The thoughts tumbled through my mind in a matter of seconds. I blinked and looked away, not wanting him to see them reflected there.

"Forget I asked that."

He leaned forward and gently gripped my jaw, turning my face to his. "I won't forget, and I swear to you, I will answer when the time is right."

His words left me breathless, his touch, although gentle, was firm and commanding. He made me feel safe and I liked it.

He released me and sat back, smiling with his eyes. "Sit back and enjoy the journey. We'll be there soon enough."

I didn't bother asking him where we were headed again. I was sure I'd enjoy wherever we went if I was with him.

I sat back and watched the crimson dunes beneath a bruised, darkening sky. The sand glittered beneath the rays of the dying sun, a billion crimson grains.

"The view is beautiful."

"Yes, it is," Ignatius said.

I knew without looking at him that the view he was referring to was me.

Corny as fuck. But when it came from him, I didn't mind.

Didn't mind at all.

THE MOON WAS out by the time the carriage swerved and picked up speed. Upbeat, jovial music drifted in through the windows and shapes appeared on the horizon. Shadows that took form and bled to color.

A huge wheel ringed with tiny lights turned slowly somewhere amid a mass of colorful tent tops. A cocktail of sweet and savory aromas hit me, and my mouth watered, despite the fact I'd demolished a feast for two earlier.

The carriage dipped, and I lost sight of the vista for a few minutes, but in the next the carriage was sliding to a halt by a red and orange tent.

A djinn with laughing eyes approached the window. Ignatius leaned forward and spoke to him.

"A silver to water my karrak and a gold to watch my carriage."

"A sound deal, traveler. Enjoy the festivities." He nodded and smiled and nodded some more as he stepped back.

The door opened. Ignatius climbed out and reached for my hand. I slid my palm into his and allowed him to help me from the carriage.

The music, aromas, and atmosphere of excitement closed in around me. So many colorful sights and vibrant sounds. So many djinn and demons milling about, eating, drinking, playing games at stalls, or purchasing goods.

A carousel made up of fantastical beasts turned lazily, carrying young demons accompanied by older ones. There was a tent with the image of an eye emblazoned on it and so much more I couldn't see from here.

I wanted to explore it all. "It's a fairground." I turned to Ignatius, excitement bubbling in my chest. "I haven't been to a fairground since I was a child." Not strictly true because I'd been to one recently, but it had been in the dead of night and not for fun. But this...This was delightful.

Ignatius grinned down at me. "I hoped you might like it. This is the Grand Mela. It passes close to the Court of Flame twice a year and I've heard that it's a most popular event."

"You've heard? You mean you've never *been* before?"

His smile dimmed and he shook his head slightly.

"Why not?"

"I hear these things are more fun when you have someone to share them with."

I covered my fluster with a smile. "I see why Levistus put you in charge, you sweet talker, you."

He chuckled softly. "Come, let's go and explore." He offered me his arm and I hooked mine around it, allowing him to draw me close.

We set off into the crowd, blending in and becoming one with the revelers. People smiled at us as we passed, and vendors offered us sweets and treats, urging us to come look at their stalls, to play the game of throw the hoop or hook the fish.

We dove deep into the throng. Time slipped by as we enjoyed delicious meat on skewers and sampled the many sweet offerings laid out colorfully on trays. I spotted the wheel hung with lanterns. Demons and djinn hung from the wheel in two-person carriages, taking in the view.

"Can we?" I pointed at the wheel.

He reached out and swiped his thumb across the corner of my mouth, then brought it to his lips to suck it clean.

My heart stuttered at the action. But he was already looking away, across the mela to the big wheel. "Of course we can. There are seats empty now."

I slipped my hand into his easily, as if we'd been doing it forever, and we set off toward the wheel.

A man hurried into our path, babbling excitedly and pointing at me. "Beauty for the eyes. I would love to capture this."

Ignatius tensed, his grip on my hand tightening. But it relaxed a moment later, and he leaned in to speak to me.

"He wishes to paint you."

"Me?" I looked over at the man, noting the palette in his

hand and the dabs of color on his white tunic for the first time.

He grinned widely at me, earnest and expectant.

"Oh, I dunno."

Ignatius shook his head at the man, who pouted and gave me sad eyes.

"The lady has given her answer." Ignatius's tone was stern, and a flash of fear crossed the painter's face.

I squeezed Ignatius's hand. "On second thought, it might be nice to have a souvenir to take back. I'll do it, but you'll have to pose with me."

I spoke to them both and the painter beamed and nodded, clearly understanding me. My ability to switch to demon tongue was working without my even realizing it.

Ignatius's brows flicked up. "You want him to paint us both...together."

I canted my head coquettishly at him. "Is that a problem?"

His gaze warmed. "No, Nyx. I would like that. I would like that very much."

The painter seemed more than happy to accommodate us both. He sat me on a stool and placed Ignatius behind me with his hands on my shoulders.

I grinned up at the duke. "This is a far cry from the last time we were out together."

"Oh?"

"No one's running from you in fear."

"Because they have no idea who I am." His tone was flat, but I recognized the sadness hidden behind it.

"Do you like this? Being accepted as one of them. Having them smile at you and approach you?"

"More than I expected to."

I reached up and covered his hand with mine. "Then

you can have it all the time. Just show them the man I see. They won't be able to help but fall in love with you."

His fingers twitched beneath mine and my words registered.

"And will *you*?" Ignatius said softly. "Will *you* be able to help falling in love with me?"

The breath rushed from my lungs, my mind going into a spin. No. I probably wouldn't be able to help it. I was already on that damned road, walking steadily toward the inevitable. But before I could say anything, the painter rushed over clutching his canvas and speaking rapidly. He pointed to the sky and then held out the canvas to Ignatius.

Around us the music died, and voices rose in alarm.

"We have to go," Ignatius said.

"Go? Why? We just got here."

"There's a storm coming. It wasn't anticipated but it's headed this way."

Around us people were rushing away, leaving their tents and stalls behind.

"Where are they going? Shouldn't they get into their tents?"

"The storm could tear the tents away. They're headed to their carriages and carts, as should we."

He grabbed my hand and we set off through the chaos, weaving between frightened djinn and demons.

The carriage was way back, at least a thirty-minute walk, and a horrible realization dawned.

We weren't going to make it on time.

TWENTY-FIVE

The wind picked up, tearing at the pins in my hair and whipping tendrils against my cheek. The sand swirled off the ground, cutting at my skin. It was hard to breathe, hard to push against the pressure of the elements.

Ignatius scooped me off my feet without breaking stride.

"Close your eyes," he yelled over the howl of the wind.

I wrapped my arms around his neck and turned my face into his shoulder as he broke into a run. The journey seemed to last forever, but it couldn't have been more than a minute or so at the pace Ignatius was going.

We came to a halt, and the next moment I was inside the safe confines of the carriage. Ignatius climbed in after me and slammed the door shut. He shoved the canvas against the back of the carriage, then proceeded to close and latch the shutters.

The angry roar of the wind surrounded us. "What about the karrak?"

"They'll be fine," he said. "They're born to withstand these elements. The carriage is heavy enough to stay put."

The carriage chose that moment to rock slightly. "Are you sure?"

"Fairly."

"Great." I sat back and closed my eyes, breathing, just breathing, until my heart rate slowed. Long seconds passed, and when I opened my eyes, Ignatius was watching me with an amused expression. "What?"

"You..." His tone was gruff and indulgent.

"What about me?" I couldn't help my defensive tone.

"Come here." He patted the seat next to him.

I studied him warily.

"Do you trust me?" he asked.

I sighed and crossed the carriage to sit beside him. "What is it?" I turned to face him, trying valiantly to ignore the flutter in my belly.

He reached up and plucked something from my hair.

One of the pins holding my hair up. Oh fuck, I probably looked a mess.

"These will need to come out." He reached behind me, his fingers deft as he found every pin. My hair tumbled down my back. He tutted softly, then slid his fingers into my hair, combing from scalp to tip again and again. A tingling lethargy swept over my limbs.

His touch felt so good.

My head fell back, mouth parting on a sigh. My nipples turned to aching peaks, breasts swelling desperately in need of his mouth. How was this such a turn-on?

"Sand gets everywhere." Ignatius's tone thickened as he massaged my scalp with one hand and kneaded my nape with the other.

I might have made a soft purring sound. I wasn't sure, but the world felt far away, as if all that mattered was inside this carriage, here between us.

He dipped his head, lips whispering against my jaw and

across my cheek. I wanted his lips on mine, fuck, I ached for it. Pulse beating at the base of my throat like an erratic drum, I clutched at his bicep, pressing my fingers into his taut flesh to urge him to complete his journey and kiss me already. But he didn't. Instead, he drew back to look at me, those luscious lips so close I could have claimed them myself, but for some reason I needed him to make the move. To break this *almost* situation between us.

His gaze flicked from my eyes to my mouth, then back again. "You have no idea how much I want you."

Frustration tightened my throat. "Then do something about it."

His jaw ticked and his eyes flared bright in the gloom of the carriage. "If I start, I won't be able to stop."

The pulse slammed harder. "Who says I'd want you to?"

"You have no idea what you're setting in motion."

My palm grazed a path up his bicep and over his muscle-rounded shoulder, reveling in the dips and hard planes. I paused at his neck and pressed my palm to the pulse that thrummed just as hard and erratic as mine.

I wanted him to break. To lose his grip and just take me. I wanted the explosion, the heat, the desire, all of it, everything that had been simmering between us for days now to come to a head.

I leaned in so our lips were a hairbreadth apart. "Show me. Show me what I'm setting in motion."

He sank his hand into my hair, fisted and tugged, forcing my head back, and my eyes fell to half-mast. My mouth parted, breath coming faster, shallower. "Please."

He dipped his head, his sweet breath skimming across my lips, and for a moment I thought he was going to back off again, leaving me twisted and wanting, but then his mouth crashed down on mine and I forgot how to breathe.

This was a kiss of possession, a ravaging plunder that left my head reeling, my thoughts fractured, and my body pliant and in his control. There was nothing but his lips and his tongue wrestling with mine, nothing but the cinnamon-and-sugar taste of him. I tore my mouth free, lips grazing the stubble on his cheek, his jaw, his throat. I nipped and he growled, hands clenching, fisting my hair again to yank me back so he could stare down at me with blazing eyes.

I stared back, chest heaving. "Don't stop."

"I don't intend to." He pressed his mouth to my throat, to the pulse jumping eagerly beneath my skin, then trailed kisses down the column of my neck to the sensitive dip on my collarbone, then lower, the heat of his mouth seeping through the light fabric to kiss my breast.

I wanted him to taste my skin. To tear the dress off and claim me. Instead he dragged me onto his lap so that I was straddling him and took my nipple into his mouth, sucking hard through the thin fabric.

My head fell back, and a low moan escaped my lips. "Please..." I tore at the collar of my dress, wanting, needing it off.

He gripped my wrist and bit down slightly, dragging my nipple between his teeth. My pussy throbbed and wet heat bloomed between us.

He hooked his arm around my waist and held me firm, rolling his hips up against me to give me a taste of what was to come.

But I didn't want a taste, I wanted it all. "Fuck, stop teasing me."

He chuckled softly against my throat as he lowered me to the ground, then hovered over me. His thighs were trapped between mine, his golden hair falling forward to shield his face.

I reached up to brush it back, running my fingers through it as a tender feeling bloomed in my chest.

He leaned in to nudge my nose with his. "I didn't want the first time to be like this. You deserve to be pleasured on silk sheets. To be fed grapes and wine."

I reached down between us, slipped my hand into his pants, and wrapped my fingers around his cock.

He sucked in a sharp breath, dipping his head so his lips brushed the corner of my mouth. "Nyx..."

I pumped him, once, twice. "I don't give a fuck about silk sheets, Ignatius. All I want is right here in this carriage. All I want is you."

He broke with a growl and his mouth collided with mine in a kiss that shattered all thought, leaving only need. We tore at each other's clothes until we were skin to skin, sinking against each other, heat to heat, finally touching the way we needed to, but then he pulled away.

"What?" I reached for him, but he grabbed my hips and lifted me easily onto the seat. The plush fabric caressed my naked skin as he pushed me back and spread my legs, exposing my wet center.

"Oh..."

He buried his face between my thighs and claimed my pussy, tongue lashing against my clit until I was swollen and weeping with arousal, hips bucking against his face, hands buried in his hair to hold him to me. I was so close, so fucking close to coming.

"Please... don't...don't stop."

He buried his tongue inside me, curling it up and flicking. I came hard, hips rolling against his mouth as he sucked and lapped.

I couldn't breathe...Oh fuck...I couldn't breathe.

IGNATIUS

She tastes like honey, sweet and fragrant, and I can't get enough. Mine. She's mine and I don't care about caution, not while she comes undone in my arms. Not when I have her screaming my name.

Part of me warns that I should stop, but I no longer care. I must have her. I must stake my claim.

I lap at her sweet cunt, hungry for every drop of her arousal. She tugs at my hair, thighs quivering, body tight as she orgasms.

But I'm not done with her.

I give her one final lick and surface.

She's slumped on the seat, her eyes at half-mast, lips full and swollen from my kisses. I pull her against me and then down onto the floor. I need her beneath me. I need to hear her scream my name again, but this time while I'm inside her.

She's soft and silken beneath me, the perfect form of a warrior. Taut and tight. I slide against her heat, opening her wide to me, teasing her until she's crying out my name and begging me to take her.

I need to remember this. I need to commit this moment to memory. Every inch of her glorious bronze skin. Her tight, high breasts bob as she moves against me, desperate for the wet friction against her center. The wave is almost upon us. The tightening at the base of my spine and the tingle beneath my cock warn me that I won't be able to hold off for much longer.

She grabs at my arms. "Please. Ignatius..."

I pull back and she lets out a whimper of protest, which inflames me even more.

I grab the top of her thighs and hold her still as I press myself to her entrance.

Our gazes lock and she's holding her breath, waiting, and for a moment I'm riddled with doubt. Am I wrong to take this? Am I wrong to keep the truth from her? No. I can do *this* and not complete the process, because her abilities are muted. We can have this taste without consequences.

She chooses that moment to push her hips up, taking me into herself. My mind shuts down and primal instinct takes over as I bury my cock inside her.

NYX

My pussy was full, but a strange hollow feeling opened in my chest. A sob clawed at my throat. I needed something... Something more. "Please." I met his thrust with mine, opening wider, taking him deeper, hurtling toward release and knowing that there was more that he could give me. "Ignatius... I need it."

I didn't know what "it" was. I just knew that he had it. "Give it to me. Oh earth. Please."

Another sob broke from my lips.

Ignatius made a rough sound, part moan, part growl, and lifted my hips, adjusting his angle. My mind went blank as sensation ripped through me, deep and satisfying.

"Please." I was crying, and I didn't know why. "Please." I slid my hands down his back and clutched at his buttocks, digging my nails in, desperate to haul him back, to stop the release, because it was nothing without the *other* thing. It was incomplete, and I had to have them both. "Damn you." I shoved at his chest, suddenly enraged.

He stilled, our bodies remaining locked together, vibrating with sensations that begged for culmination.

"You don't know what you're asking for," Ignatius said finally.

"I don't care. Whatever it is, it belongs to me, so fucking give it to me."

His eyes blazed bright and golden patterns flared across his skin, moving over his pectorals and up his neck. "You're right. It does belong to you." He pinched my jaw, forcing my head up, his expression almost angry. "But once you have it, there is no going back."

Something fluttered in the back of my mind, a warning, my wary hunter mind trying to wake up, but my body was in control, wrapped tight around his huge, thick cock and balanced on the precipice of an epic orgasm.

Caution seemed light years away, but still my mouth asked the right question. "What is it? What do I need?"

"Me..." Ignatius said. "You need me." He bowed his head and pressed his forehead to mine. His silken hair fell forward to kiss my temple. "It's all right, Nyx," he said against my mouth. "You'll have it soon enough, I promise." He kissed me and the anger and desperation melted beneath his lips.

His grip on me flexed, fingers caressing and kneading, one hand sliding up to cup my breast and pinch my nipple.

"Yes." I nodded. "Please." I squirmed beneath him, rolling my hips to take him deeper, to find that spot again.

He obliged with a low growl, moving slow, each thrust deep and deliberate, reigniting the heat and building it into an inferno, until I was panting and sobbing with the need for release. Only then did he break and pick up the tempo, fucking me so hard that it was no longer the storm that rocked the carriage and the sound of our bodies meeting rose above the howl of the wind. I came in rolling waves, cresting the rise over and over, the sensation edging on pain, until he found his release, burying his face in the crook of my shoulder to stifle his gruff groan.

The hollow feeling melted away, and heat spread through my limbs before receding. As if it was waiting.

But for what? I didn't know.

Twenty-Six

T he patterns beneath Ignatius's skin moved beneath my fingers, making it impossible to trace them. Didn't stop me from trying, though. It was cozy curled up naked against his golden frame, his silken skin pressed to mine, his heat cocooning me. He played with my hair, twirling tendrils around his fingers then letting them go only to do it all again.

The storm continued to rage outside, but it was safe here with him, and for a little while I allowed myself to forget what waited for me back at Morningstar.

I tipped my head up to look at him. "How long will the storm last, do you think?"

"Could be hours." He looked down at me with a smirk. "Or days."

I arched a brow. "Really?"

"Oh yes. These storms have a mind of their own." His hand skimmed up my side. "But I'm sure we can find something to keep us busy."

The pulse between my thighs fluttered. "Uh-huh? What about food and water?"

He turned toward me, forcing me onto my back, and slid his thigh between mine, pushing up so he was pressed to my core.

"Oh..." I closed my eyes and rubbed against him.

"I will be your sustenance, and you..." He kissed the hollow of my throat. "Will be mine." He trailed kisses up my neck and nipped at my earlobe.

"I'm not sure that will work."

"No?" He arched a golden brow. "I ate quite well a little while ago."

Ate? Oh... The dirty bastard. I grinned up at him. "Yes, you did. But I haven't." I licked my lips, and his eyes darkened.

"No, you haven't." His voice caught, and fuck was that sexy as hell.

I ran my hand down his gorgeous body, over his cobbled abs and down to his Adonis belt, tracing a finger back and forth, closer and closer to my prize until his breath was fast and shallow. I loved this. This control. This effect I had on him.

I kissed his pectoral and then slid down his body. I was going to blow his mind.

"Nyx, wait." He grabbed my nape and I looked up to find him staring at the roof of the carriage. "We have to get dressed."

"What?"

He smiled down at me, but his eyes held shadows. "The cavalry has arrived."

THIS WAS one time I would have been happy not to have been rescued too soon. But Hrath and the sylphs found us and carried us back to the keep by flying us above the storm.

I guess it wasn't protocol to leave the Duke of Flame stranded in a sandstorm. By the time we made it to Ignatius's quarters it was gone midnight.

Hrath hovered at the door as Ignatius led me into his bedchamber.

"Get some rest, I'll be back soon."

"Where are you going?"

He stroked my cheek. "Court business."

"Like earlier?"

He sighed. "Merihem is looking into how the fawda could have infiltrated Libidine. The only ways in or out are through portals sanctioned by Merihem. We believe the marid possessing Merihem may have sanctioned the portals, but we have no idea how the marid got into Libidine in the first place."

"You think there's a spy at the fortress?"

"Possibly, or...there's a breach we're unaware of somewhere, and as the Court of Flame is connected to Libidine, that breach could be here."

I glanced at Hrath by the door. "You think you've found it."

"Maybe. The conji have been sweeping the lands looking for anomalies or any mystical signatures that do not belong. They detected one."

"I'm coming with you."

"No. You can't."

I bristled. "Excuse me?"

He placed his hands on my shoulders and met my gaze earnestly. "Not because I don't want you to. The suspected breach is in the far east, an area where lava runs beneath the sands. You won't be able to withstand the heat."

My stomach knotted. "Is the breach dangerous?" I looked to Hrath.

"We won't know until we explore it."

"You think there might be fawda there?"

Ignatius squeezed my shoulders to reassure me. "I'll be fine. I have Hrath and my guards. It may be nothing."

Or it could be something.

"Get some rest," Ignatius said.

Yeah, like hell would I be sleeping, not until he got back.

IGNATIUS

The flight to the suspected breach takes almost an hour, and I can't help but be resentful of this task that takes me away from my *Qalbi*. This night was mine. To keep her close, to know her, hold her. But instead I'm tied up in duty.

I land on sand that's so hot the air shimmers. The sylphs, Hrath and Ugar, remain airborne, and my efreet guards join me on land.

"Up ahead," the conji being carried by Ugar calls out.

The sand gives way to black, jagged, rocky terrain. The remnants of the effects of lava. The hairs on my body quiver.

Yes, there is something here.

My guards take the lead, running ahead toward the shimmer hidden in the heat waves rising off the ground.

It's a breach all right. Unsanctioned. It would have gone undetected indefinitely if Nyx hadn't brought the fawda symbol to me. If she hadn't confided in me. Trusted me.

"Is it live?" Hrath calls out.

"Yes," the conji says. "I feel it."

"Shut it down," Hrath calls out.

"No!" I run forward to join the guards closest to it. "We must investigate. Find their base."

"And walk into a camp filled with fawda?" Hrath says.

"No. We stake it out." I turn to the guards. "Set up a

perimeter and make camp." I look up at the conji. "I'll need a doorway from here to just outside the fortress walls so that the guards can take shifts without having to travel too far. Make sure a conji is on watch at all times. Do you have enough allure to make the door?"

"I do, but I'll need help maintaining it if it is to be temporary."

I don't understand how a conji allure works but I know that our permanent portals don't need to be constantly maintained.

"Very well, do it."

The conji gets to work and Hrath flies to hover a few feet beside me.

"I'm sorry," he says. "Maybe I should have kept this information for the morning."

"No. You did the right thing."

"But you're upset."

"Selfishly, yes."

"It is time you were selfish, brother. You've given yourself to your people, to the court, to Merihem, for too long."

"Maybe. But it is my status and my connections that will save my heart now."

"What will you do if the conclave votes to execute?"

A vise grips my heart. "Whatever it takes." I meet his gaze, and he nods at me then echoes my words.

"Whatever it takes."

NYX

"Are you sure you don't want to sleep?" Tipta asked for the fifth time.

"I'm sure."

She drifted ahead of me, leading me to Ignatius's library. He'd given me a tour the last time I'd been here. Shown me his collection of paintings depicting the abyss and Soreena, the daimon queen. I wanted to study those paintings again. See the world I was meant to belong to and the person I was meant to be related to.

I wanted to understand how I was a possibility. If Satan was my father, then who was my mother?

Yeah, I'd avoided thinking about that one.

Until now.

Tipta stopped at the library doors and stepped back so I could enter.

I crossed into the cool, dark confines of the library, lit only by the moon. She didn't follow.

I paused to look back. "Everything all right?"

She bobbed her head. "Sprites are not allowed inside. Books." She smiled and bobbed her head again, her purple flame hair flickering.

"Ah, yeah, of course. You can go if you want. I'll find my way back."

She shook her head. "Tipta will stay as long as Nyx needs her."

Something told me that trying to change her mind would be a waste of time. "Okay, then."

I crossed the room to the portrait of the daimon realm, but it was much too dark to see the details. I needed a lamp. There was one on a table in the center of the room, the small flame glowing valiantly in the dark.

So, fire was okay if contained behind glass. I turned the lantern up and carried it back to the painting, allowing the soft amber glow to dispel the clinging shadows around the painting.

Ah, there it was. Silver spires stretched up to the sky like metal fingers desperate to claim the purple clouds. Tiny walkways jutted out here and there, linking the buildings. It was a technologically advanced metropolis, but if what I'd learned so far was true, also a mystically powerful one.

This place was where my kind had come from.

But what about me?

I sighed and moved across the room to the other painting of interest. The print I'd found Ignatius studying the last time I'd been here. A picture of the daimon queen herself.

Soreena. Regal, powerful, and honorable, if Dhuma was to be believed.

She stood with her back to the painter, dark hair whipping about her shoulders, surrounded by her mates.

I studied them now, looking for Dhuma. Ah, there he was. The height and breadth of his shoulders gave him away. There was an efreet too. What was his name? Erebus. Ignatius's mentor. What had these males been like? What had Soreena been like when not playing queen? She'd loved her mates, all three of them, and they'd accepted that. Shared her heart and worked as a team. A family.

A warm feeling unfurled in my chest. Hope...possibility. Permission. To care for, to want...To love more than one male. To accept it as a part of who I was. To hope that maybe this time I wouldn't get my heart crushed. That this time, I wouldn't be rejected.

If I could live through the next few days, if I could convince the conclave to let me exist, then maybe I could have the kind of connections she'd had, not just with my siblings but with the males who'd slowly found their way past my defenses and into my heart.

THE SKY WAS GRAY, and I was losing my fight with sleep by the time Ignatius returned to his quarters.

A warm flood of relief washed over me. He was back and unharmed. "Is everything okay?"

He nodded and began to shuck off his clothes. "The breach is active, and I've set up a watch. If anything or anyone comes through, they'll get a nasty surprise."

"I'm glad you didn't go through it."

He climbed into bed and lay beside me. "Roll over." We settled with his chest to my back so that I was little spoon. "You smell good." His voice was a weary purr.

I smiled, eyes heavy with sleep. "And you sound exhausted." I drew his hand to my lips and kissed it. "Sleep now."

His sigh ruffled my hair. "Everything is under control. Close your eyes. Sleep and let me hold you."

But I forced myself to stay awake a little longer. Long enough to commit this moment to memory, because despite my earlier surge of hope, there was no denying the dark kernel of dread inside me. The voice that warned me that nothing good ever came without a price.

At least not for me.

Twenty-Seven

SEV

The struggle to train my body to be awake a few hours before sunset continues. If I can succeed, then I can spend more time with Nyx before she falls asleep. But tonight, I fail, waking to a moonlit room.

I sit up, rake a hand through my hair, and frown at Chase. "I thought we had a deal. You were supposed to wake me up mid-afternoon."

Chase gives me a hard, flat look, as if to say, *you think I didn't try?*

I can't even argue with him. I sleep deep when the sun is up. "Next time bite me."

He bares his teeth as if to showcase how bad of an idea that would be.

"I have a tough hide and if you break the skin, I'll heal." I climb out of bed and head to the washroom.

We didn't have showers in the stables, just a pump to drink from and wash. Thrown in stalls like beasts. My brethren are still trapped there, being treated like animals, while I'm here, bathing, sleeping, eating, fucking, all in the lap of luxury.

Why do I deserve this and not them?

I step out from under the spray and dry off before entering the bedroom again. "I'll get them out, Chase. Once Nyx is Satan, we'll get them out from under Umbrane's rule."

Chase chuffs in agreement.

I glance at the door to the Court of Flame. Nyx is with the efreet right now. What are they doing? I'm no fool. I know she's attracted to him. It doesn't bother me. When she's with me, she's mine. Wholly mine. I reign over her body and soul. I have her mind. And as long as that remains true, I'm happy to share.

I cross to the door. "Time to do some sleuthing, Chase. You up for some shadow work?"

He pads over to me and nudges my thigh, as if to say, *get on with it, then*.

I crack a smile, open the door, then slip into shadows.

WE TRAVERSE the keep like ghosts, stopping here and there to listen in on conversation, hoping to catch something that might help us learn more about the conclave. More about who'll be chosen to vote.

But as the hours crawl by, I'm beginning to think it's a waste of time. The demons and devils who'll be voting probably aren't in the keep yet. They'll arrive the day before, or the day of.

The halls and corridors are empty and silent, the staff probably holed up in their quarters, preparing for bed.

I doubt I'll find any useful information tonight. Best to go back to the spawn quarters and check in on the others. I continue past the kitchens and take a different route back, one that cuts through the staff quarters, because, heck, if there's gossip to be had, this is where I'll find it.

Sure enough, I get a hit.

"...wants silk sheets. Silk? Where are we meant to get those at this hour?" a female voice complains. Probably a zuni. Most of the keep staff are zuni. Zuni or imps affiliated with one of the courts.

"Just take them from the Seneschal's linen closet," a male voice says gruffly. "He won't know."

"Why must he stay here now?" the female whines. "The conclave is days away."

"Hush, you fool. If anyone of note hears your words, you could lose your position here. Or even your head. The Duke of Shadows has been known for taking tongues and wings."

"I'm sorry." Her voice trembles.

A sigh. "Get the linens and take them to Duke Umbrane's guest chambers."

"The west wing?"

"Yes, child. The west wing, the ivory room. Go."

I look down at Chase, and he nods once.

It looks like we're headed to the ivory room.

Ten minutes later we're outside the guest room, looking at an ivory door gilded in silver. I move past it and duck into one of the deep recesses that line this corridor. Each holds a decorative plant and enough shadow for me to cloak myself and Chase.

I close my eyes and focus. My sense of smell and hearing are heightened compared to the demons and devils of Morningstar. I'd wager they could rival that of an incubus or even a fallen. My kind were born for stealth.

Long seconds pass before I catch Umbrane's smooth, imperious tone. My skin crawls but a twisted yearning flares in the pit of my stomach too.

I've been his pet for too long and old habits die hard.

His voice has accompanied my pain and pleasure for too long. It's tangled and twisted inside me. A part of me, like a disease I'll need to cut out. Eventually...with time.

But for now, I grit my teeth and listen. For Nyx. Anything to protect my woman.

"You almost ruined everything," Umbrane says. "All the spawn were in that carriage, including *my* custodia. Have you *any* idea what it would have meant if they'd all been killed?"

"I brought you what I knew." This voice is a sibilant hiss that makes my scalp tighten.

A low growl drifts up from beside me and I place my hand on Chase's head to calm him.

"You said the Nephilim and the incubus would be in the carriage," Umbrane snaps.

"That is what I heard."

"Maybe spying isn't for you."

The scuff of shoes on marble shatters my concentration. I push further into the shadows as the footsteps draw closer.

A cloying feminine scent tickles my nostrils. The person stops before they can reach my hiding place and there's a knock on a door.

"Enter," Umbrane calls out.

A visitor. But who? The maid with the sheets, maybe? I tune my senses back onto the room.

"Do you have everything you need?" The female voice is easily recognizable as Erinea.

"I requested silk sheets," Umbrane says coolly. "I prefer them against my naked skin."

"Oh?" Erinea's tone drops. "So do I."

"You're welcome to share mine once they arrive."

A shudder passes through me at that tone. The one that

promises delicious pain. I close my eyes and breathe through my nose.

Chase presses closer, his heat grounding me.

"I might take you up on that offer," Erinea purrs. "After all, we have much to celebrate."

"Oh?"

"I've spoken to each dignitary chosen to vote at the conclave." A glass clinks. She's pouring a drink.

"And?" There's a hint of impatience in Umbrane's tone.

"And...they all agree with us. The daimon abomination must die."

Ice fills my veins.

"And how did you convince them?" Umbrane asks smoothly.

"Don't worry. No threats were used. No physical bribes that could be traced back to us. Simply the promise of a favor once our choice of Satan is on the throne."

"Good. Very good."

"And you're sure the zuni is a good choice?"

"Well, your daughter obviously isn't."

Silence reigns for a moment. "I wasn't suggesting—"

"I'm aware. But I don't like my choices being questioned."

"I apologize. It's just...we almost lost her, and all the others."

"What do you mean?"

"You haven't heard?" There's no mistaking the thread of glee in her tone at having one up on Umbrane, but she has no idea how much he already knows.

"Spit it out, woman."

I can't help but admire his acting skills. He sounds genuinely annoyed.

"Artimus's carriage was sent to the old forest. The spawn

were almost killed. The Minorax is still recovering from his wounds."

"Who would do such a thing?" Umbrane says.

This, right here, is why he's such a fucking snake.

"I don't know," Erinea says. "But the portal was set from Libidine, so whoever did it may not have known all the spawn were in the carriage."

"They were targeting Artimus." Umbrane maintains his solemn, thoughtful tone. The deceptive son of a bitch.

"It would seem so."

"And that angers you?"

"He belongs to me. An attack on him is an attack on me," Erinea says simply.

"I see...and if there was an attack on me?"

Erinea gives a low, sexy chuckle. "Oh, Umbrane, who would *dare* to attack you?"

"Hmmm, so true."

Erinea lets out a soft gasp that is cut off by wet sounds. Oh, fuck, they're kissing and...no. I'm out of here.

I hurry away down the corridor and back into the main keep, my mind spinning with what I've learned. Umbrane is somehow responsible for the carriage attack. But that would mean he has a contact in Libidine who fucked with the portal, which makes sense because he's Merihem's duke, but Merihem was possessed by a marid so...Shit, does Umbrane know about Merihem? Or does the marid have nothing to do with the portal thing? Why would the marid want to kill Artimus? He won't have a motive. But he might have a motive for Nyx. She's fucked with his shiqq and the fawda and...wait, does that mean that Umbrane's working with the fawda?

Oh, fucking hell.

My thoughts are all over the place. I momentarily lose

my grip on the shadows and a figure chooses that moment to step around the corner.

Artimus.

He freezes at the sight of me, his gaze dropping to Chase then flicking up to the shadows clinging to my frame.

I shake them off. No point hiding now. He glances over my shoulder, noting the direction I'm coming from. "Do you want to talk?"

I'm working with Loke because I know Nyx trusts him, but after everything she's told me happened in Libidine, I'm sure she trusts Artimus too. I know he wants to protect her as much as I do.

I nod. "Yes, let's talk."

Twenty-Eight

MALLINI

I t feels like an age since I was in this room. It's a mess, as usual. Charod was never a neat person. I always tidied up after him, and truth be told, I'd been relieved when Mother had given us separate chambers, but even then, he'd snuck into my room at night to curl up beside me. We'd slept holding hands every night. No liaison or conquest had kept us apart. We'd never stayed with any lover overnight.

We'd returned to each other, unable to settle without hearing the other's heartbeat. I'd often wondered what would happen when one of us fell in love. Moved in with our mate. Got our own life. But the thoughts were always fleeting because we'd had time. So much time to figure it out.

But then the truth of our heritage had come out. The ascension happened and now Charod is gone, and I know...I know the pain of never hearing his heartbeat again.

I've slept holding his shirt the past few nights. His scent

was on it, comforting, a part of him, but the shirt no longer smells like him. One of the zuni took it. Washed it.

I swallow my rage. It's fine. There are more shirts here. More of his things strewn all over the floor.

I shut the door behind me and pick my way through the whirlwind of debris. A smile tugs at my lips because when I'm here, in this space, it feels like I'm close to him. I pick a gray shirt off the floor by the bed and hold it to my nose. My eyes well. Charod...There you are.

The door opens and I step back, tucking the shirt into the belt at my back and shaking out my plumes to hide it.

I expect a zuni, sent to maybe tidy the room, or clear it out, but my mother steps inside. She stills at the sight of me, and the look on her face might be comical if the sight of her didn't evoke rage. It surges up my throat, leaving a bitter taste on my tongue.

She recovers her composure quick enough. "What are you doing here?"

"I could ask you the same question." I give her a thin smile. "Come to clear out the room? Put it to better use."

If I didn't know better, I'd say there's a flash of hurt in her eyes. But I *do* know better. I know that she stood by and let the trials murder her son.

"I know you must hate me," she says.

"You're right. I do." I want to get out of here, but she's standing between me and the door.

"I didn't have a choice. The contracts were clear."

"I don't want to hear it." I move to the dresser where more clothes are strewn and start to gather them. "If you want to clear the room out, fine. But I'm taking his things."

"I didn't come here for that."

I round on her, anger buzzing in my veins. "Then why the fuck are you here?"

"To be close to him…" Her voice is small. So unlike the boisterous, bossy female I know that I'm left stunned.

I don't want to see it, but it's there. On her face. Finally. The look that a mother who's lost her child has. Devastation. Grief.

If she'd shown me her pain before…earlier, after it happened…if she'd shared her grief with me then…then maybe I'd have been able to accept it. To forgive her. To mourn with her, but not now.

No. Now, it's too late.

"You chose your path, Erinea." She flinches at my use of her name. "And now I have to walk mine." I stride toward her, and she steps aside to let me pass.

I'm almost out the door when she speaks. "If you lose the seat, you fail him. If you lose, his death would have been in vain."

Her words are a noose around my neck. This is her power. This has always been her way, and for a moment I almost fall back into the pattern of listening, of allowing those words to poison my mind and my intentions.

Just for a moment.

But then I turn and give her a cold smile that drains the color from her face. "You better hope I don't win, Erinea. Because if I do, it'll be your last day on this earth."

GUS

It's all right. Everything is all right. I can do this. I just need to stay calm, ask the question, and not piss myself. Yes. Perfectly fine.

The long, dark corridor stretches out before me like an inky snake. Silver forests flank me, and the sky above is a multitude of stars. The House of Luna holds the southern edge of the Court of Shadows even though it isn't under Umbrane's rule. No history book can tell us why the House of Lunar is permitted such liberties, why Satan gave them these lands. It makes no sense. They ran and hid during the Chaos War. They barricaded themselves in their underground city until it was all over, and Satan rewarded them?

It makes no sense.

But I'd have been a fool to reject Lady Minera's hand of friendship, a gesture asking for forgiveness from one of the last surviving descendants of House of Solar.

My people are mostly gone, my breed scattered amongst the courts, our blood diluted, but we hold our heads high because we didn't run and hide. We fought.

And I'll continue to fight for what I believe in. I may not be seven feet tall. I may not have strength of body, but I have strength of mind, and I'll use that in any way I can to save my family.

My throat tightens as I approach a set of double doors that seem to be fifteen feet high. This is my first time visiting the House of Lunar and my stomach quivers and twists, but I take a deep breath, press my palm to the wood, and push.

The doors swing open easily, admitting me into a pretty courtyard dotted with silver blossom trees. A fountain sits in the center, gurgling and bubbling happily, and Lady Minerva perches on the stone lip, feet dangling a foot off the ground, fingers trailing in the water. Her mahogany hair is swept off her face and into a braid, leaving her beautiful ivory horns on display. They curve away from her forehead and over the top of her head like a crown of bone.

She looks up at me with slanted violet eyes and something in my chest squeezes. This close I can see she's younger than I thought. She smiles and my stomach flips.

"Gustov, how lovely of you to come visit me."

I look back at the door, but it's gone. There are only trees. "You knew I was here."

"Of course. I know everything that occurs in my home. Come sit." She pats the stone lip of the fountain.

My pulse quickens the closer I get to her.

"Do not be afraid," she says.

"I'm not afraid."

"Your heartbeat tells a different story."

"Hearts race for many reasons."

She blinks at me in surprise and my nerves are gone. Lady Minerva may be the head of this house but she's no ancient. She can't be much older than me, but she gives the impression of age and wisdom, and there's no denying the power beating off her skin.

I hop onto the edge of the fountain a couple of feet from her. "I wanted to thank you for your sponsorship."

She runs the tips of her fingers across the water, leaving ripples in their wake. "I should thank you for your sacrifice. House of Solar was valiant in the wars."

"Why did your house not fight?" The question's out before I can stop it. "I'm sorry. I shouldn't have—"

"No. I understand. I would ask the same question if I were you." She gave me a wry smile. "Unfortunately, I don't have the answer. It was before my time and the elders don't speak of it. No one does."

"Did you sponsor me because you feel bad about it?"

"Partly, yes, but mostly because you're an imp. You're one of us, no matter what house you come from. We weren't at your side in the Chaos War, but I won't abandon you now."

Good. "I'm glad to hear that because I need your help."

She arches a delicate brow. "This is about the conclave, isn't it?"

"Yes. Have you been invited to vote?"

"I have. And I've accepted." She smiled. "The daimon blood will not have our vote to exist."

I stare at her dumbly for a moment. "But...you haven't heard the arguments for or against yet."

"There is no argument that would justify allowing such an abomination to exist. We can't allow her the opportunity to take the seat. All that power..." She shakes her head. "No. I've made up my mind." She smiles. "Your path to the seat will be much clearer once she is gone."

My heart sinks. "I don't want her gone."

She sighs. "Yes, I've heard the rumors about your sibling bond. The fact that she's turned the trials into a farce and enchanted you all into protecting her."

"Enchanted? She hasn't done anything but be herself."

"A daimon blood." She arches a brow. "They had abilities, you know."

She thinks Nyx is using allure on us. The concept is ridiculous. "Nyx didn't come into any power until she died a couple of days ago. Everything she's done up until now has been without any abilities. She's protected us, saved our lives, risked her own." I blink back tears of frustration. "I can't lose her. We won't lose her."

Minerva's expression smooths out. "Your duty is to your people. To the imp race. You have the opportunity to be Satan, to speak up for the weak and persecuted. To make Morningstar glorious once more. You can't let anything stand in your way."

My cheeks heat with anger. "The imp race? Where were your people when the imp race needed you? Where were you when your Solar brothers fought the beasts that crawled from the pit? You speak of duty, what about your duty? To the truth. To finding the best Satan for the seat? If I'm worthy, then I'll have that seat whether my sister lives or not." Coming here may not have given me the results I want, but it's opened my eyes. I know what I must do. I hop off the fountain and move away from her. "I, Gustov of House Solar, renounce your sponsorship."

"What are you doing?" She slips off the fountain and reaches out to me. "You'll be defenseless."

I shake my head. "I'm not defenseless. I have my family." I lift my chin. "I have Nyx."

She sighs and her expression shutters. "Not for long."

TWENTY-NINE

ORINA

"Oh, come on, Micah, there's got to be something you can do."

"I'm sorry. The Morningstar keep is on lockdown for the ascension," Micah says over the phone.

"My friend is trapped there."

"From what you told me, it's where she belongs," Micah says coolly.

"They're putting her through trials. Probably some kind of gladiator shit and she's not...she's basically human."

His tone grows clipped. "I'm sorry, Orina. There's nothing the Order can do, not without breaking the Accords. Maybe once the trials are over you can petition to visit Morningstar through Mageri channels."

"Why Mageri? I thought the Order could—"

"I'll see you tomorrow." He hangs up, and I resist the urge to hurl my phone across the slick, rain-coated streets.

I hate the smell of the Fringe after rainfall. All the shit from the air gets brought to ground level, all the crap from the alleys that's been baking for days releases pungent odors. My heightened senses can't take it. That, coupled with Micah's call, leaves me itching for a brawl.

I cross the street to where I've parked Pea, my green mini bug. She's been with me for years, with us—the Trio, as we named ourselves when we met studying at the Ministry. Seems like an age ago. Nyx, Quinn, and me. Best friends for life. Pea was our first purchase together. Our get-about vehicle when we ran our business, helping the helpless from a shitty back office right here in the Fringe.

That time feels like a simpler time, but in hindsight we had a lot of growing up to do, and we did it separately, splitting up only to reunite properly again a year ago.

I've got my friends back. The Trio reformed, and now Nyx is in danger. I dial Quinn.

She answers on the fourth ring. "Hey, Orina. Is everything okay?"

"Why would you assume it isn't?"

She chuckles softly. "You know why. Nyx calls to catch up, and you call when we need to kick ass."

I can't even argue with that. "I think Nyx is in trouble."

"Shit, I tried calling her a couple of times over the past week and she didn't answer. I thought she was on a case."

"Yeah, so did I, until I got the note."

"What note?"

"She's in Morningstar. In the keep doing some kinda trials. She's Satan spawn, Quinn."

Silence greets me. I catch the rumble of male voices in the background. "Hush, wait..."

"Quinn?"

"I'm here. I'm getting dressed. I'll be with you in a few hours."

The knot in my belly eases. "You don't have to come. We

can't do anything. The Morningstar keep is in lockdown until after the ascension is over."

"Okay, so we wait. Together."

"You're gonna come all this way just to wait with me?"

"It's what we do, right? It's part of the sisterhood pact. We come together in times of need. Times of trouble. You guys were there for me when I needed you the most, even after we hadn't spoken for years. You came to Hawthorne when I called."

"Of course we did. We love you."

"And I love you guys." She drops her voice to a whisper. "Besides, I could do with some testosterone-free time."

"We heard that," a deep, rumbly male voice says.

I can't help but smile. "Hi, guys!"

Quinn found her place with the wolves of Hawthorne Cove last year and in doing so she found herself. She's stronger for it.

"I'll be with you soon," she says. "Love you."

"I love you too."

I climb into Pea, reveling in the scent of lemon zest and coffee, and shove my carrier bag of snacks onto the seat beside me.

Yeah, I stress eat when I'm anxious. I just hope that the salami sticks, jelly bears, mega-bags of crisps, and an extra-large bar of dark chocolate will suffice until Quinn gets here with a much-needed hug.

I turn the key and the engine purrs to life, but the thought of going home and doing nothing makes my stomach twist. There's no way I'll sleep tonight, and I know the perfect person to keep me company.

I hope she's home.

BABS'S HOUSE is a three-story terraced affair on the edge of the Fringe. If you climb up onto the roof you can see the dusty red line that's the beginning of the Rim—the land that falls outside the reach of the Accords.

Nyx and I sat up on the roof for hours speculating about what lay beyond the city. What horrors and adventures we'd find if we decided to take a trip past the wards and into unknown territory, but whenever we mentioned it to Babs, she always said that the Rim was a place for people with no place, and as we both had a place it was no place for us. Which always made us giggle because of the number of times she said the word "place."

It's been too long since my last visit. Working for the Order takes up all my time and it's a rare moment when I get a day off. Still, I should have made the time.

I knock on the green door and wait. Yes, it's late, but Babs is a night owl. Never up until mid-afternoon and never asleep till dawn.

Sure enough, the door opens to reveal an empty hallway. Nothing unusual there. Babs has a way about her.

"In the kitchen!" she calls out.

I follow the smell of freshly baked something into the warm, cozy kitchen where Nyx and I spent hours cutting cookies into shapes, eating ice cream and, when we grew older, cleaning and sharpening our weapons.

Babs stands at the stove, perched on a footstool, stirring a huge pot of something. Her silver hair is piled on top of her head and her cheeks are flushed. "Sit, sit, child. Soup's almost ready."

"That's a lot of soup."

"It's for the children's home down the street, but you can have a bowl."

It smells delicious. "Thanks."

I've barely taken a load off when Babs places a bowl of vegetable soup in front of me.

"Eat up and tell me everything." She takes the seat opposite.

It doesn't matter that I haven't seen her in over a year, or that I've come over unannounced. It doesn't matter that I've mud on my boots or that my clothes are damp. Babs makes me feel welcome and at home, as if she's been expecting me.

I scoop some of the delicious soup into my mouth and it instantly warms my belly.

"Good?" she asks.

"Very." I eat in silence until my spoon scrapes the bottom of the bowl.

"Now, tell me what's wrong," she says.

I sigh and sit back. "Nyx is stuck in Morningstar. She's at the keep. They think she's Satan spawn, a...Nephilim." I shake my head. "I thought Nephilim were a myth."

Her smile is indulgent. "Is that what the Order told you?"

"You know different?"

She sighs. "I know many things."

My scalp pricks. "Did you know what Nyx was?"

"Yes."

I exhale sharply. "And why didn't you say anything?"

"It wasn't for me to say. My job was to keep her safe. Give her the love and home she very much needed, and it's been more of a comfort to me than I could ever have expected."

There's something off about her tone but I can't place my finger on it. "Babs?"

She blinks at me. "Don't worry about Nyx. She's strong, stronger than anyone could have imagined, and she's in the place she needs to be."

"Wait. What do you know?"

Babs scrapes back her chair and stands. "You've been a

good friend to her, Orina. You and Quinn, you're just what she needs."

"What are you talking about?"

She gives me a weary smile. "Make sure the orphanage gets the soup for me, will you, dear?"

"What?"

The lights go out, and when they flicker on again Babs is gone.

I'm alone in the kitchen with a pot of simmering soup, an empty bowl, way too many questions, and the clawing conviction that I've got to get to my friend sooner rather than later.

THIRTY

NYX

Why was I surprised that breakfast at the Court of Flame was just as elaborate as supper? Why was I surprised that I ate most of what was on offer...again.

Ignatius helped by placing more food on my plate or feeding me directly. I didn't want to leave here. Leave him. But I missed my siblings, Sev, and Chase. I wanted to see them before I went to stay at the Court of Ivory.

I sipped the dark, heady coffee provided. "What'll happen at the conclave? Run me through it. Do I get to speak?"

"You'll be present throughout," Ignatius said. "The charges will be read out."

I snorted. "The charges? You mean the fact I exist?"

His jaw flexed. "Yes. The conclave members will then discuss. They may ask you questions too. After that, you will be given a chance to speak and then they will cast their votes. The princes will then deliberate and make their decision."

"I need at least two of them to back me, then?"

"Yes. But you won't be going through it unless I'm sure there's a real chance of the vote going in your favor."

"How can you possibly know that?"

"Artimus is making inquiries and..." He looked away. "We've prepared an exit plan for you."

"Wait, when did you have time to do that?"

"Yesterday when I left you at lunch. I met with the Seneschal on safe ground."

I smiled. "Ah. Sev is doing some snooping too."

He nodded. "Then we will know for sure by tomorrow morning."

My stomach dropped. "I don't want to leave."

He took my hands. "Sometimes we must retreat so that we can live to fight another day."

As much as it grated to think I may have to turn tail and run, he was right. Survival was key here. My siblings would be safe from the contracts no matter if I was here or not. One of them would become Satan, and then...Then maybe they'd make it so I could come home...

Home...

"This is my home now." I stared up at him, realization blooming hot in my chest. "Ignatius..."

He cupped my face and kissed me hard on the mouth. "Yes, *Qalbi*, this is your home."

I covered the backs of his hands with mine and kissed him again. "What does that mean? *Qalbi*?"

He brushed the tip of his nose against mine. "My love. It means my love."

"Dammit, Ignatius, you're going to make leaving you so much harder."

"There's time yet before you leave." He ran his tongue along the seam of my mouth. "Time enough for pleasure."

"Yes please."

SEV WAS WAITING for me when I returned. His eyes were bloodshot. He looked exhausted.

Crap, he'd been waiting up for me. "Sev..." I should have come back at dawn. "I'm sorry."

His jaw tightened but he shook his head. "It doesn't matter. You need to speak to Artimus before you leave for the Court of Ivory. It's vital." His eyelids drooped. "Dammit. I can't stay awake much longer so—"

I crossed the bed and wrapped him in a hug. "I'm *so* sorry."

He sighed and hugged me back. "It's all right." He pressed his nose to my neck and inhaled, then tensed. When he spoke, his tone had dropped an octave. "I can smell him on you."

I'd showered before leaving Ignatius, but with Sev's powerful senses it probably didn't make a difference.

He cupped the back of my neck and squeezed. "Did you fuck him?"

I met his gaze levelly. "Yes. Is that a problem?"

He closed his eyes and exhaled through his nose, as if trying to rid himself of Ignatius's scent. "No. I meant what I said before. I can share you. But when you're with me, you're mine." He licked a trail up my neck and pressed his lips to my jugular. "When you're with *me*, you're *mine*," he said again.

Then he bit me.

I swallowed my cry of pain and clutched his shoulders, digging my fingers in and breathing shallowly until...ah, oh yes...there it was...My body melted, euphoria flooding me, spreading over my body and down to the apex of my thighs, where it settled and throbbed invitingly.

My back hit the mattress, and Sev was on top of me, his mouth still at my throat, one hand between us, yanking up my skirts then tearing off my panties before entering me hard and deep. I took him greedily, wrapping my legs around his waist to anchor myself as he pounded into me, rough and primal. A claiming, a marking of his territory.

He retracted his fangs and closed the wound on my neck before claiming my mouth, never breaking stride with his thrusts.

"Mine," he growled against my lips. "Mine."

I'D TAKEN TWO LOVERS, both alpha males, both possessive in their own way, even though they were open to sharing me. I guess I'd have to get used to taking extra showers to avoid the whole "you smell of him" deal. But then, I probably wouldn't be here long enough to have to get used to anything.

Sev was out cold on the bed in his favorite position, on his front, head to one side, silver hair mussed.

Chase returned from his wanderings a few minutes ago and was already asleep on the floor at the foot of the bed, also on his side, snoring loudly.

At least Chase would come with me if I had to leave. I stroked Sev's hair off his face, anxiety unfurling in my chest. What would happen to Sev if I left? Would Umbrane take him back? No. I'd have to take him with me. There had to be a way. We were bound by a blood oath, after all. I'd speak to Artimus about it.

I tugged on my boots and quietly let myself out of the room.

The plan was to go find Artimus, but raised voices coming from Gus's room drew me there instead. The door was open.

"You shouldn't have done that," Tristeene said. "It was impulsive."

"It was honorable," Dhuma said. "And he has me for protection now."

"What's going on?" I stood in the doorway. "Gus?" Gus's ochre cheeks were flushed, his sapphire eyes bright with... anger? I was immediately on the defensive for him. "What happened?"

"He told Minera to shove her sponsorship up her ass," Mallini said with a satisfied smirk. "Who knew my imp brother had balls."

Tristeene glared at her, but Gus seemed to relax, some of the tension dropping from his shoulders. "I won't be her puppet."

Puppet? "What did she say?"

"Stupid things," Gus said.

"She's on team kill Nyx," Mallini said.

Fucking fabulous.

"What's going on?" Keelan appeared behind me, one hand clutching his torso.

I turned to him. "What are you doing out of bed?"

"Being nosy." He snorted. "You could have been considerate and brought the drama to my room."

"Gus just sacked Minera," Veena said, her eyes wide with awe.

He did it for me. To show his solidarity. But it left him without a sponsor, and although Dhuma was here, he couldn't be watching everyone at once.

"Gus..." I trailed off, lost for words as a warm, gooey feeling battled with common sense.

The tiny wings at his back flexed and he gave me a half smile. "I can't be affiliated with anyone who means my family harm."

Tristeene cursed softly under her breath and shook her head. "How am I meant to argue with that."

"You're not," Keelan said. "We stick together. No matter what."

How could I leave these guys? I blinked against the heat building behind my eyes. "I've got to go. I have to speak to Artimus."

"I'll come with you," Dhuma said. "The rest of you remain in the quarters. I've spoken to Nugen and the Lady Zinichi. Extra Minorax have been posted outside your quarters sent directly from the Court of Flame. If for some reason you must leave, then you will take a Minorax guard with you."

No one argued with him.

Dhuma followed me to the main doors of the spawn quarters but slowed when we passed my room. "Is your maras inside?"

"Yep, you haven't met yet?"

"No, but that is not surprising. A skilled maras can move in the shadows and take a willing passenger with him."

"Yes, Chase seems to have grown attached to Sev." I pulled open the doors and stepped out into the corridor where five Minorax stood guard. They inclined their heads in Dhuma's direction as we passed.

"Chase?" Dhuma asked.

"My hound. He's been with me since I was a child." I smiled up at him. "He's my best friend."

A small frown dimpled his forehead, but he didn't say

anything for a moment and then, "I'd like to meet them both."

"You'll have to catch them in the evening. Sev sleeps during the day and Chase seems to have adapted to that now."

The frown deepened. "I see. Interesting."

"It is?" I chuckled. "If you say so." I took the stairs, then a left onto the corridor where a hidden passage could get me to Artimus unseen. "You might have to duck to get in." I pressed a recess in the wall, invisible to anyone who didn't know it was there. The wall slid open.

Dhuma made an appreciative sound. "After you."

I climbed in and he followed. The door closed behind us with a snick and the passage lit up, activated by our presence.

Now which way was it again?

THIRTY-ONE

Artimus answered the door almost immediately. "What took you so long?" He ushered us in, not even batting an eye at the fact I'd brought Dhuma with me. "It's almost midday. Zepar will be coming for you soon."

I strolled into his neat, minimalist chambers. "You make it sound so ominous."

Dhuma stayed by the door as I followed Artimus deeper into the room to stand by the seating area.

Artimus's lips pressed in a thin lin. "Sometimes I wonder if you realize how much danger you're in."

My smile faded. "Oh, I know. But crying and cowering isn't going to help me, is it? Besides, that's not my MO."

He sighed. "No. I suppose it isn't. Another trait you got from your father."

I didn't know or care what Satan had been like. "That male was simply a sperm donor and being told I'm like him means nothing to me."

Artimus's jaw ticked. "Noted."

I'd hit a nerve. Of course I had. He'd worshiped Satan. "Why did you want to see me?"

"To tell you the plan. We can talk freely in here. It's secure."

"Okay. What plan?"

"Your escape plan."

This again. "The plan B."

"No, the plan A."

"What?"

"Things have changed. Sev overheard Umbrane talking to someone last night. The bastard orchestrated the carriage detour into the old forest."

Why wasn't I surprised? "We should have figured that out sooner."

"Probably. But he keeps a low profile. It's obvious now that he wants us both dead. He wasn't aware that all the spawn would be in the carriage with us, though." He held up his hand before I could ask any questions. "We don't know who his spy is or who he's working with in Libidine. We can't know for sure if this has anything to do with the fawda." He smiled dryly. "It's unlikely. I can't see Umbrane being anyone's lackey. He isn't the kind to give up power."

"So, you're worried Umbrane will come after me? We already know he wants me out. That's nothing new. We can handle him."

"That's not the problem."

My brows went up. "It isn't?"

"No. It seems that he and Erinea have teamed up. She's convinced all the lords and ladies invited to vote at the conclave to vote *against* your existence."

"Bribery?" Dhuma boomed. "How can the princes stand for such a thing?"

"There's no proof," Artimus said. "No physical bribe. Just a promise of a favor."

This was bullshit. "But Sev *is* a witness."

Artimus snorted. "You think they'll take his testimony as proof? Your nightmare was Umbrane's pet. His torture toy for decades. He has every reason to want to discredit the duke."

I stared at him, dumbfounded. "So that's it?"

His throat bobbed. "It would seem so."

"Then we leave," Dhuma said. "Now."

"Leave, yes," Artimus said. "But not yet. You'll leave tomorrow."

"Why wait?" Dhuma asked. "She can leave today. Nothing can stop her. I will not allow it to."

"You think there aren't eyes everywhere? Erinea is anticipating such a move. She's upped the guards around the keep and at the bridge and instructed the Eyes to attack if Nyx tries to leave."

"Then how do we leave?" Dhuma asked.

"Nyx will get severely sick and be taken to the infirmary, where a portal will be waiting to transport her to the market on the edge of the golden bridge. You'll get her onto the shooting star and back to mortal soil."

"Whoa...you want me to pretend to be sick?"

"Not pretend." He handed me a paper pouch. "You'll take this tomorrow morning when you return from the Court of Ivory. It takes thirty minutes to start working, so make sure you're with someone *after* you've ingested it because once it starts to work, you'll be in no condition to move."

Okay, that sounded worrying. "What kind of symptoms are we talking about?"

"Painful. Excruciating, but they will pass in a few hours. Long enough for everyone to believe you're sick."

My mind spun. We were discussing my escape. Discussing leaving everyone behind.

"There is no other choice," Artimus said softly. "Nyx, you must live to fight another day."

"I know. I just... I hate running away."

"This is not a surrender," Dhuma said. "It is a tactical retreat."

"You'll be safe on the mortal side of the bridge," Artimus said. "As part fallen and part daimon you're exempt from the extradition laws in the Accords that allow Morningstar to demand your return. The princes can't force you to come back."

"Fallen and daimons were never added to that law, were they?"

"No. Fallen are free to come and go as they wish, and daimons...Well, aside from Dhuma here, all the pure-blood daimons are gone, trapped behind the abyss gates."

So that was it? I'd have to leave. "What about Sev? I won't go without him. If Umbrane gets his hands on him..." I couldn't bear to think what that fucker would do to my lover.

Artimus seemed to chew this over. "You have a blood oath so you're within your rights to keep him with you, *and* as an abyssblood with more daimon than demon blood in his veins, he'll able to withstand the pure mortal atmosphere. It's pure demons that struggle with it."

Ah, yes. "I heard there are only a few bloodlines of pure demon left, and they refuse to procreate with the fallen."

"Yes, there are a handful."

"So I can take Sev with me? Sev, Chase, and Dhuma?" I smiled up at the hulking daimon.

"Yes," Artimus confirmed. "Once you're safe, just lie low. I'll find you eventually."

My throat tightened. "Why?"

"Why what?"

"Why are you doing so much to help me? I know you

said it's because you loved Satan, that you wanted to give all his spawn a fair chance, but that's bullshit. Tell me the truth. Heck, Arty, it might be the last chance you get."

His jaw ticked and he looked away. "You're right. It is bullshit. I came to find you that day in the market. I knew you'd be coming."

My pulse raced, blood rushing to my head as my suspicions were confirmed. "How?"

He took a shuddering breath. "Because it was me who sent the helhunters after you that night."

My mind flashed back to the night weeks ago when three huge beasts, a cross between hounds and lions, had attacked me. The glowing mark on their heads had appeared on my hand, labeling me as their target.

A band of betrayal wrapped around my chest. "Why? Why would you do that? I could have been killed!"

"They weren't sent to kill you, just to scare you. To make you angry enough to come searching for answers."

Fucking hell, how did he know me so well even back then? "You wanted me to find out I was Satan spawn."

"Yes, but now, in hindsight, I think I may have been mistaken."

I was so confused. "I don't understand. You knew where I was...Who I was? You knew I was in the mortal realm?"

"Yes, because, Nyx...I put you there."

THIRTY-TWO

His confession rang in my ears. "Excuse me? *You* put me in the mortal realm?" When we'd met, he'd acted like he didn't know me, like he was helping me figure out how I ended up in the mortal realm. "You lied to me!"

There was no emotion on his face. No guilt, no remorse as he told me his truth. "I gave you to a human female to raise. She was paid handsomely for her efforts. I checked in on you a couple of times a year for the first three years, but then business of state kept me busy. Time runs differently for us. Weeks seem like days and years like months, and by the time I returned you were gone."

"Yes, my mother dumped me in the Fringe like garbage." The words sat bitter and hollow between us.

Dhuma made a low sound of disgust in the back of his throat, but I didn't look at him. My attention was reserved for the man responsible for the clawing, hungry, desperate years of my childhood. *He'd* done this to me. He'd abandoned me in the human world.

His chest shuddered on a sigh and his careful

unrepentant mask cracked, showing me a glimpse of the torment beneath it. "When the human confessed what she'd done to you, I was going to kill her. That wretched woman who'd vowed to take care of you had betrayed you and me. But then her children came in, bright-faced, innocent. In the end I chose to let her live. For them. I went looking for you, and I found you'd been taken in by a kindly female. You seemed happy."

"So you left me there."

"It was the safest place for you."

Silence stretched between us for long seconds before I broke it. "Satan asked you to take me away, didn't he?"

"He did. It was...*You* were a secret he desperately wanted protected. He made me vow to take care of you. He said you were the key to everything. He said that once the deed was done, he and I would part ways. That we couldn't be seen to be close any longer, but he promised...He promised that when the time was right, he would reveal all to me."

"But then he died."

"Yes."

"But he never told you who my mother was?"

"No."

"And all this time you faked being estranged because he asked you to?"

"Yes."

"Do you see how insane that is? Do you see how fucking pathetic it is?"

"Maybe... But what would you do for the ones you love, Nyx?"

Dammit! "Fuck you, Artimus. Fuck you for making it so hard for me to hate you."

He didn't say anything, which was good because I needed a minute to get my shit together. "Why did you bring me here, then? Why bring me back if you didn't know for sure that was what he'd want?"

"I couldn't let you miss out on your birth right. Maybe I was wrong. Maybe that wasn't his plan for you, but I couldn't take the risk."

"Or maybe you should have backed off and let me make my own plans. Maybe you should have stopped fucking moving me around the board like a chess piece." My anger was back, rising like a wave. "I'm sick of the secrets and the lies. I'm sick of other people thinking they know what's best."

Dhuma placed a hand on my shoulder and my clawing wrath ebbed. "There will be time for vengeance, little one," he said. "But first, you must live."

I tucked in my chin and breathed through my nose. "Yeah...okay." I lifted my gaze to meet Artimus's sapphire one. Arguing about his actions was pointless. Raging at him would achieve nothing, and I was all about the results. Besides, the fact remained that I needed him. Not just for me, but for my family. "Promise me that you'll look out for my siblings. Promise me that you'll take care of them. Don't let Umbrane or Erinea poison their minds against each other. Remind them that they're stronger together. Do that, and I'll forgive you for the lies."

"I'd watch out for them whether you forgive me or not."

I pocketed the herbs he'd given me. "I better go. I need to say goodbye to my siblings."

"You can't do that," Artimus said.

"Why the fuck not?"

"The less they know about our plan, the better. You don't want them implicated and I don't want the princes finding out that I was involved. They might suspect me, but they can't act without proof. I won't be much help to your siblings from a cage."

I wasn't going to get to say goodbye? Shit.

"I'll make sure Sev and Chase make it to the infirmary," he continued. "The portal will be inside the washroom, in the shower stall."

"What about the conji you're using to make the portal?" Dhuma asked. "What if they talk?"

Artimus's lips curved in a thin smile. "That isn't something you need to worry about."

Dhuma moved to the door suddenly and pulled it open to peer outside.

"What is it?" Artimus asked.

"I thought I heard something." He stepped out of the room. "I'll stand guard while you say goodbye."

He closed the door behind him, leaving me alone with Artimus, and it hit me that it wasn't just my siblings and Ignatius that I'd be leaving behind. This would probably be the last time I'd see Artimus in a long while.

I'd be leaving him too.

The look on his face echoed my revelation.

He bridged the distance between us in two strides and hooked a finger under my chin, tipping my face up to his. "I'm sorry for lying to you."

The final vestiges of anger toward him melted away. I understood his motivations and didn't doubt his sincerity now.

"I believe you." My gaze dropped to his lips, then flicked back to his eyes. "Is it kinda weird that you knew me as a baby."

The corner of his mouth lifted. "In our world of immortals and longevity it hardly matters. Besides, I didn't *know* you until you came to Morningstar. It was here that I saw you for the formidable woman you are." He grazed my cheek with his fingertips. "Honorable, with the heart of a warrior and the compassion of a mother. You did something that no one expected. You brought the spawn together. You made them into a family. We expected bloodshed in a thirst for power, but instead we saw unity."

"That was them. Always them. I just gave them a reason to trust. But I will say, none of this is what I expected."

"No…no, it probably isn't, but this place fits who you are, Nyx. Maybe I shouldn't have dragged you into the ascension, but I don't regret meeting you. I don't regret the way I feel about you, only that we never had a chance to fully explore it."

My heart thudded painfully against my ribcage.

He smiled, soft and wistful. "I wish we had more time."

My throat pinched, and I forced my lips into a cocky smile and injected a teasing note into my voice to hide the very serious question beneath it. "You mean you'd have dumped that witch Erinea?"

His attention settled on my lips. "In a heartbeat. Once you were safe."

I pressed my palm to his chest, allowing the heat of his skin to seep into mine through the fabric of his shirt. "I'll be safe soon enough…"

His eyes darkened. "You're right. She's served her purpose. It's over." My stomach flipped as his mouth brushed mine. "I can't trust myself to taste you and then let you go."

It took everything I had not to press my mouth to his and take the kiss I'd been craving. Instead, I held back, reveling in the soft caress, trying to memorize the shape of his mouth as it tantalized mine.

His bottom lip brushed my top one, catching for a moment. "Arty…" His name was a breathless explosion between us.

He gripped my nape, a low, sensual groan slipping from his lips. "Nyx…"

Our mouths finally met, and a jolt shot through me. I let him in, licking at his tongue, moaning into his mouth as his honeysuckle flavor hit the back of my throat. My hands sank into his hair, fingers twining in the silken strands as I pushed up on my toes to deepen the kiss and bring our bodies together. Heat seared my torso where we touched, and his need pressed against me, hard and hot.

The kiss, which started so gentle and soft, devolved into something carnal and primal. Hands pinched and squeezed. Tongues wrestled. Our teeth clashed and nipped at flesh.

I tasted copper and Artimus's chest vibrated in a deep growl that made the hair on my body stand to attention in warning. His grip tightened, sudden and painful, then his mouth crashed down on mine so hard tears sprang to my eyes.

In the next moment I was free and he was standing across the room, shoulders heaving as he sucked in huge lungfuls of air.

His lips were tainted crimson with my blood and his eyes were black as night. "Fuck...Nyx..." He touched his mouth, then licked his lips, moaning softly. "Your blood..."

He'd reacted oddly to my blood when I'd been hurt getting out of Umbrane's stables. I knew he had an issue with feeding. Understood how he could easily lose control, but this reaction was intense.

"Are you okay?"

He turned away. "I'll be fine. Give me a moment."

His voice had that deep and gruff timbre like when he'd come to find me in the old forest.

Long seconds ticked by before he turned to face me. He tugged a handkerchief from his pocket and dabbed at his mouth. "That was careless of me."

And there he was, back to his reined-in, composed self. Which was good, but also disappointing, because peeking under the veneer, the thrill and dance with danger was an aphrodisiac to my twisted soul.

"Do you always react that way to a teeny taste of blood?"

He adjusted his cuffs. "No."

But he did to mine. To my messed-up fallen and daimon blood. We'd talked about this—about how little he knew about his bloodline. The Bsar bloodline. His reaction to me could be a clue.

He shook his head slightly, his expression turning wistful again.

A fist gripped my chest. "I wish I didn't have to go."

"So do I." He kept his distance.

"Does Ignatius know I'll be leaving?"

"Yes. He and Loke both know."

"You spoke to Loke about this?"

"You'd be surprised how many people want you to live. Unfortunately, none of us have the power to overturn the princes' decree."

"But the new Satan will."

He smiled fully, showcasing pronounced canines.

My breath caught in my throat. Damn, he was dangerously sexy.

"I have no doubt you'll be given his full protection once he or she is seated," he said.

Not long, then.

I just had to get out and survive long enough for one of my siblings to claim the seat's power.

Which was good, because not dying was my forte.

THIRTY-THREE

Not being able to say goodbye, not being able to tell my siblings what would happen tomorrow morning, sucked. It wasn't even as if I'd get to spend any time with them before my escape.

Escape.

I hated the word.

Running away.

Hiding.

So much needed to be changed here. This fear of the unknown, the creatures that were different. Creatures like me. It needed to change, and I had confidence that my siblings would make these modifications, whoever took the throne.

Dhuma left me at my quarters with a promise to watch over my siblings until I returned. I'd considered asking him to stay with them when I left for the Fringe, but with me gone, they'd no longer be in any danger.

I was the problem here. The princes, Erinea, Umbrane, all of them wanted me gone. With me out of the way, the trials would continue, and a Satan would be chosen without any more drama. As much as I hated to admit it, it was for the best.

Sev was still sleeping soundly when I got back to my room, but Chase stirred and raised his head to greet me.

"Hey, buddy." I crouched and stroked behind his ears the way he liked.

He chuffed softly, then nudged my knee before looking toward the door to the Ivory Court.

"Yeah, I have to go soon. But it's more than that."

He looked up at me with his intelligent brown eyes as if to say, *I know. I know it all.*

"This time tomorrow, we'll be home." But the word felt hollow and untrue, because this was my home now.

Chase whined softly and then did something he rarely ever did. He licked my hand. A comforting lick. His equivalent of a kiss.

I touched my forehead to his. "You want to hang for a bit? I have a half hour till midday?"

Chase tensed, his attention flying to the Court of Ivory door again. The frame was glowing. The portal was live. Early.

I guess Zepar was impatient to see me.

The door opened and a zuni appeared. He stood with his hands clasped in front of him, eyes downcast. "Duke Zepar will see you now."

This male was different from the one who'd escorted me to Zepar the last time I'd visited. His dark hair was long, tied back in a braid, and he was sporting a neat blond goatee.

"Looks like our hangout session will have to wait." I patted Chase's head. "I'll see you later."

I grabbed the overnight bag I hadn't bothered to unpack and slung it over my shoulder. "Lead the way."

THIS TIME the doorway led us into a sunlit circular courtyard. The gray stone walls were covered in ivy and several stone benches bordered a path leading to an arch in the wall. The zuni led me through an arch and onto a wide stone walkway that led to another arch cut into an ivory tower. Mist surrounded us so it was almost like walking through a cloud. It didn't take me long to realize that we were doing just that because this was no walkway but a bridge across the vast expanse of nothingness.

Thank fuck I wasn't afraid of heights.

The closer we got to the arch, the taller it grew until I was a gnat in the presence of a giant.

I'd seen this place from afar when Zepar had flown me into the night sky, but I'd underestimated its magnitude. This was a court that housed mainly fallen, and it was obvious they were all about the philosophy of go-big-or-go-home. My assessment was confirmed as we stepped through the ivory arch and onto a vast platform facing a maze of bridges. Several exits shot off the platform, jutting out to become steps and more bridges until even those disappeared through glowing arches suspended in nothingness.

Figures scurried along the bridges that crisscrossed and joined only to separate again. It was a fucking highway, and we were at a junction.

"This way." The zuni set off down one of the bridges, then hopped up a flight of stairs to another platform and another bridge.

"Are those portals to different parts of the Ivory Court?"

"Yes," he said.

"And my room has a portal connected to it, right?"

"That is correct."

"So why not just port me directly to Duke Zepar like last time?"

The zuni didn't answer. Instead, he picked up his pace.

My scalp pricked. "Hey! Wait up."

I jogged and caught up to him at the foot of a flight of steps.

He hurried up them, then stopped on a platform housing an arch. "This is the duke's tower. He's expecting you."

My gut told me something was wrong, and then it hit me. "This arch isn't glowing. Doesn't that mean it's not active?"

The zuni made a pained sound and then the fucker shoved me.

Hard.

Right through the dark portal.

The inactive portal.

Which meant it was just a fucking arch that led to nothing.

Nothing but a long plummet to death.

THIRTY-FOUR

I was a lead weight in the grip of gravity hurtling through mist, a scream stuck in my throat. The air rushed past too fast, pressing in on me and sucking me down.

How many bones would break when I hit the ground?

I'd never get to see my siblings again.

Chase...

Sev and Ignatius...

Artimus...

Orina would never know what happened to me.

Would I die on impact?

Wait, if I died, then I'd be back, right? I had to, even if it was just to beat the crap out of the zuni. I'd stick my boot so far up his a—

My descent sped up and terror hit hard, stealing my rage. I squeezed my eyes shut. No need to watch death rushing up to meet me. No need to see.

Any minute now?

Fuck, I hated pain.

Please be quick.

Something slammed into me, and my scream finally flew loose, coming out as a pathetic squeak. Bands wrapped around me. I was no longer falling. I was rising.

"I've got you," Zepar said.

Oh my fucking earth and stars. I hugged his neck, tucked my face into his shoulder, and breathed, finally breathed. He took us back into the clouds, his scent filling my head, potent like the electrically charged air before a storm.

I was safe.

He had me.

ZEPAR DIDN'T TAKE me back to the bridges. Instead, he flew us through a twenty-foot aperture into a tower room with a ceiling so high you'd need wings to dust the cobwebs. Which, considering where we were, made sense.

We touched down on the hardwood floor, but Zepar didn't set me on my feet straight away. He held me tighter, his heart beating hard and fast against me.

"I'm okay." I'm not sure why I said it. He knew I was okay. He'd just made sure of it. I guess I just needed to hear it said out loud in my own voice.

"Why did you leave without me?" he asked.

"What?" I stared up at him in confusion for a moment before the pieces clicked into place. "You didn't send the zuni to get me, did you?"

"What zuni?"

Anger spiked beneath my relief. Not aimed at him, but at my situation. At the fact that I was a target. "Put me down. I can stand."

He did so, reluctantly. But when my boots hit the ground, my knees buckled. I grabbed hold of him to steady myself. He scooped me back up and carried me across the room.

There was no point fighting it. My mind was sharp, ready for action, but my body obviously needed more time to recover from its plummet to almost-death.

The damn cuffs must be messing with my ability to bounce back from an adrenaline rush.

He lowered me onto a chaise with no back. "Lean against the arm."

I settled on the soft fabric as he knelt and reached for my boot.

I pulled my foot away. "What are you doing?"

"Taking off your boots so you can get comfortable."

"I can do that myself. Just... Just give me a moment."

But he already had my ankle in his grasp and the next moment my boots were off. He gripped my foot and pressed his thumb to the arch, sending a warm tingle up my leg to wake it up. A soft moan fell from my lips.

"What happened?" he asked. "Tell me everything."

His tone was calm and even, but his tawny eyes were hard and cutting and his mouth was tight at the corners. He was pissed, but in control.

I admired that.

"A zuni came to pick me up and bring me to you. He took me high up on those bridges and then shoved me through an inactive portal." It sounded so ridiculous when I put it into words and my anger resurfaced, this time aimed at myself. "I had a gut feeling something was off. I should have listened to it. I usually do." I tugged at the cuffs. "These things are fucking with my instincts."

He gently gripped my wrist, covering the cuff and stroking a thumb along the inside of my arm soothingly. "What did he look like?"

I took a moment to rein in my rage. "Dark hair. A blond goatee. He was wearing the uniform."

He nodded curtly and stood. "Stay here. Do not go with anyone. Wait for me to come for you."

He strode to the huge window and launched himself into the air. The shadow of his wings stretched across the stone frame for a moment, then he was gone.

I should have gone with him, but that would mean flying, and I'd had enough of the sky for one day. I had no doubt that if the traitorous zuni was still around, then Zepar would find him.

I put my feet up, stretched out on the chaise, and closed my eyes. It was barely midday, and I was exhausted.

"Nyx?"

"Huh?" I stared up at Zepar blearily. Hadn't he just flown out the window? But the gathering shadows in the room told me time had passed. "I fell asleep."

"You obviously needed it." He crouched beside the chaise.

Were those bloodstains on his shirt?

I reached out and touched the spatters. "You found him."

"Yes."

I sat up. "What did he say?"

"Nothing. He refused to speak, no matter what we did to him."

"I want to speak to him."

"He's dead."

I slumped back on the chaise. "Dammit! I don't get it. Why try to kill me? Everyone knows what I am now. If I die, I'll come back and—"

"Not necessarily," he said. "I spoke to my mother about high daimons when we found out what you were. There are ways to stop a high daimon being reborn. Shattering its

211

body irreparably is one of them. Tearing it to shreds is another. Burning it...If there is no body for the soul to come back to, then..."

"Oh..." An awful thought filled my mind. "Is that what they plan to do to me? Pull me to pieces? Burn me?" Panic squeezed my chest, and for a moment I forgot that I didn't plan to stick around to give them a chance.

"No. No." He cradled me in his lap.

When had he picked me up? Mmmm, this felt good.

"Those methods were used when there was no other option," he said soothingly. "The fallen aren't unnecessarily cruel."

I allowed him to rock me and calm my panicked body while my mind worked. "What *will* they do?"

"They have a weapon. It would be quick," he said softly. "But it won't come to that."

"You don't know that."

"No, I don't, but I can promise you, I will fight for you. I will do everything in my power to sway that vote into saving you. I can be extremely persuasive."

"Thanks for not lying to me. And I don't doubt your persuasion skills."

"Good."

His face was close to mine, his tawny gaze warm like honey and filled with shadows. "Are *you* all right?"

His throat bobbed. "I could have missed you. If I'd flown back a different route..."

My lungs grew tight. "But you didn't. You saved me."

But the look in his eyes echoed the tremor in my belly because there was no overlooking the fact that I could have died today.

THIRTY-FIVE

By the time we sat down to eat, my body had recovered from the shock of my fall. Just like before, there were several courses on offer, and with my increased appetite I was happy to indulge.

We ate beneath the stars on a large, enclosed balcony lit by lanterns. The air tasted of summer and vanilla and the anxieties of the past few days melted away for a little while.

Zepar had changed into a teal T-shirt and loose black pants, his feet were bare, and there was an air of chill about him that helped me unwind. He entertained me with stories about his childhood in Superbia. He mentioned his mother several times in his tales, but Ramiel was absent to a point that it felt significant.

"There's a river that sits on the edge of Superbia," he said. "Filled with all manner of horrors."

"Like Lake Morbidus?"

He considered my question for a moment. "No. The creatures that swim around Morningstar's keep are something entirely unique. Able to kill demons and fallen."

"What about high daimons?"

He frowned, then looked up at me. "I'm not sure."

I could see I'd thrown him off. "So about this river in Superbia?"

"Yes. Only the most skilled fishermen take to the water there, but when I was barely fourteen a fallen challenged me to catch a ratka."

"And what is one of those?"

He smiled smugly. "A large predatory fish able to shred the flesh from any creature's bones in seconds."

"Sounds like a piranha, except they're smaller and tend to hunt in shoals."

"Ah...yes, maybe."

"So, you caught one?"

"I did. But I lost my hand in the process."

I stared at him in horror. "What?"

His eyes twinkled with mischief. "Luckily for me my mother is a very powerful conji. Even then, it took a week for allure to grow it back." He held up his right hand. "But good as new."

He obviously had a strong bond with his mother, despite the tension I'd picked up on between them in Libidine. But once again, there was no mention of Ramiel.

"Why didn't you tell me your father was one of the princes?"

His jaw tightened. "Why? Should I have?"

I shrugged. "We spoke for hours the other day. It's the kind of thing you might disclose to someone you want to be friends with."

He looked away into the night. "Ramiel may have sired me, but he was never a father. He refused to claim me publicly and announce me as his heir."

"But why?"

"Because my mother is merely a consort. Not his chosen mate, which makes me illegitimate and unworthy."

"Wait...what? That's ridiculous. You're still his son."

"By blood maybe, but not in name. Not in status. Not *officially*. Ramiel's tryst with my mother was a fleeting thing. He keeps her close now because he needs her power. She has value to him. I do not. My mother raised me. Alone." A bitter smile curled his lips. "Ramiel's only concession to my existence was giving me the title of Duke and handing me this court to run, and I'm certain even that was under duress from my mother." He picked up his fork and stabbed a piece of meat on his plate. "He needs her. She's the most powerful conji in the realm."

I shook my head. "I really don't understand the fallen."

He picked up a napkin, then put it back down again. "Well then, allow me to explain. There are many original fallen, but there were only nine powerful enough to call themselves princes."

"The nine realms?"

"Yes. Six of them were killed in the Chaos War, including the most powerful of them all..."

"Lucifer."

"Correct. Now all that remain are Levistus, Merihem, and Ramiel. Satan is simply a seat of power. One that contains a fraction of each prince's power, given willingly. A collaboration that ensures a balance throughout our world."

So the seat had a bit of all their power in it. It explained why they were so gung-ho about protecting it. Why it mattered so much to them who sat on that seat and claimed that power.

"Why did you choose me, Zepar?"

He blinked sharply. "Excuse me?"

"Why did you choose me as your custodia out of all the other spawn? Was it because you thought I'd be easy to manipulate because I was half human? That if I got the seat, you'd be able to control the power through me?"

His tawny eyes flashed and then he sighed. "I can't blame you for coming to that conclusion, especially after what I just told you about my life. But no. That wasn't why." He smiled wryly. "I saw a fiery, proud female with a sassy mouth that would probably get her killed if someone didn't step up to shield her. I saw a female thrown into a world she didn't belong in. I saw an underdog, and, well...I have a soft spot for the underdog."

"And now? Now that you know what I am? Now that there could be enough power inside me to be a threat?"

"Now I see a woman who, if allowed to flourish, could be truly formidable." His smile was soft and intimate, spawning butterflies in my belly. "You fascinate me, and—"

A gust of wind threw my hair back over my shoulders. The flap of wings killed the candlelight and a moment later a figure landed on the balcony by the stone barrier.

The shadows parted and Prince Ramiel stepped forward.

And it didn't take a body language expert to deduce that the fallen prince was furious.

Thirty-Six

Zepar slowly set down his fork. "Ramiel, to what do we owe the pleasure?" His tone was stony and unwelcoming despite his words.

"Tell me, Duke Zepar, who do you answer to?"

Zepar's jaw ticked. "You, Your Grace."

"That is correct. So why did you not report the attack on Nyx to me?"

Zepar's brows flicked up. "I—"

"Quiet!" Ramiel's command was a boom that made my stomach hurt.

Zepar's hand curled into a fist on the table.

Ramiel turned his focus on me. "What happened?"

I looked to Zepar, and I swear he was grinding his teeth. "A zuni tried to kill me." I gave Ramiel a tight smile. "Your *son* saved me."

Ramiel flinched.

Maybe it was pushy to emphasize their relationship, but he was acting like a dick, treating Zepar like he was lesser. An underling.

I didn't like it.

Indignation formed a knot in my chest. "Like Zepar said, I'm fine now."

"You should have reported this to me," Ramiel said to Zepar, acknowledging his presence once more.

"Why?" I sat forward. "Isn't my death exactly what you all want?"

His brows pinched. "There are protocols. A conclave."

A farce. "What does it matter to you *when* I die? Today or after the conclave, it's all the same, right?"

Ramiel stood tall, wings snapping at his back as if in agitation. "A zuni attempting murder on a Satan spawn will not be stood for. I want his—"

"Head?" Zepar finished. "You can collect it from the interrogation chambers in the west tower."

"You killed him?" Ramiel glared at his son. "You fool. We need to know who's behind the attack."

"You think I don't know that? He was tortured for hours. He would not yield."

Ramiel's lip curled in disgust. "A better fallen would have *made* him yield."

His words hung in the air like a barb, but to give him credit, Zepar didn't flinch. He didn't react at all.

Instead, he picked up his fork, jabbed at a chunk of meat, then looked up at his father. "Will you be staying for dinner?"

He seemed outwardly chill but his white-knuckled grip on his knife told a different story.

Ramiel didn't seem to notice. He simply stared at his son for several beats, his mouth turning down, before launching himself up into the night air and away into the stars.

Zepar sagged in his seat, breathing through his nose.

I wanted to say something. To ask if he was okay, but it felt intrusive. Zepar—proud, controlled, and powerful –

didn't need a reminder of the cracks in his armor when it came to his father.

I sat back and patted my belly. "You know, I think I'm ready for course number five."

His gaze lifted to mine, tawny eyes warming to honey, and a small smile played on his lips. "Are you sure you can handle it?"

"I can if you can?"

The smile bloomed, lighting up and softening his angular, chiseled features.

I returned the smile. "How about we have some dessert instead?"

"It's a deal. And then I'll give you a tour of my court."

THE COURT OF IVORY was a large, echoing place filled with thirty-foot ceilings and fifteen-foot doors. There were apertures everywhere, not windows covered in glass, just wide spaces cut out of the white and gray stone to allow the fallen to fly in and out as they pleased. Intricately carved, sturdy balustrades and gleaming golden beams held it all together. Each room was a cavernous space that made me feel small. The floors were cold white marble threaded with silver filigree patterns. It was a detached place. Beautiful in its simplicity.

Not my kinda décor, though. I preferred the rustic cozy vibe. But the pride on Zepar's face as he showed me his home was enough to keep my mouth shut.

We strolled through corridor after corridor, past fallen and zuni going about their business. Everyone stopped to bow to Zepar, staying bent over until he passed. He commanded respect here. This was his domain. Here he was king. A king who wore T-shirts and joggers and walked barefoot through the halls of his castle.

"You don't dress like the other fallen."

"I prefer comfort to pomp. Cotton is comfortable. T-shirts are comfortable and easy to customize for wings."

The air behind him shimmered where his wings hid from sight.

"How do you guys do that? Hide your wings?"

"I'm not sure. It's just something we can do, like clenching or unclenching your hand."

We stepped through a vaulted arch into a stairwell that wound up to a large tower room. This room was different from the others, all dark wood and worn sofas. Two doors led out of this central room that smelled faintly of paint, which made sense when I spotted the easel by one of the wider windows. A small table littered with tubes of paint, brushes, and supplies sat beside it, and several canvases were propped against the wall with their backs to the room.

I glanced up at him. "Is this your space?"

"Yes." He dropped into an armchair and indicated I take the sofa. "I know it's not as opulent as the rest of the court towers, and if you like I can find you a guest room."

"We're staying here?"

He looked suddenly unsure. "Not if you don't like it."

"Like it? I love it. It feels...comfortable."

He relaxed. "It's not as large as the other towers but it's cozy. No one comes here but me."

But he was sharing it with me and that meant something.

"What would you like to do for the rest of the evening?" he asked.

I glanced at the easel and the painting things. As a child I'd loved to draw, but I'd never painted before.

"You could teach me to paint."

He blinked in surprise. "You want to paint?"

I shrugged. "Sure. I always wanted to try, but the life of a bounty hunter never left much time to learn."

"Painting isn't something that can be taught, exactly, more...facilitated."

I grinned at him cheekily. "Then facilitate me."

TWO HOURS LATER, I was covered in paint. I'd gone for abstract, adding color and patterns and blending where I felt it needed to be worked.

The image screamed turmoil.

"You really did put your emotions onto the canvas, didn't you?" Zepar studied my work, his leonine gaze bright. "May I keep it?"

"Really? You want it?"

"I do."

"Okay. On one condition..."

"Name it."

"You paint me something to take with me." As soon as the words were out, it hit me that I may not be able to take anything with me but the clothes on my back and the people Artimus had promised to send with me.

"Nyx? What's wrong?" He studied me shrewdly.

I plastered a smile on my face. "Nothing. I'm good. So? Will you paint me something?"

I indicated a blank canvas propped up against the window.

"Yes. We have a deal, but I'll have to owe you. What I have in mind will take a few days to paint."

Regret jabbed at my chest, but I maintained a carefree demeanor. "I can wait." A yawn tugged at my jaw, and I swallowed it, but not before Zepar noticed.

"You're tired. You should sleep." He plucked at my paint-covered shirt. "This won't do. We best find you something to sleep in."

"I'm good. I'll be taking it off anyway."

His brows flicked up and then his tawny gaze heated. "Oh…"

I gave him a slow-burn smile. "Yep."

"Won't you be cold?"

In the time before I would have come back with something like, *why? are you offering to keep me warm?* And that would have led to some epic sex. But things felt different now. I'd held off on getting physical with Zepar due to trust issues, but he'd been honest, candid, and saved my life. The attraction between us was strong, but that was no longer enough for me.

Somewhere along my journey from bounty hunter to high daimon, my heart had changed.

I was in love with Sev, had deep feelings for Ignatius on a level I didn't quite understand, and Arty… I wanted to explore our connection. Loke's face filled my mind, but I pushed the forbidden fruit away. My heart and body were taken, and sharing them with anyone else outside of the males who'd already wriggled their way under my skin felt wrong.

This fallen just wasn't there yet.

I tipped my head to the side. "You're right. I best borrow something to wear."

Zepar's eyes dimmed but he smiled and nodded. "I'll find you something. You can have my bed."

"You don't have a guest room?" Ah, he'd been hoping to share a bed with me tonight. Presumptuous and kinda annoying. But I was beginning to understand that Zepar had an ego. I recognized it, even respected it, because I could relate to it.

We were, in many ways, the same.

He looked out the window. "I think I'll take a dip through the sky, tour the perimeter, then I might start on that painting for you." He reached out and tucked a tendril of my hair behind my ear. It was the first physical contact we'd had in hours, and a tingle radiated out from where his fingers brushed my cheek. He dropped his hand, his smile wistful, almost...lonely. "I'm not much for sleep anyway."

I was tempted to ask him to stay, but that might give the wrong message. A message I wasn't ready to give him.

"Thank you." I pressed my palm to his chest and looked up into his face, wanting him to know how grateful I was for his presence tonight. For his sponsorship and his friendship. "For everything."

"Always, Nyx. Always."

But would he feel the same way about me when I ran? Would he still be here for me when I finally returned?

And why did the answer to those questions matter so much to me?

Thirty-Seven

Tea for Three

Three figures sit quietly sipping tea in a cozy firelit room. The world beyond the windows is dark and starlit as if their cabin floats in the night sky, and who knows, it may be doing exactly that.

The tea is strong and dark, and the flickering flames almost hypnotic. It's an obligatory meeting of siblings, held once every hundred years.

In the beginning, eons ago, they would have bantered. Laughed even. Marveled at the progression of life around them. At their part in guiding the fates of the creatures within.

But that time is long past.

Like the world around them, the sisters too evolved. Took many names and roles over the centuries. But deep beneath it all, they clung to what they believed to be their inherent purpose. They held on to their beliefs.

Well...two of them did. The third... She changed.

Loss can do that to a person, even one who was forged in

the darkness of an infinite abyss by hands that have no master.

Now there are unspoken words between them. The bitterness of betrayal and the clawing need to know why? Why the betrayal cannot stop.

But no one speaks.

They merely sit and drink their tea.

Long minutes pass and the youngest of the three, in appearance and in time, leans forward to refill her cup from the metal-topped teapot on the table around which they sit.

Her gaze flicks across to the middle child, the one who's the reason for the silence, the one who refuses to conform, and a wave of sadness washes over her.

"Mayhap we should speak about it?" The question is put to the oldest. The heart-shaped one. The glowing one who sits head bowed, fingers tapping on the rim of her cup.

Older in time, the first of the three is their anchor. Their voice. At least she was before...

The oldest shakes her head slightly. "That would be up to *her*."

The *her* in question sighs. "Unless you're willing to concede, then there is nothing more to say." Although younger than the eldest and older than the youngest, the middle sister holds the appearance of age, with a softly lined face and silken silver hair. But her eyes are bright, filled with wisdom and infinite youth.

The youngest makes a sound of exasperation. "Please. This has gone on for much too long. Does it matter? Why can we not continue as we were? Why can we not believe what we wish?"

Her naivety is part of her charm. But the eldest has no patience for it today.

"Because we have roles. Roles that we were created to perform. A purpose we were given life to serve."

"You don't know that," the middle sister says. "We don't know that for certain."

"I feel it," the eldest says.

"But I do not. Not anymore."

"You are tainted by loss, sister," the youngest says. "If you would only—"

"No," the middle sister snaps. "This is about more than that. This is about freedom. I will no longer contribute to the bars that hold the flesh-and-blood beings of this world to account."

"You would give up the threads?"

"I would hand those who are bound the means to cut them if they so desire and have the will. I would give them the true choice."

"And in doing so you invite chaos," the eldest says.

"It matters not," the youngest says. "You will not win the wager."

The eldest smiles in agreement.

The middle sister shrugs a shoulder. "Maybe not, but I will be content knowing that I tried." She sips her tea. "While you play jailer in the realm of your creation, I shall take the role of guardian and liberator for those who wish to forge their own paths."

"Paths are there for a reason," the youngest says in a hushed tone. "Straying brings danger to us all."

"How can we know that when we have never allowed for it to be so? All we ever do is give the *illusion* of choice. We whisper lies and they believe it. They believe they are thwarting fate, that they are forging their own destinies, when in truth we have already woven the intricate pattern of their lives and bound them to it, leading them exactly where we wish them to go."

The eldest slams her hand on the table. "It is our purpose!"

The middle sister's lip curls. "Oh? And was it our purpose to gift them the thread of magic too?"

The eldest flinches. "That was not my fault. It was an accident."

The youngest places a hand on the eldest's shoulder. "They stole from her. They stole a thread and bound it to their world. She does her best to keep order and you're not helping. Give up the wager. Come home. Please."

Doubt flickers across the middle sister's face, and for a moment she wonders if she's in the wrong. If maybe her grief has made her callous. If maybe her quest is selfish, but then she recalls the face of the one she wishes to liberate.

A creature she has grown to love.

She drains the dregs from her cup and pushes back her seat. "Until next time, sisters. I have a wager to win."

THIRTY-EIGHT

NYX

I woke to the strangely comforting aroma of coffee and fresh paint. Someone, probably Zepar, had left a tray on the bedside table. There was pot of black coffee, a mug, two small pots of cream and sugar, and some delicious-looking pastries.

My stomach growled, but I ignored it in favor of the washroom. Zepar's shirt whispered across my skin with every movement, the cotton so soft it was a caress. I needed to find out where he got these made.

I came out of the bathroom a few minutes later, grabbed the breakfast tray, and padded into the central tower room.

Had Zepar eaten yet? If not, there was plenty on the tray to share.

The circular room was edged in darkness, the center bathed in the gray light of dawn, but the gloom didn't seem to bother the duke.

He stood facing away from me, dabbing paint onto the

canvas, his tapered back blocking my view of what he was painting.

"Hey." I set the tray on the table by the sofas. "Did you sleep at all?"

"No." He glanced over his shoulder, a frown of concentration on his beautiful face. "I wanted to keep painting."

What *was* he painting? I approached but he picked up the easel and flipped it. "Not yet."

"Spoilsport."

His short dark hair was ruffled, and he had paint on his chin and nose. I reached up and rubbed the turquoise spot on his jaw. "Paint."

His eyes dropped to half-mast. He gently gripped my wrist, then swept his thumb back and forth across my pulse. "Did you sleep well?"

I swallowed to moisten my suddenly dry mouth. "Yes, that mattress is perfection."

I was acutely aware of how close we were standing to each other, of the warmth of his fingers around my wrist and the rasp of his stubble against my fingers because, yep, I was still stroking the spot where the paint had been.

He slow-blinked, his pupils dilating, and leaned in. He was going to kiss me.

My pulse kicked up.

But his lips never made it to mine. "You should eat and then I'll take you back to Morningstar. The Seneschal will be waiting." He released me.

I had no reason to be disappointed. I mean, I didn't want him to kiss me, right? "Have you eaten?"

"Not yet."

I indicated the tray. "Then join me."

It was only as we were tucking into the pastries that the wisdom of that decision hit me. I'd be taking the herbs to make me sick as soon as I got back. Was it wise to eat so much?

Artimus hadn't explained the symptoms.

But it was too late now.

Let's hope one of the symptoms wasn't vomiting, or worse, the shits.

ZEPAR TOOK me on the scenic route through the Ivory Court grounds. I'd been nervous about the possibility of having to fly again, but so far so good. Our feet remained firmly on the ground. I hated the fact that it bothered me. That an activity I'd enjoyed the last time I was here was now tainted by my fall.

I'd have to get over it at some point. I drew Zepar to a halt. "Look, we can fly if we need to. You don't have to worry about me."

The corner of his mouth tipped up. "I know. You're not the kind of woman to run from your fears. But there is no need for a flight today. I've already made other arrangements."

I arched a brow. "You're not just saying that to make me feel better?"

"I wouldn't dare."

"Fine, lead the way."

We entered a room containing three glowing doorways. A robed figure sat at a desk scrawling on parchment with a quill.

He looked up at Zepar, his expression one of polite inquiry. His eyes were silver like the conji I'd met in the Court of Flame, but his skin was pale, not metallic.

"Have you attuned it?" Zepar asked him.

"I have indeed," the conji said in a soft, melodious voice.

"The portal in the spawn's room will be cleansed and recalibrated. In the meantime, she may pass through the main doors to Morningstar."

I frowned up at Zepar. "The main doors?"

"The portal that we usually use."

Ah, the room with the bricked-up arches and all the carved images of winged beings and demons. "Got it."

"There's a Minorax guard waiting for you on the other side to escort you to your rooms. Do not use the portal in your room until I tell you it's safe to do so."

I wouldn't be using it again at all, but he didn't know that, and I couldn't tell him, so I smiled and nodded.

"The central doorway is ready for you," the conji said.

Zepar cupped my face in his large warm hands. "Stay safe, Nyx. I will see you before the conclave. I will be there, and I will fight for you."

I believed him. Believed that if I planned to go through with the conclave, he'd have been there to support me. "I thought you don't get to vote."

"No, but we do get to address the conclave members."

It was clear after spending some quality time with him that Zepar wasn't as totally up his own ass as I'd first thought. He was a product of his past like all of us, and his wounds were just as deep as mine.

It was a shame I wouldn't have the chance to get to know him better. I could only hope he'd understand why I hadn't shared my plan with him.

"I'll see you soon." He drew me close and tipped my chin down to press a kiss to my forehead.

The tender gesture left my throat too tight to speak. I nodded mutely and walked into the portal.

I NEEDED to get back to my quarters, check out where everyone was hanging, then take the herbs Artimus had given me and join them in time for the pain to hit.

I wasn't looking forward to that part.

Did Sev know the plan?

Artimus must have told him.

The Minorax guard escorted me to the spawn quarters and joined the other guards outside the room while I went inside.

A sharp yell pulled me up short. The commotion was coming from Veena's room.

"What the hell?" I ran toward the cacophony of sound, and Keelan stepped out of his room, falling in behind me.

We entered Veena's room to chaos. Too many people, all tense, all ready for a fight. Veena clung to Sev where they crouched against the large armoire across the room. Tristeene, Mallini, and Gus stood in front of them, as if trying to shield them. Chase growled menacingly from beside the bed, his attention on the other end of the room.

I tracked his gaze to Dhuma. He had his back to me, his body a wall blocking off the dark, menacing figure of Umbrane.

The duke stood beside the portal to the Court of Shadows. Dressed in a fitted black rollneck and slacks that accentuated his wiry flame, hair swept back to showcase his horns, he looked the picture of casual nonchalance. As if none of the hubbub in the room had anything to do with him, even though every gaze was trained on him.

"What's happening?" I moved instinctively to stand beside Dhuma. "What are you doing here, Umbrane?"

He dragged his attention away from Dhuma and settled it on me. "Why, hello there, Nyx. So glad you could join us. I'm here to collect my custodia."

"She doesn't want to go with you," Mallini snapped. "Just leave. Now."

He studied his fingernails, unperturbed. "I'm afraid she doesn't have a choice."

But she did. She most definitely did. "She's no longer your custodia." I looked across the room to Veena cowering in Sev's arms. "Tell him. Tell him you no longer want or need his protection."

"It's not about that," Tristeene said softly.

Veena broke into heart-wrenching sobs.

What the fuck was happening here? "Then what?"

Both Tristeene and Mallini looked as if someone had killed their pet puppy.

"What is this about?" Keelan demanded. His arm brushed my shoulder as he came to stand next to me. "If this isn't about the custodia status, then what?"

Behind us Veena sobbed harder, the sound so broken and despondent that it made my heart ache and my fists clench against the desire to punch Umbrane in his smug bastard face.

"It isn't safe for Veena here," Umbrane said. "Not until *after* the conclave. Anyone could use her to get to you." He smirked.

Bullshit. We had Dhuma, Sev, Chase, and all the Minorax, including Keelan.

Umbrane paused long enough for these thoughts to pass through my mind, then continued, "Veena will be coming with me, because it is my duty and right to protect her, not as her sponsor but as her betrothed."

THIRTY-NINE

B etrothed?
The word rang in my ears and the implications sank in.

Veena let out a wail of despair, but it was drowned out by the rush of blood in my ears. Veena's mother did this. She gave her daughter to a monster.

Again.

"No." I took a menacing step toward Umbrane.

He let out a bark of laughter. "No?" All mirth died, and his expression turned stone cold. "*You* don't get to tell me *no*, spawn. I am the Duke of Shadows. You might have daimon blood, but it won't be long before it stains the marble of the Convectus Locus. You. Mean. Nothing. You *are* no one."

I crossed my arms and glared back at him. "Sticks and stones, Umbrane, sticks and stones."

The look on his face was pure confusion. He had no idea what I was referring to, the phrase too mortal for him.

"I owe no fealty to you, Umbrane," Dhuma said in a rumbling voice. "Your head would crack easily between my palms."

I liked the smooth way he laid out the threat.

Umbrane's gaze whipped to Dhuma. "You may owe no fealty to me, but you live in our world and by our rules. I am within my rights."

"To claim the zuni, yes, but touch my kin, and I *will* kill you."

Chase's growl punctuated Dhuma's sentence, and Umbrane's attention flicked to my hound for a moment. Was that a flash of unease on his face?

"You're not taking her," Mallini said. "Not until the Seneschal confirms your claim."

Artimus had gone to check up on Umbrane's claim?

Umbrane shrugged a shoulder. "I can wait."

"It's all right," Sev said softly to Veena. "You'll be all right."

"My, my," Umbrane drawled. "The torturer becomes the comforter. How quaint. The daimon blood bitch has made you—"

Dhuma punched Umbrane in the face.

The duke's head rocked back, but the blow didn't knock him off his feet. With his dark shock of hair, wiry form, pointy horns, and dark, demonic air, it was easy to forget Umbrane's true nature. But the way he took Dhuma's blow was a clear reminder of his power. A reminder that he may not be an original, but he was still a fallen.

He tipped his head to the side. "Did that make you feel better?"

Dhuma smiled thinly. "Much."

The clip of boots on marble drew all our attention to the doors. Artimus walked into the room with a grim expression that made my stomach hollow out.

"Artimus? Please." I wasn't sure what exactly I was pleading for. For him to make shit up and lie to us, maybe.

His gaze found Veena and his mouth turned down. "You must go with your betrothed."

Mallini cursed and Tristeene sucked in a shuddering breath.

"This is insane," Keelan said. "Why are you doing this?" he demanded of Umbrane.

Umbrane's gaze slid my way. "I'm merely protecting my investment. She'll be returned, safe and sound, once the conclave is over." He gave me a pointed look.

A chill swept up my spine.

Umbrane knew about my escape plan.

This wasn't about Veena. It was about me.

Claiming Veena, taking her with him, was his way of making sure I stayed. He knew how much I cared about her. Loved her. He knew I wouldn't risk her being hurt. He knew...knew I wouldn't run when she was in his clutches. In danger.

I wasn't sure how he'd found out, but it hardly mattered now. I could feel Artimus's gaze on my face, but I couldn't bring myself to look his way because I wasn't sure I'd be able to hide my devastation that our plan was fucked.

Umbrane had me backed into a corner. "Do I have your word she'll be safe?"

He smiled, thin and wicked. "Yes, Nyx. You have my word. Veena will be returned to her quarters, *unharmed*, once the conclave has concluded."

"And afterwards? Will you let her go? Release her from the betrothal?"

He shrugged a shoulder. "I'll consider it."

It was the best I'd get from him. I nodded, then crossed the room to Veena, who was huddled against Sev. His silver eyes swirled with angry shadows.

I crouched and stroked Veena's hair. "He won't hurt you. You'll be fine. I promise. I'll make sure of it."

She stared up at me with tear-stained cheeks. "I'm scared."

"I know, sweetheart."

She wiped at her cheeks. "Why? Why would Mother do this?"

"I don't know." I kissed her temple and dropped my voice to a whisper. "But I'm going to find out."

FORTY

I'd fought demon bloods, suckers, and shifters. I'd died and come back, but watching Veena leave with Umbrane was one of the hardest things I'd ever done.

The look on her face, the despair and fear frozen into her expression...

As soon as the portal closed behind them, I turned to Artimus. "I have to get to the zuni town. I need to speak to Veena's mother."

"You can't," Artimus said. "The princes agreed for you to stay with Ignatius for one night and Zepar another, but that was all. They won't agree to you visiting the zuni settlement."

"I'll go," Tristeene said. "I'll speak to her. She can't possibly want this for her daughter. At least she won't once I impress upon her the depravity that is Umbrane."

But she'd have to find their home and... "Take Hrath with you. He knows where they live. He can fly you there in a blink."

Her expression froze for a moment. "I don't think—"

"Please." I gave her a terse smile.

She nodded. "Of course."

"Artimus, can you get a message to the Court of Flame?"

"I'll do it right away."

I blew out a breath. "All right, then we wait."

"We need to be there," Mallini blurted out. "At the conclave tomorrow. All of us."

Tomorrow...My stomach dipped.

"I'll speak to the princes when they arrive tonight," Artimus said. "Meanwhile, I'll get a message to Hrath. If we can get Veena back, then..." His gaze flicked to me. He didn't need to finish his sentence. I got it. If we got Veena back, the plan to get me out of Morningstar might still be viable. "Freshen up and pack some things. I'll be back to collect you in a couple of hours." He lifted his chin in Sev's direction. "Sev, I could use your help with something."

My nightmare pressed a kiss to the spot below my ear and whispered, "I'll be back before you have to leave."

I couldn't ask where they were going, but I suspected it was either to get rid of any evidence of the escape plan Umbrane had rumbled or to plot a fresh one. But if I ran while Umbrane had Veena, he'd make her pay. I couldn't do it. I wouldn't.

Unless Tristeene could convince Veena's mother to cancel the betrothal, there was no way out for me.

I was doomed.

DHUMA STOPPED me outside my room. "Nyx, may I have a word?"

"Sure."

"Your hound...Chase. Where did you get him?"

"I didn't. He found me when I was a child. Why?"

"He reminds me of an infernal hound native to Inferis.

239

I've seen pictures of them and there were paintings in Soreena's gallery in the abyss. Infernal hounds were apex predators among the beasts in Inferis. There are stories of how the first high daimon saved the life of their brood queen. In turn she gifted him protection. That high daimon was a Knightwood."

"What are you saying? That Chase is an infernal hound?"

"No, he can't possibly be. Aside from the fact that infernal hounds were twice his size, none made it out of Inferis. I just...He looks so much like the depictions."

I patted Chase's head. "Well, that's another mystery. We can add it to the question of who my mother was and whether some miracle will happen and the princes will decide to let me live long enough to find out."

"You could still leave," Dhuma said. "I'm certain Artimus has a failsafe plan."

"I'm sure he does. But unless Umbrane releases my sister, I'm not going anywhere."

"You'd die for her?"

I smiled brightly at him. "Maybe it won't come to that. Erinea may have swayed the votes against me by promising favors to the voters, but who is she anyway? What power does she truly have?"

His lips bloomed in a slow smile. "Not as much power as Satan."

"Exactly."

If Erinea could sway the vote against me, then maybe me and my siblings, the true candidates for Satan, could sway it back in my favor.

I SHOWERED and changed into fresh clothes, pulled on boots, and donned my weapons. Despite my bravado earlier, my stomach was in knots, for Veena, for what was to come.

Someone knocked at the door.

I answered to Tristeene. "Did you hear back?"

"Yes, I have a summons to the Court of Flame. I'm leaving now, I just...You were going to escape today, weren't you?"

"You've always been perceptive."

"Nyx, if this meeting with Veena's mother doesn't work, you should still go."

"Are you crazy? Have you any idea what he'll do to her if I leave?"

She gave me a small, sad smile. "She'll live. But if you stay, you may not." She cupped my shoulders. "Veena would never forgive herself if you died because of her."

My belly felt tight. "I can't let him hurt her."

"Would you take the hit for one of us? Take the pain so we could live?"

"It's not the same. I can take it, but Veena—"

"Is stronger than you know. She survived a shiqq, she can survive Umbrane. He can't kill her. He needs her. She's his custodia. She's his link to the seat." She squeezed my shoulders. "If Artimus has a plan B, promise me that you'll take it."

She was right. Umbrane needed Veena. He needed her on his side. Hurting her would make her hate him and do him no good if she got the seat.

I breathed through the vise around my chest. "I promise."

Forty-One

ARTIMUS

S ev and I don't speak until we're in my quarters and the bedroom door is closed. Savi, my zuni footman, doesn't even blink an eye. He's aware of my varied appetites. I keep him with me because of his loyalty and discretion.

Did I consider he could have betrayed me to Umbrane? Yes, of course. But the day I spoke to Nyx about my plan, Savi was visiting with his family on his one day off a week.

"How?" Sev asks. "How could Umbrane know?"

I've been wondering the same thing. I've been extremely discreet. The only thing that jumps out to me is my meeting with Nyx and Dhuma. "Dhuma heard something outside my quarters when I met with Nyx yesterday. He checked but no one was there. I think it may have been Umbrane's spy and he may have heard enough to figure out our plan. My conji contact is missing. Probably dead."

"I've been sweeping the grounds and I haven't come across this spy," Sev says.

"Maybe he's invisible." I meet his gaze. "Like the spies at Merihem's court."

He's silent for several beats. "I thought you said that Umbrane wouldn't work with the fawda. That he wouldn't be an underling to anyone?"

"I stand by that. But we can't discount the possibility. Who knows what kind of deal he has with them, or even if he intends to keep it."

Sev snorts derisively. "I doubt he'd have a problem double-crossing anyone."

"*You* know him best. What do you think?"

He considers my question for a moment. "I think Umbrane will do whatever it takes to achieve his goals. Right now, his goal is a connection to the seat. He chose Veena because he feels she'll be easy to manipulate. He's never warmed to Nyx because she's headstrong and therefore a threat. Now even more so. I doubt the betrothal to Veena is a new thing."

"You think he was betrothed already?"

Sev shrugs. "It makes sense. If he's mated to Veena, then he has a forever connection to the seat. Veena is strong, but Umbrane has broken stronger." He looks away.

"Fuck."

Does Nyx know how smart her nightmare is? How sharp and insightful?

Sev takes a deep breath. "We've got to get Nyx out of here. We can worry about Veena afterwards."

He's right. "You don't think Tristeene will be able to convince Veena's mother to break the betrothal, do you?"

"Miracles do happen. And we need to pull one off now. Please tell me you have a plan B."

"Always."

TRISTEENE

Hrath meets me on the other side of the portal to the Court of Flame. The heat is immediate but nowhere near as bad as I expected it to be. We're at the end of a stone corridor with huge, vaulted windows on either side giving a view of golden sand and red dunes far in the distance.

But the view pales in comparison to Hrath.

I can't help but stare at him. He steals my breath every single time. With his ember eyes and sun-streaked dark hair, he's beautifully forbidding.

He looks down his nose at me with granite features. "You wish to visit the zuni settlement."

It isn't a question, but I answer regardless. "Yes."

"Something has happened. Tell me."

"Umbrane has secured Veena's hand in mating."

His eyes flare. "Ah. I see." His mouth presses in a thin line. "Then we must convince her otherwise." He holds out his hand to me.

My stomach flutters as I slip my palm into his warm calloused one. His fingers tighten around mine. He draws me close and wraps his arms around me, holding me against his body, and for a moment I'm scared to breathe, frightened to inhale too much of his evocative bergamot and saffron aroma, in case I lose myself in it.

"Put your arms around me," he says gruffly. "You must hold on. Tight." He pulls me flush against his body, as if to emphasize.

Heat spreads through me and I melt against him, yielding eagerly to the contact. He tenses, his heart beating faster against me.

Neither of us speak, both frozen.

Slowly, carefully, I raise my arms and hook them around his neck.

"Good." His tone is thick. "That's good."

I keep my head down, afraid to look at him in case he sees how aroused I am right now.

His lips brush my ear. "The air around us will keep you from burning in the heat. But you must hold on."

I tighten my grip on him. "Got it."

A breeze whips up around us, quickly turning into a gust and then a whirling wind. My feet leave the ground and we're airborne.

THE ZUNI SETTLEMENT is buzzing with activity when we arrive, but they stop to stare as we stride past. My body is still humming from contact with Hrath's solid frame and I'm grateful that we're no longer touching. I need a moment to recalibrate my senses.

He leads me to a small house with red shutters and knocks briskly on the door.

It's opened a moment later by a female who looks so much like my sibling that I have no doubt who she is.

Her gaze flicks between Hrath and me. "What do you want?"

Hrath nods to me. I have the floor.

"Hello, I'm Tristeene, Veena's sister."

She frowns slightly. "What do you want? Why are you here? Is Veena all right?"

"May I come in?"

She steps up to fill the doorframe. "No. You can say what you want to right here."

"Very well." I clasp my hands in front of me. "I'm here to ask you to rescind the betrothal blessing you gave to Umbrane."

She stares at me blankly for several seconds. "Why would I do that?"

I tamp down on my anger. She obviously doesn't understand how much of a bastard Umbrane is. "Umbrane is a cruel male. He enjoys inflicting pain on others and Veena is very unhappy with your choice."

"Veena will do as she is bid as is the zuni way. I did not give my body to Satan so that the product of our union would be left behind in the race for her birth right."

Is she serious?

"You change your tune quickly," Hrath says. "The last time we spoke you cried and pleaded to see your daughter. You expressed remorse for giving her to the shiqq."

Her eyes flinch. "I *am* sorry for the pain that caused Veena, but we must all sacrifice for the greater good. This is her purpose. To be Satan and elevate her people."

"Her people?" My eyes burn with rage. "And you think *you're* her people? The family who throws her to the wolf? You think she'll favor you once this is all over? Once she's been violated and abused by a monster?" I rake her up and down with a fiery gaze. "You're delusional. You are no longer her people. *We* are. Her siblings. Her family. But there's still time to change things. Still time to free her and regain her trust."

Her lip curls. "I know what you're doing. You want her weakened and out of favor with the duke so that you can win the seat."

"You know nothing about how things are. How we are. I love my sister. And I will stand by whoever wins the seat proudly."

She lifts her chin. "And thanks to me, that creature will be Veena. Duke Umbrane assures us of it, and Veena will understand. She will thank us. She is zuni; forgiveness is in her blood." She steps back. "Now go. Do not come here again." She slams the door in our faces.

Hrath is the first to break the stunned silence. "And they say that the zuni are a peace-loving race."

I take a shuddering breath, blinking back tears of rage. I can force the zuni female to comply, bend her to my will, but then what? Once I leave, she'll be free of my control. Free to give Umbrane whatever he wants.

I curl my fingers into fists, fighting against the primal urge to punch and claw, an instinct I've succeeded in controlling for most of my life. "Take me back, Hrath. Get me out of here before I hurt that female."

He pulls me into his arms, wraps us in a whirlwind, and whisks us away.

I've failed to save Veena from Umbrane, but I won't fail in saving Nyx.

FORTY-TWO

NYX

Sev hurried into my room. "We have to go. Now."

"What? Where?"

He gripped my elbow and steered me to the mirror. "Chase, come on."

"Sev, what are you—"

"Loke," Sev said to the glass.

The smooth silver rippled.

"You knew?"

"No, but he told me. We've got to go this way. I'll explain later."

He urged me through the mirror, his grip tight on my arm. We stepped into Loke's room to find him waiting.

"What took you so long?" Loke asked Sev.

Sev made a sound of exasperation. "I got to her as quickly as I could."

"Can someone please tell me what's happening?"

"We're getting you out of here," Loke said.

"I thought you couldn't interfere in my fate."

His jaw ticked. "I'm making an exception."

He hurried across the room to the wardrobe up against the wall, flung it open, and shoved the clothes to one side.

A soft click was followed by a cool gust of air. "Through here. No one knows about this but me and Satan. These quarters were built for me. This passage leads to outside the keep walls. There'll be a carriage waiting to get you to the town and the station."

"Wait, what about Dhuma?"

"He'll follow in a few days," Loke said. "Artimus has arranged it all. Ignatius has been informed too."

"And where is Artimus?"

He grabbed something off the dresser and handed it to me.

A flashlight.

"Making sure no one interferes in your escape. But you need to go. Now. The Eyes only leave their posts once a day for about twenty minutes during a shift change in about..." He glanced at his watch. "Five minutes. Hustle. Go."

"Veena... I have to know she's okay."

"There's no time," Sev said. "We need to get you out of here. Now. Nyx, please."

Tristeene's words filled my mind, her logic that Umbrane wouldn't hurt his investment.

"Okay, let's go."

I stepped up to Loke and hugged him, pushing up on tiptoes and turning my head into the hollow of his neck. "What will the source do to you when she finds out about this?"

"I don't know and I don't care." He pulled away, cupped my face, and kissed me hard on the mouth. "I just want you to live." He released me and stepped back. "Now get out of here."

I allowed myself one last lingering glance his way, then

dove into the passage.

It was time to escape this place.

ARTIMUS

The princes are due to arrive in a few hours. I need to keep Erinea and Umbrane distracted until then. Because of course he's here, the smarmy cunt, his gaze roving all over Erinea.

Nothing strange there considering they've been fucking. I would be relieved if not for the fact that their fucking leads to their plotting Nyx's demise.

But if they're here, it means Nyx's route to freedom is uninterrupted.

Erinea pores over a map of the guest wing.

Rooms must be prepared for the dignitaries who'll be sitting in on the conclave. But political etiquette needs to be observed and quarters befitting station need to be allocated. Not to mention the fact that we need to avoid the faux pas of putting certain lords or ladies close together.

Umbrane sidles up to her and leans over her, his chest pressing against her back. "We could put Lady Minera here." He points at a spot on the map. "It has a balcony so she can watch the moon."

"Oh, fabulous idea." Erinea gives him her kitten grin. I don't give a shit who she fawns over, but I know she prefers to be her conquest's main focus. So I can't help but drop a bomb I'm sure she isn't aware of.

"I should congratulate you on your betrothal, Umbrane."

He tenses, and her smile freezes.

He's quick to recover. "Thank you. I believe it will be a

good match." He steps away from Erinea, wisely so. The woman can be lethal.

"And who is the lucky female," Erinea says, the smile still frozen in place.

I answer for him. "His very own custodia. The zuni Satan spawn, Veena."

Erinea's smile drops. "You're betrothed to one of the spawn?" Her eyes narrow. "What are you playing at?"

Ah, the façade is gone. The claws are out. I sit back and nurse my whiskey, not bothering to hide my smile of satisfaction, because right now Nyx will be in the carriage with Sev and Chase, on her way to freedom.

Umbrane sighs heavily. "I did what needed to be done to stop Nyx from executing an escape. She loves her siblings and that love is her only weakness."

"You can't harm the zuni," Erinea says, but she doesn't sound too sure. "You wouldn't."

"Yes, well, I hoped the threat would be enough to keep the high daimon spawn put, but..." His gaze slides my way. "Unfortunately, I was wrong. It seems she favors her skin dearly and has a plan B."

He knows...

Oh, fuck, he knows.

"What? She's trying to run?" Erinea's eyes flare in panic.

He smiles thinly at me, then turns to Erinea. "Don't worry, my sweet. I have *eyes* everywhere. She won't get far."

The Eyes. The shift change...

Umbrane must have tampered with it.

I push my seat back and stand.

"Where are you going?" Erinea asks.

"To make sure our Satan spawn doesn't escape."

Umbrane smirks. He knows my involvement. Knows everything, but it's his knowledge, not to be shared with Erinea but to be held over me, because if he shares it with her, she'll want to know how he knows. She'll want to know who his spies are, and his secret will be out.

We're in a state of mutually assured destruction.

But it hardly matters.

All that matters is stopping Nyx from getting out of the keep, because if the Eyes see her, they'll attack. No questions asked.

NYX

"How long is this fucking passage?" The words puffed out of me as we jogged.

The musty, unused smell filled my nose, making me want to sneeze.

"It can't be much longer," Sev said. "At least there are no turnoffs to confuse things. Just one way out."

"Or in."

"Hmmm."

"I can see natural light." I flicked the torch off, and sure enough, the passage was gray.

Sev picked up speed and shot off ahead, but Chase kept pace at my side.

Sev's voice drifted around the corner. "There's a metal grill."

I rounded the bend and joined him as he fumbled around the small grill high up. "I think this is a lever."

He tugged on something I couldn't see. There was a soft snick and the stone wall opened with a low grinding sound. The afternoon sun streamed into the passageway, burning my eyes and forcing me to squint.

Sev slipped out first, and I ushered Chase to go next, following him into the fresh Morningstar air.

"I see the carriage," Sev said. "Come on." He held his hand out to me and we broke into a jog toward the dark shape on the bridge.

Lake Morbidus seethed either side of us, as if the creatures beneath the water sensed our presence.

"Stop!"

The voice came from behind us. Artimus? I tried to slow down but Sev hauled me along.

"Nyx, stop!" Artimus yelled.

I glanced back to see him sprinting toward us, his face twisted in panic.

"The Eyes!" he yelled. "The Eyes!"

My gaze whipped up to the keep walls and the alcoves that held the dark-robed figures of the Eyes. The alcoves that should have been empty but weren't.

Heads angled down toward me in unison, like lasers activated by motion. Red pinpricks bloomed in the inky ovals of their hoods.

They were about to attack.

Sev ground to a halt, yanked me against his body, and spun us so that his back blocked me from the Eyes.

So that he could take the hit.

"NO!" I punched at him. "No! Sev, no!"

The air crackled with power.

I craned to peer around Sev's bicep in time to see Artimus skid to a stop between us and them.

He turned and raised his arms. "Stop. Stand down. That's an order."

But the red pinpricks had grown to fill the dark oval of each hood.

They were about to fire.

My stomach hollowed and my heart shot into my throat. "Artimus, no! Move!" A hum filled the air. "Arty!"

He looked at me then and our gazes locked, his dark

with apology, with goodbye.

Pressure built inside me, sharp and thick, pushing outward from my solar plexus to singe my wrists.

A figure shot over the top of the walls, batlike wings flared to catch the air, dark hair blowing back in the breeze.

Umbrane.

Suspended high above, wings beating the air slow and easy, sunlight gleaming off his horns, he looked every bit the devil mortals feared.

"Stand down," Umbrane bellowed. "By order of the Erinyes."

The red lights glowing under each hood winked out on his command and the pressure inside my chest vanished.

Oh, fuck. Oh, earth and stars. I blinked back tears of relief.

Artimus lowered his arms and backed toward me. I reached for his hand and our fingers twined.

The gates to the keep trundled open and several Erinyes marched out, led by none other than Erinea. She took in the three of us, standing together. The two guys flanking me. Protecting me.

Her lips thinned. "Nyx, Satan blood and daimon blood, you will be remanded into the custody of the Erinyes until your conclave. Come with me."

"Erinea, there's no need for that, surely," Artimus said.

Her eyes flashed in rage, pinning him to the spot. "Hold your tongue, Seneschal, lest I be tempted to incarcerate you along with her."

I squeezed his hand in warning. "Don't." Then to Erinea, "I'm coming."

I pulled out of Sev's grasp, slipped my hand from Artimus's, and walked toward them.

There'd be no escape today.

It was over.

FORTY-THREE

The last place I expected to find myself when I woke up this morning was a dungeon cell, and I'm talking a proper sublevel deal with fire sconces bolted to the wall, gray stone floors, and thick iron bars. They took my weapons, leaving me with a scratchy blanket and a narrow cot for the night.

At least the cell was clean, dry, and didn't smell...much. The rest of the cells in the square room were empty. Either these were special dungeons for the higher-ups in Morningstar or Morningstar's crime rate was non-existent. With the Erinyes in charge, and with what I'd seen of the people living here so far, it was easy to believe the latter.

But the ascension had brought out the worst in everyone. Power corrupted after all.

Were Sev and Chase okay? They'd separated us at the gates. And Artimus...the way Erinea had looked at him, betrayal etched on her face. Which was hypocritical considering she was fucking Umbrane.

There were several hours until dawn and I was wide awake. Sleep would be welcome right now, a quick way to get through the night and cut to the conclave tomorrow. Were the princes here yet? How many hours would it take them to sentence me to death tomorrow?

I sat facing the stone steps that led out of the dungeons. How long had I been down here?

The scrape of a lock was loud in the silence. Someone was coming. I tensed at the sound of voices, more than two. Three, maybe? My scalp pricked in awareness. If someone wanted to bypass the whole conclave and end me sooner, now, right here, while I was alone and unarmed, was the best time to do it.

Bootfalls echoed on the stairs. I pressed myself into the shadows at the back of my cell.

"Watch it," a female voice said. "You're standing on my blanket."

Mallini? I left the shadows and approached the bars, pulse quickening.

Gus came into view a moment later, valiantly trying to peer over the pillow and blankets he was carrying. Mallini was close behind, followed by Tristeene.

The knots in my belly eased. "What are you guys doing here?"

Gus dropped his bundle of bedding by the bars. "We thought we could have a sleepover."

Tristeene placed the basket she was carrying on the floor. "I brought snacks."

My throat pinched. "What? How...Who let you in?"

"The guards. They checked everything first, though," Gus said. "Made sure we weren't planning a third escape for you."

They'd come to stay with me. To keep me company the night before my judgment. Do not cry, Nyx. Don't you dare fucking cry.

I cleared my throat. "I don't understand. How are you allowed to be here?"

Tristeene and Gus looked to Mallini, and the Erinyes shrugged, all nonchalant.

"No big deal," she said. "I spoke to Erinea and reminded her that she owed me. Big time." She sniffed and placed her load of bedding on the floor. "She wants to make amends so badly she agreed."

Mallini had grated on my nerves the most when I'd gotten here, and now I understood why. Out of all my siblings she was the most like me—in your face, blunt, and unforgiving when it came to betrayal.

"I love you, Mallini." The words spilled out before I could check them.

She blinked sharply and her eyes widened.

Fuck it, I wasn't taking it back. "I love you all." Damn the tears. I blinked them away. "Look what you're doing to me, you fuckers."

Mallini reached through the bars and gripped my hand. "I love you too, Nyx."

"We all do," Tristeene said.

"Impossible not to," Gus said.

I pressed my forehead to the iron and closed my eyes, gathering my thoughts. "Promise me that whatever happens tomorrow, whatever they decide, you'll stick together. You'll support one another and whoever becomes Satan." I opened my eyes to look at them one by one. "Promise me you won't let them tear you apart. You won't let them corrupt your bond."

Gus's sapphire eyes shimmered behind a sheen of tears. "Never."

"I promise," Tristeene said.

"You can bet on it," Mallini added.

This was right. Being with them. Be it in a dungeon, in

the middle of a trial, or in the luxury of our quarters, it felt right.

I squeezed Mallini's hand, then let go. "Where's Keelan right now?"

"With Artimus," Tristeene said. "He's making sure we get a say at the conclave."

"And Veena? Did you speak to her mother?"

"Yes. It didn't go well," Tristeene said. "She doesn't care what happens to Veena as long as she has a shot at the seat."

"That bitch."

"Yeah..." Tristeene's delicate jaw tightened. "It took everything I had not to hurt her."

Veena was stuck with Umbrane...for now. But maybe he'd break the betrothal after the conclave, after I was... Nope, not thinking about it. Not yet.

"Are Sev, Chase, and Dhuma okay?"

"Dhuma's standing guard outside," Mallini said with a wicked smile. "You should have seen him when he found out you'd been captured. I thought he was going to rip Erinea's plumes out."

"He insisted on guarding the dungeons to make sure you were safe," Gus said. "But Erinea's made it clear he isn't allowed down here."

"Why not?"

He shrugged. "Maybe she thinks you guys will do some high daimon allure and escape."

I rolled my eyes. "If that was possible, I'd already be out of here."

"Sev and Chase are being kept in quarters close to the Erinyes wing," Mallini said. "You know, to make sure they don't try anything either." Her mouth tipped up in a wry smile. "I guess us three aren't a serious threat."

"Oh, wouldn't it be fabulous if they'd underestimated us?" Tristeene said, her eyes lighting up with glee.

"Yes, imagine their faces if we were the ones to bust you out of here," Gus said, catching on.

But reality was around us, in the cold gray stone walls surrounding us and the thick iron bars creating a barrier between us.

There was no escape.

"Let's set up," Tristeene said quickly.

My siblings arranged their bedding and settled down in a cozy nest outside my cell.

I pulled my cot up close to the bars and gathered my blanket around me. "Have the princes arrived yet?"

"No, but Ignatius turned up about an hour ago," Mallini said. "I was with Erinea when he stormed in with his second, what's his name..."

"Hrath," Tristeene said softly, eyes downcast.

"Yeah, Hrath. The duke demanded you be released into his custody, but Erinea shut him down, quoting some bullshit Morningstar law. He had to concede, but boy, did he look pissed."

Ignatius was here, and even though that didn't mean he could get me out of this, it made me feel better knowing he was here in the building. Close.

Tristeene opened the basket and began taking out neatly wrapped packages of food. The smell had my mouth watering, reminding me that I hadn't eaten since Zepar fed me this morning.

"Zinichi packed us some meat rolls in fresh bread." Tristeene passed me one through the bars. "There's fruit too."

I unwrapped it and chowed down, stomach gurgling appreciatively.

"They haven't fed you?" Gus said softly.

I shook my head.

"Bastards," Mallini sneered. "All of them. When this is

over, when one of us is Satan, we can kick their asses."

I made a fist and pushed it between the bars toward her.

She stared at it in confusion.

Gus made an exasperated sigh. "You're meant to do this." He bumped fists with me.

"Why?" Mallini asked.

"It's a mortal thing," he said. "It can be used as a handshake or a greeting or in this case can indicate approval."

Mallini grinned. "In that case." She held out her fist to me and I bumped it.

Tristeene did the same.

Then Gus and Tristeene bumped fists, and after that Mallini bumped fists with Tristeene.

Oh boy, what had I done?

FORTY-FOUR

SIN

Time slows and ebbs, then passes at the speed of light with little meaning aside from those shining moments—the pearls that stand out among the countless grains of sand. She is one of those pearls.

One of those moments.

The most poignant and the most precious.

It's time, Sin...time to wake up. The voice is familiar. The voice of my savior.

My blood tingles with awareness.

No time to waste.

Yes, I feel it now. So close. Too close.

Wake up!

I open my eyes.

FORTY-FIVE

NYX

"Are you all right, Nyx?" Zinichi asked as she braided my hair.

"No. This..." I plucked at the cuff of my tunic, indicating the fine silver embroidery. "It's ridiculous."

"You don't like the clothes?"

The clothes in question were a fitted black tunic and pants in the kind of material that made love to your skin. The cuffs and collar were decorated in delicate silver thread woven into intricate patterns. My sandals were silver too and Zinichi had woven silver beads into my hair.

I sensed a theme. "The clothes are fine, but hardly appropriate for a conclave where they're going to discuss..." I drew my index finger across my throat and stuck my tongue out the side of my mouth.

"Don't!" Zinichi tugged on my hair mid-braid. "You'll be fine. This will be over soon, and we can get back to the trials." She continued to braid my hair, humming softly under her breath, the sound so soothing it was almost possible to forget that I was sitting on a stool in a cell.

Was everyone already in the Convectus Locus? I needed to pee. The next few hours could be my last.

My chest tightened in panic.

Zinichi draped my braid over my shoulder and stood back. "There. All done."

I stood and pulled her into a hug. "Thank you for everything. Take care of them for me."

She opened her mouth, then snapped it closed and nodded, eyes welling.

Yeah, she knew it too.

Bootfalls echoed down the stairs. My gaze whipped up to see Zepar descending.

He paused at the foot of the stairs, gaze going from me to the cells around me then back. I'd seen him in his casual wear so often that I'd forgotten how formidable he looked in his court colors of cream and gold that contrasted beautifully with his bronze skin, tawny eyes, and dark hair.

Was it wrong to just take him in for a moment? To forget about what his being here meant?

"You don't belong in here." He strode across the room and unlocked the cell Zinichi and I were in. Yeah, they'd locked her in here with me to get me ready. Truss me up for the carving.

Ha.

Oh earth, keep it together, woman.

Zinichi squeezed my hand, grabbed my dirty clothes and her bag of hair things, and left the cell.

I was alone with the fallen, and for a moment I didn't know what to say. "They sent you to get me?"

"I insisted."

I swallowed the lump of emotion in my throat. "The others?"

"All in place," Zepar said. "All ready to fight for you, but Nyx...You must fight too. You must believe that you can win this." He bridged the distance between us and cupped my face tenderly in his hands. "You are special. A light in the dark. And it doesn't matter how you came to be, all that matters is that you are. Don't let them snuff you out."

I couldn't speak past the lump in my throat, so I turned my face in his hand and kissed his palm.

He leaned in and pressed his forehead to mine. "Breathe, and then we go. We do this and we win."

I'D BEEN in the Convectus Locus twice. Once for my custodia ceremony where I'd leapt into the battle ring to save Sev, and the second time after we'd lost Charod.

I knew the room from above and below, but this time I was led through a tunnel toward the battle chamber. The circular pit where Sev had fought. I'd be left vulnerable. Forced to look up to meet the eyes of my judges.

To them, I'd be small and insignificant.

Zepar brought me to a halt by the archway that opened into the battle pit. "Keep the fire. You are not an insect to be trodden on."

"Maybe that's what they want to see. A weak creature. Someone who isn't a threat."

"They know what you are, and that's enough of a threat. My kind respect strength of character; we believe that power should be in the hands of those who are strong of mind and body. If they think you're weak, it will go against you."

"Okay."

He nudged my chin with the crook of his finger. "I'll see you when it's over."

The confidence in that statement fueled the hope in my chest, and when he dropped his hand, my chin stayed up.

I'd come too far and fought too hard in my life to lose it all because these fallen feared the unknown.

Deep breath, Nyx. Let's do this.

I strode into the pit, head held high.

They might have me standing in a hole, but I didn't have to look small.

But I'd barely gotten into the center of the chamber when the floor began to move.

Forty-Six

T he chamber shuddered and shifted. I stumbled and caught myself as we rose to meld with the ground floor.

They'd brought me out via the battle pit to rattle me. To show me how insignificant they thought I was, which was bullshit, because if that were true, we wouldn't be having this meeting.

Four males and three females sat to the left of me, Lady Minera among them, ready with her kill vote. I made sure to lock gazes with her for a beat before moving on to scope out the rest of my judges. Faces I didn't recognize until I snagged on Umbrane. Another known kill vote.

He tipped his head in greeting and I resisted the urge to give him the finger.

My siblings sat behind a barrier to my right, all present except Veena. There was no sign of Dhuma, Sev, or Loke, and I didn't expect them to allow Chase in here so no surprise there. I'd have expected Loke to be allowed in, but I guess the source had no power over these proceedings.

Gus gave me a surreptitious thumbs up. A smile tugged at my lips but I staunched it and turned to face the princes at the front of the room. They sat on elaborate chairs that reminded me of mini-thrones, each decorated in the colors of their affiliated courts. Had they brought them here specifically for this meeting? Like, I need my own chair or I'm not doing it?

The thought made it harder not to smile. I bit the insides of my cheeks, my gaze flicking to the left where Erinea sat at a desk with quill and paper, then to the right of the princes where Artimus, Ignatius, and Zepar were seated in their smaller, very normal chairs.

"Is this amusing to you?" Ramiel demanded.

Oh, crap. "No, of course not."

"Yet you smile."

Anger squeezed my chest. "What do you want me to do? Break down and cry?"

He blinked sharply.

Whispers broke out amongst the lords and ladies.

"Your lack of respect will not serve you well," Ramiel said coolly.

"My respect is earned and given where due."

Ramiel looked like he was about to say more but Artimus interrupted. "We should begin the proceedings."

"Yes," Levistus said. "First the charges against you will be read."

Charges my ass. I'd be interested to hear this.

Erinea stood and held up the paper she'd been writing on. "Nyx, daimon blood and Satan spawn, you are charged with the crime of being an abomination. An aberration of nature who poses a threat to the balance of our world through your claim to the seat." She looked across at me, her expression giving nothing away. "How do you plead?"

The cool, detached way she laid it out, the drone of her

voice, as if she were reciting the weather report, not a ridiculous charge, spawned lava in my veins.

"Are you fucking serious?"

Shocked gasps filled the air and someone in the sibling alley groaned.

"Nyx," Artimus said calmly. "Enter your plea."

His eyes begged me to keep my head, but beside him Ignatius's ember gaze burned with a passion that matched the swirling wrath in my chest.

"You will have your chance to speak soon," Artimus said.

I sucked in a breath and exhaled to calm my racing heart. "Not guilty."

Erinea lowered her paper. "Now it is up to you, lords and ladies, to decide whether the aberration should be eliminated or not. You will hear the princes debate, and you will hear from the aberration and her witnesses." Her gaze flicked to my siblings. "Then you will cast your votes and the princes will make their final decision based upon yours."

Another wave of murmurs. Just get the fuck on with it.

Prince Levistus spoke first. "I prize the unique. The beauty of nature and creation that allows roses to bloom amidst the thorns. The existence of a high daimon blood who also shares fallen blood is unique indeed." He looked to the visiting panel. "You, the chosen few, have been brought into the circle of trust. You know the true story of our history and you are bound by death contracts not to reveal it. So, you now know that although fallen can procreate with abyssbloods and demons, we cannot sire offspring with a pure daimon." He looked down at me. "Nyx should not exist, not only because the union of a fallen and high daimon cannot bear fruit, but because there are no high daimon in the demon realm or Morningstar to have sired her." He sighed. "Her origins are in question, and thus, so is her purpose."

What the hell did that mean?

"She could be a weapon forged to end us," he continued.

"Or to liberate us," Merihem said. "A gift from powers beyond our imagining."

"Yes, she is flesh and blood," Ramiel said. "So she must have been born from flesh and blood."

"We were not born from flesh and blood," Merihem said. "And yet, do we not bleed?"

The room fell into silence and all eyes were on me.

"We must consider the facts of what we know," Levistus continued. "Her existence is inexplicable. Her power, if allowed to foster and flourish, may be almost equal to ours. If permitted to live, as Satan spawn, she has a claim on the seat. We cannot risk handing an unknown entity so much power."

Fuck, when he broke it down like that...

"But to take a life based on what *might* happen..." Ramiel rubbed his chin, his whiskey eyes slightly unfocused in thought. "It seems premature."

"Have we not been taught to strike before danger strikes us?" Levistus said.

"And where has that gotten us?" Ramiel asked.

Levistus's jaw ticked, and he raked a hand through his golden hair. "Ah, brother, you were always a master debater. But our duty now is to protect our world. This world. This home which we have built."

Murmurs in the voting alley drew my eye. Umbrane smirked at me and dropped me a wink.

If I lived through this, I'd find a way to make him pay.

Merihem took up the argument. "Yes, but to end a life because we don't understand how it could exist or what it may become..." He shook his head. "I'm unable to reconcile with that notion."

Thank you, Merihem. He was on my side.

Artimus sat stiffly in his seat, his expression giving nothing away, but his white-knuckled grip on his chair said everything. Ignatius caught my eye and warmth bloomed in my chest, feeding my hope. Zepar inclined his head slightly, as if to say, *phase one complete.*

Ramiel nodded toward Erinea. She scraped her chair back and stood to face my siblings.

"Satan spawn, you have petitioned to speak for your sibling. You will answer the princes' questions and put forward evidence in illustration of the accused's character. Have you chosen a spokesperson?"

"We have," Mallini said coolly.

Gus stepped forward and gripped the barrier.

Perfect choice. The smartest of us, the sharpest.

"State your name?" Erinea said.

"Gustus of House Solar," Gus said proudly.

Erinea sat down and Prince Ramiel leaned forward in his seat. He smiled, and his eyes warmed as they settled on Gus. "Hello, Gus, it's wonderful to meet you."

Gus's cheeks flushed. "Your Grace."

"Tell me, Gus, how long have you known the accused?"

"Since she arrived here a few days before the custodia ceremony."

"And in that time have you witnessed any flares of temper? Anger? Aggression?"

Gus's gaze flicked to me, panic widening his eyes.

I nodded to let him know it was okay.

"Nyx has a passionate temperament," Gus said. "She fights for what she believes in and protects those she loves. Sometimes aggression is needed. Anger comes when people hurt those she cares about." He smiled at me. "She makes me feel safe."

Oh...My heart. I breathed shallow and quick, blinking away my tears.

"Hmmm." Ramiel sat back in his seat and Levistus leaned forward to ask his question.

"Tell me, Gus, when did you stop wanting the seat?"

Gus looked taken aback. "Excuse me?"

Levistus smiled thinly. "When did you stop wanting the seat for yourself? When did you stop believing that you were the best candidate and start supporting Nyx's claim?"

"I...I'm not sure what you..." His expression cleared. "I see what you're trying to do. You're trying to illustrate that Nyx's affection and her sacrifices are manipulations to make us love her and root for her."

Motherfucker. I had to hand it to Levistus. That was a twisted, wicked play.

"But you're wrong," Gus continued. "I never stopped thinking I was worthy of the seat, I just learned to accept that I wasn't the *only* one worthy of it." He looked over his shoulder at the other siblings. "We all are, and Nyx...She made us see that."

I couldn't breathe with how much love was coursing through my veins right now, swelling my heart and making my eyes water.

Levistus pressed his lips together and sat back.

All attention went to Merihem, who sat with his fingers steepled beneath his chin. Long seconds passed and he finally looked up and smiled at Gus.

"Tell me, Gus, do you love your siblings? Do you love the accused?"

Gus beamed from ear to ear. "Of course. They're my family."

The voting row burst into whispers, but I had eyes only for my brothers and sisters. My family.

"Now the accused may speak," Erinea said.

I gave my siblings a nod and turned to face the princes. I hadn't considered what I'd say when it was my turn to speak. Words and emotions were a tangle inside me, but now, standing in the spotlight with my family rooting for me and Gus's words ringing in my ears, the words came easily.

"I had a life in the mortal world, but it feels like so long ago now. Since I came here, since I found out I was Satan spawn, everything's changed." I looked to Artimus. "At first all I wanted to do was prove to the stuck-up Seneschal and all the powerful beings here that I was good enough, that I belonged. But deep down I knew that was a lie. I wasn't one of you. I was an outsider. But then...day by day, hour by hour, I began to feel connections. To find mirrors and echoes of myself in the creatures around me. Creatures who were mine by blood." I turned to my brothers and sisters. "I fell in love with all of you."

Tristeene wiped at her eyes and Mallini's bottom lip trembled. A lump formed in my throat, making my next words come out thick with emotion. "I don't know how I can be what I am. I never asked for it. The status of spawn, the power of a high daimon, none of it. But I have it and—" I turned back to face my judges. "There are consequences. I understand that. I understand that power comes with responsibility. I understand that it can also breed fear." I looked at each of the princes in turn. "But I vow that if I'm allowed to live, any power I have will be used to protect this world and its many varied creations. And that's all I can do." I sighed. "Whatever happens now, I'll go out knowing I've found my place, even if I'm unable to keep it."

A deep, echoing silence followed my speech. I made sure to keep my head up and meet each prince's eye steadily. I'd be damned if I'd cower. I had nothing to be ashamed of.

"The votes will now be cast," Erinea said stiffly.

She passed an urn to Umbrane, who was sitting on the edge of the row.

The Duke of Shadows kept his gaze on me as he pushed

a folded piece of paper into the urn. Yeah, he already had his vote ready.

The urn was passed down the line, but some of the voters took their time, leaning their heads together to whisper.

Long minutes ticked by before the urn made it back to Erinea.

She didn't look at me as she emptied out the contents of the urn and counted the votes. She exhaled softly and her mouth turned down.

Wait...that was good, right?

She looked up. "The vote is unanimous."

Unanimous...Oh...wait...

"Elimination," she said.

The breath whooshed out of my lungs, even though I'd suspected as much. Even though I'd come here knowing the shit Erinea had stirred, I'd hoped. Hoped that they'd reconsider after hearing from my family and me.

"No!" Keelan stepped around the barrier, his forbidding Minorax frame bearing down on the voters. "Vote again," he commanded. "And remember who you might be answering to soon enough." His lip curled. "One of us."

In that moment he looked every bit the part of Satan. Powerful, unforgiving, ready to knock some heads.

"Enough!" Levistus stood abruptly, fire in his eyes. "You are not Satan yet, and you may never be if you cannot respect a democratic vote."

"Democratic?" Mallini stepped forward. "Bullshit. They've been paid off by her." She pointed an accusatory finger at Erinea.

Umbrane sat back in his seat, dark eyes gleaming with amusement.

The fallen was insane.

"That's a serious accusation," Ramiel said. "Do you have any proof?"

We did, but it involved Sev spying on Umbrane, and no one would believe a nightmare's word over a fallen's. Especially when the fallen was responsible for the nightmare's pain.

Mallini must have come to the same conclusion. Her jaw worked, her turmoil evident in the clench of her fists and the quiver of her plumes.

"She has no proof," Erinea said. "Merely anger toward a mother she believes failed her." She gave Mallini a tender look filled with maternal angst and longing, and I couldn't be sure it was an act. "I'm sorry, child. Sorry for the pain this process has caused you."

"Fuck. You," Mallini said.

"It's all right." My pulse was pounding so hard I could hear it in my ears. "It's okay."

"The princes will cast their votes," Erinea said.

My gaze flew to Zepar to find him glaring at his father, then Ignatius, who had his head bowed, hands gripping the armrests of his chair.

Look at me. I needed him to look at me. But he didn't and something inside me withered.

Artimus did meet my gaze, but his sapphire eyes were filled with shadows and doubt.

"The decision is clear for me," Levistus said. "Elimination is the safest option."

Ramiel spoke next. "I came here sure of my feelings on this matter. But I cannot ignore the voice within that begs me to reconsider. We faced a threat a long time ago and barely survived it. We do not know what the future holds." He looked over at Merihem as he said this. "What terrors may still rise." Was he referring to the fawda? "Eliminating a power that might aid us would be foolish." He fixed his whiskey gaze on me. "I vote to let her live. Her daimon power can be muted until we have need of it, *if* we have need of it."

Levistus exhaled and shook his head, clearly not happy about his brother's decision.

But my mind was whirring because there was only one vote left, Merihem, and he was on my side, which meant—

"You are right," Merihem said. "We cannot know what the future holds or who's placed this power in our midst. We cannot know whether it's a weapon for or against us." He shook his head.

My heart sank. No. Please. No.

"I'm sorry, Nyx. I must err on the side of caution and vote to eliminate."

FORTY-SEVEN

B lood rushed in my ears, muting the sound around me for a long moment, then someone cried out. One of my siblings.

Tristeene, maybe?

They were going to kill me.

"No!" Ignatius unfurled his powerful frame from his seat. Intricate patterns glowed through the material of his shirt, moving beneath his skin, and every strand of hair on his head burned brighter. "No one will touch her."

"What is the meaning of this?" Ramiel demanded.

"My people and I have lived by your rules and kept your secrets without resistance for centuries. But harm this woman now, and all that will change."

"You would break our covenant over a female?" Levistus shot to his feet. "Do not forget your place, Ignatius. Do not forget our power."

"No, I have not," Ignatius said. "But I believe you have forgotten mine. You have forgotten the lore around my people. You have forgotten the power a true mate can bring."

True mate? What was he talking about?

Ignatius locked gazes with me. "Nyx is my true mate."

Artimus cursed loudly and the room broke into chaos, but it barely registered. All that mattered was Ignatius, his intensity focused on me, and his words that rang true and sincere.

Yes.

How had I not known?

How had I not seen it?

I took a step toward him, needing to be close to him, to touch him.

Power slammed into me and threw me backward.

Ignatius let out a bellow of rage but was thrown back into his seat.

"I thought you might need me." Odette swished into the room. "I sensed something about these two the last time they were in the same room together." She peered across at me. "It's stronger now." Her lips curved. "Consummation can do that."

Ignatius glared at her. "Release me now."

"Only if you promise to behave."

Ignatius looked my way and nodded, then sagged as she released him. "Nyx is my mate. If you harm her, you harm me."

"And you left it till now to tell us?" Ramiel said. "Why?"

"I didn't wish to put her in any more danger. Being my mate might have put a target on her back from creatures who would see it as a power play on my part." He looked at me. "I didn't want that for her."

"Yet you did not complete your mating," Odette said. "Could not complete it because her powers are muted."

Ignatius's jaw clenched.

"There is no risk to the efreet duke," Odette said crisply.

"And no true claim, not when a mating hasn't been completed."

Ignatius glared at her. "You can't do this."

"There has to be another solution," Zepar said. "Mother?"

She shook her head. "I'm sorry, son. Your choice of custodia was...unfortunate."

The next few moments passed in a blur.

Shadows moved in my periphery—conji entering the room and surrounding me.

Mallini cursed and Tristeene sobbed.

"You're doing it now?" Artimus cried, incredulous. "Give her time. Please."

But his pleas were buried beneath the conji's chanting. The air grew heavier and pressed down on me. Someone rolled a table into the room covered in a dark velvet sheet.

Ramiel looked away as Levistus pulled something from beneath the cloth. A sword with a glowing blue blade.

My chest tightened and the urge to run coursed through my veins. I fought it, locking my knees and raising my chin as the fallen approached.

I wouldn't cower.

"This is a celestial blade repurposed to take a daimon soul." He held it up so I could see. "The pain will be fleeting, and your death will be like falling into a dream."

I wanted to scream in his face. To demand I get a chance to say goodbye to Sev and Chase. Demand that I get to hold them one last time, but all I'd be doing was giving them pain by prolonging the inevitable.

I grit my teeth. "Enough with the words. Get it over with."

Levistus gripped my shoulder and pressed the tip of the blade to my chest. I closed my eyes, and every person who meant something, every moment that mattered, flitted through my mind.

A tear slipped down my cheek. "Do it! Damn you."

A loud crack like lightning filled the room, followed by silence so complete that for a moment I thought I'd gone deaf, but then a smooth baritone, gruff around the edges, filled the void.

"It seems I arrived just in time."

My pulse stuttered. That voice. I knew that voice.

My eyes snapped open to Levistus lowering the blade, his face drained of color, his gaze on a spot across the room.

I tracked it to a broad-shouldered beast of a male dressed in black. His dark hair was loose around his shoulders and thick, powerful horns pushed out from his forehead.

Dark eyes swirling with starlight zeroed in on me and a smile curled his luscious lips. "You seem to have gotten yourself into quite a predicament, haven't you, Nyx?"

Oh, fuck. Oh, fucking hell. "Sin?"

His smile widened, showcasing wicked canines. "Call me Lucifer."

FORTY-EIGHT

I was used to seeing Sin half naked, torso bare and glistening from sweat. Used to gripping his horns while he claimed the price for whatever it was I'd come to him for. We had an unspoken connection that I'd taken for granted until he'd severed it.

The Sin I knew was bestial and gruff, and I'd seen a glimpse of his lethal side the last time I'd visited. The kiss he'd claimed was seared in my mind, as was the echo of the imprint of his hand on my throat.

He'd told to me to leave, to never come back, and now... Now, he was here. A beast in tailored clothing. Regal, powerful, but with an I-will-tear-your-head-off energy that had the room in stunned silence.

Yes, he was here, and he was called Lucifer.

"How is this possible?" Merihem asked. "How?" He stood slowly, staring at Sin with wide eyes. "It's you. Really you."

Sin didn't take his attention off me. "The fact that you could believe I was gone is frankly insulting."

"You led us to believe it," Ramiel snapped. "You expelled

your celestial light, and you were gone. What did you expect us to think? Where have you been all these years?" he demanded.

"Here and there. I had business to attend to."

What the hell? He ran a workshop. He was a blacksmith. I was so confused right now.

"Why did Nyx call you Sin?" Levistus asked.

"It's the name she knows me by." Sin gave him a flat look. "In fact, it's the name I would prefer you use for me now."

Odette sidled up to Ramiel and whispered something.

Ramiel's brow pinched and his mouth flattened. "Sin? Is that the name of the entity inside you?"

Sin transferred that flat gaze to Ramiel, then dropped it to Odette. "Come here. Take a closer look, Conji."

Odette shot Ramiel a panicked glance, but he nodded.

"Go."

She approached Sin cautiously, peering up at him curiously.

"Touch me." His voice was a delicious rumble, the kind of tone I wanted whispered in my ear.

But it seemed to frighten Odette. Her throat bobbed nervously as she tentatively placed a hand on his bicep. A soft gasp slipped from her lips, and her eyes rolled back in her head for several seconds.

She snatched her hand back quickly and stepped away from him. "It is you...but not you."

"What does that mean?" Ramiel asked.

Sin answered before Odette could. "It means that closing the pit may not have killed me, but survival came with a price. I was weakened after ejecting so much celestial light, but in the moment before the rift closed, I found Sin." He tipped his head to the side slightly. "Or he found me. He was...is a high daimon." His gaze was on me again. "A powerful one. We melded, and for a while there was only darkness. When we woke, we were one entity."

"Entwined," Odette said. "A being made of two souls forged into one. I have never felt anything like it."

The corner of Sin's mouth quirked. "I am unique."

"Why not come back sooner," Levistus demanded. "What was so important you had to stay away?"

"All in good time, brothers. I will explain it all to you soon." His gaze slid to the voting panel. Was that an indication that he didn't want to reveal stuff in front of the other lords and ladies?

Levistus must have taken it as such because he didn't press. "Yes. Later. But for now, we must deliver the judgment of the conclave."

Sin arched a brow. "Without my vote?"

"The conclave is over," Levistus said. "It was conducted when you were believed to be dead and therefore remains valid. You do *not* get a vote."

Sin sighed and shook his head. "In that case." He strode across the room toward us, and Levistus took several steps back because Sin was at least a head taller than him, bulky as fuck from all the anvil swinging, and inherently menacing even in his fancy clothes.

I caught a whiff of his aroma, earthy and fragrant, and the pulse between my thighs throbbed. How could my body want to fuck when I was about to be executed. There was something seriously wrong with my libido when around this male.

But Sin was bearing down on me, his body blocking me from the princes' view.

He leaned in, warm breath kissing my cheek, and dropped his voice to a low, intimate whisper. "You took me at my word, Nyx. You didn't come back." The stars in his eyes bloomed brighter, swirling like a cosmos inviting me to explore it.

"You said—"

He gripped my jaw and pinched gently, forcing my head up and bringing his lips close. "Do you *always* do what you're told?" His voice vibrated around me, through me, leaving delicious tingles in its wake, and in that moment, despite the fact we were surrounded by people, we were completely alone.

My breath came fast and shallow with the tumult of emotions and sensations coursing through me. "Not always. But I make an exception for you."

He smiled with his eyes. "Good girl."

My stomach flipped. Hard.

His gaze dropped to my mouth for a long beat and then his hand slipped away. "No one touches her," he said. "She belongs to me."

Silence followed his declaration.

Ramiel broke it. "This is a legal proceeding."

"Oh, I'm fully aware," Sin said. "And this female is *legally* mine."

He gripped the front of my tunic and tore it, exposing my chest. Thank the earth I was wearing a bra. "What the fuck, Sin?"

"Hush," he crooned, then held his hand up a foot from my chest.

Heat pricked my skin. "What are you..." I looked down. There was a silver whorl glowing on my chest.

The whorl gleamed between my breasts, the spot above my heart. The memory of our last moment together filled my mind. The moment he'd thought I was trespassing.

"You'll pay with something you prize dearly...You'll pay with your heart...I don't need to tear it from your body to own it, Nyx.

And then he'd kissed me for the first time.

Just a kiss. But had it been more than that?

The room broke out into gasps and exclamations of shock.

"She belongs to me because I've claimed her as my electus," Sin boomed.

Ramiel fell back into his seat and the others looked just as shaken.

"What is that?" I tugged on Sin's sleeve. "What does that mean?" I needed to understand. To be sure.

He unbuttoned his shirt and slipped it off, revealing his epic torso. Muscle and sinew rippled beneath his skin with every move. He held it out to me to push my arms through, then buttoned it closed to cover my chest. Only then did he answer me.

"It means you're under my protection. It means you're my chosen mate."

FORTY-NINE

The next few moments were a blur of overlapping conversations, and the next thing I knew Umbrane and the voters were being ushered out of the room on one side while my siblings were being led out of the chamber on the other.

I looked up at Sin. "What's happening?"

He ran his calloused thumb across my bottom lip, leaving a tingle in its wake. "You're safe now." He slow-blinked, keeping his cosmic eyes on me. "Seneschal, take my electus to her quarters."

He was sending me away? "Wait. That's it?"

"You'll come to me later." It wasn't a request, and although a part of me wanted to snap that I didn't take orders from anyone, the other part, the part that wanted to bend to his will and comply with him, clamped down on my retort. The corner of his mouth lifted in an almost-smile and his eyes warmed. "Good. Now go."

Artimus ushered me through a side door, but not before I caught the raw look of devastation on Ignatius's face.

"Later," Artimus said. "You can speak to him later."

Artimus took my hand and hurried me down the corridor away from the Convectus Locum. I wasn't familiar with this part of the keep, so I let him take the lead.

We took a left down a flagstone corridor hung with tapestries and paintings, but we were moving too fast for me to get a good look at anything.

He ducked into a room, pulling me in with him.

The door closed and darkness pressed in. He let out a soft groan and wrapped me in his arms, squeezing tight.

"Fuck, fuck, fuck." His heart beat fast against me. "I thought I lost you. I thought it was over. Nyx...Oh, fuck..." He turned his face into the crook of my neck. "Thank the earth."

The reality of my close shave hit hard, and a shudder racked my frame. I'd had the tip of a blade pressed to my chest moments ago. Levistus would have stabbed me in the heart and taken my soul.

I would have died.

"It's okay." Artimus stroked my hair and kissed my neck. "I've got you. You're okay."

But I wasn't. I felt sick. The kind of sick that came after an adrenaline rush. The kind that squeezed your lungs and your windpipe and turned your stomach inside out. I gripped his shoulders and fought the urge to hyperventilate, using his honeysuckle scent to ground me.

Long minutes passed where we just held each other, and finally my tremors subsided and my senses switched on to other things. Like the hard, flat planes of his torso pressed to my softer parts and his warm breath skimming across my skin where his mouth brushed the spot beneath my ear. I slid my hands up into his hair, twining my fingers deep and clenching to force his head back. His stubbled cheek grazed my lips and our mouths met, soft and questing, each contact punctuated by a shared breath. I'm not sure how long we kissed, but it was long enough to leave my body lethargic and charged at the same time, to make me swollen and wanting, long enough to have me pressed to the wall, his hips pinned to mine, his arousal rolling against my desperate core. I kissed him, eager to learn the rasp of his tongue against mine, the smooth planes of his teeth, and the sharp graze of his fangs.

I didn't want this to end.

But he squeezed my nape and broke the kiss. His mouth was still close enough for me to claim if I wanted. And fuck, I wanted it. I wanted him. All of him. But now wasn't the time. No matter how much I wanted it to be.

I nudged his nose with mine. "What happens now?"

His voice was gravelly and thick with desire. "Now we take you to your quarters and wait for the princes' orders."

"Okay." I grazed his mouth with my lips, reveling in the tingle that the contact evoked. "Fuck, Arty, I want you."

"You can have me, Nyx. You can have all of me once we know...Once everything is settled." He kissed me one last time, then stepped back. "Come, we should go."

My siblings surrounded me in hugs as soon as I stepped into the quarters, and the final dregs of fear lingering in my mind fell away.

"I can't believe it," Mallini said. "Lucifer fucking Morningstar himself is back. It's insane."

"And he's claimed you," Gus said, his gaze dropping to my chest where the whorl was hidden by Sin's shirt.

I touched the spot absently. "It would seem so."

"And you know him?" Tristeene asked.

"It's a long story."

"We have time," Keelan said.

Nugen, our satyr training master, bustled into the quarters, eyes wide, his short, stocky frame practically vibrating. "Is it true? Is the Morningstar back?"

"It is," Artimus said. "He's back and he's claimed Nyx as his electus."

Nugen sucked in a sharp breath and stared at me for several seconds before nodding curtly. "Good. His protection will keep you safe."

I still didn't understand how Sin could be Lucifer or why he'd chosen me as his electus, but those were questions I'd have to ask him. "Where are Sev and Chase?"

"I'll get them and Dhuma," Artimus said. "You need to stay here."

"What about Ignatius? I need to see him."

"I'll find him." He hurried off.

"Well?" Mallini grabbed my hand. "Come on, spill it. When did you meet Lucifer?"

It was strange to hear him called that. "Sin. His name is Sin."

FIFTY

SIN

The efreet's ire hits me in waves of passionate indignation from across the room. He's wise enough not to voice it.

I should have considered the possibility of another male in her life. Possibly more.

But it doesn't matter who she allows into her bed.

She belongs to me.

I focus my attention on the efreet duke. "You were willing to fight for her. To turn your people against the fallen to protect her."

They aren't questions but he answers anyway.

"Yes." He raises his chin and fixes his fiery gaze on me. "I still am."

I can't help but smile at that. I like him. "Good. You are already her sponsor, but you will now also be her secundarium."

The embers in his eyes flicker and flare. "As you wish, Your Grace."

He recognizes the power in that title. The trust I'm putting in him by naming him as her protector in my absence.

I contemplate ordering him not to fuck her. Not to complete their mating, but it doesn't affect me if they do. It may even work in our favor.

"Go now. Make sure my electus is taken care of. Tell her I'll be with her soon."

"Your Grace." A female approaches me. An Erinyes. "I am Erinea, the head council for Morningstar. If I can be of any service, then—"

"You can leave. Now. I wish to speak to my brothers. Alone."

She ducks her head and hurries from the room, but the conji stays. I arch a brow and stare her down until she too ducks her head and leaves.

"You have a lot of explaining to do, Lucifer," Ramiel says coolly.

"Sin is my name now. Lucifer died at the pit."

"But it *is* still you," Merihem says, raking me over warily. "You, but with...horns..."

"What have you set in motion, brother?" Ramiel, the ever perceptive one, asks.

Beelzebub was my friend, but Ramiel was my comrade in arms. We have a history, a closeness, and hiding my purpose from him all this time has not been easy.

What I plan to tell them now cannot go further than the four of us. Lives depend on it. "How safe is this room? Can we speak here freely?"

"Not here," Levistus says. "We go to the atrium."

"Then lead the way, brother. Lead the way."

FIFTY-ONE

NYX

We were all gathered in Mallini's room, and I'd barely finished filling my siblings in on Sin and our backstory when Zinichi burst in.

"Duke Ignatius wishes to see you," she said.

My pulse kicked. "He's here?"

"Go!" Tristeene urged with a smile.

I climbed off the bed and headed out into the hallway with Zinichi. "Where is he?"

"He went into your chambers."

I hurried down the corridor and into my room to find him sitting on the end of my bed. He shot to his feet, crossed the room, and swept me into his arms in a crushing hug similar to the one Artimus had given me.

I wrapped my arms around his neck and hugged him back, boots dangling a couple of feet off the floor.

"I should have told you." He spoke into my hair. "I should have solidified our bond."

"There's still time." I pulled back to look at his face. "I

want to be bound to you, Ignatius. I've felt our connection from the start, I just didn't understand it."

Flames swayed in his pupils. "Once the trials are over, we will consummate this bond properly in the Court of Flame before the Ibris flame."

I offered him my mouth and he pressed his to it softly, once then twice. The third time was harder, deeper, and our lips parted, sliding against each other in carnal delight. I swallowed his groan—an aching sound of need—and licked at his mouth, sucking on his tongue and drawing another moan. Oh, to make him unravel. To have him beneath me, mine to take from, mine to drive insane with desire. I could have him now. Right here.

He must have sensed my thoughts because he gripped my ass and lifted me so I could wrap my legs around his waist. One hand went to my nape, the other pressed to my ass as he rolled his hips against my greedy core.

It was my turn to moan now, to pant against his mouth as he thrust against me through inconvenient layers of fabric. The hard length of him...The friction... Oh...Oh, earth...

"I want to be inside you," he growled.

"Yes...Yes, please."

A sharp rap on the door tugged me out of my soupy haze of desire. "Shit..."

Ignatius looked over my shoulder at the closed door.

"Nyx?" Sev called through the door.

He was back *and* he was knocking, which meant he knew what was going on in this room. Our room.

His domain.

Shit.

I climbed off Ignatius and exhaled to calm my pulse. "Come in."

I was expecting him to be pissed with me for getting

freaky with Ignatius in our space, but all I caught on his face was relief. A moment later I was enveloped in the fourth epic hug of the evening.

I breathed in his leather and cinnamon aroma and squeezed him tight before crouching to give Chase some love.

"Have you spoken to Loke?" Ignatius asked Sev.

"No, Artimus is going to see him now." He took my hand and laced his fingers through mine. His way of marking his claim on me in our space.

Ignatius's gaze flicked to our joined hands. "Lucifer coming back changes the whole dynamic."

"Do we know *why* he's back now?" Sev asked.

"No idea," Ignatius said. "But we need to find out."

They continued to plan as if I wasn't even there. I looked down at Chase and he cocked his head as if to say, *yeah, this is a thing now.*

"When did this happen?" I wagged a finger between them. "You two..."

They broke off their conversation and turned to me.

"How else were we going to keep you safe?" Ignatius asked. "We work together to protect what we hold dear."

"Exactly," Sev agreed.

A rush of warmth filled my chest. Gratitude. Love. All the mushy things I'd kept at bay for the longest time.

I exhaled and shook my head. "I think everyone is determined to make me cry today."

There was another knock on the door. Sev opened it.

Dhuma blocked the doorway. He zeroed in on me and nodded once. "Good. You're alive."

I grinned at him. "And what would you have done if I wasn't?"

His brows came down in a frown. "I've lived a long and lonely existence. But something inside me whispered that my life would mean something. That I'd been sentenced to live while my mate and my brothers were slaughtered for a reason. Finding you *is* that reason. If they'd taken you from me, then I would have wreaked vengeance and gone out of this world in a blaze of glory."

Well, I hadn't expected that. I took his hand and peered up into his hard-as-granite face. This male had fought hard and loved harder, but he was ready to die for me simply because I carried the same blood as his late lover. I couldn't let him do that.

"No, Dhuma. No blaze of glory. This world needs males like you. And whether I live or not, Soreena will go on, as long as you draw breath. She would have wanted you to live and maybe even love again once more."

His frown deepened, then melted. "I appreciate your words. You are truly a Knightwood. You do the bloodline proud."

Gus appeared between Dhuma's legs. "There's a message from the council. The final trial takes place tomorrow."

"What?" Ignatius and Sev exchanged glances.

"Final trial? Aren't there meant to be two?" Dhuma asked.

"It says final," Gus said. "We're to meet at the gates at dawn."

"Nyx? Hello?" Zinichi called from somewhere behind Dhuma.

The high daimon grunted and stepped out of the way to allow Zinichi to enter the room. Gus yelped, darting to avoid getting squished.

"Nyx, Prince Lucifer has summoned you," Zinichi said. "There's a zuni waiting to escort you at the doors."

Ah, the summons was here. "I'll get some answers. I'll be back soon."

ARTIMUS

Loke is gone.

The wardrobe is empty and so are the drawers.

He warned me this might happen if he helped. If he interfered in Nyx's fate in any way.

I close the door to his chambers behind me with a heavy heart.

It's up to us to keep her safe now.

I hope it'll be enough.

FIFTY-TWO

The zuni urged me over the threshold of a fancy room, then left quickly. This room was huge, the size of a penthouse suite, all marble and clean lines with a balcony peeking through whispering drapes. The room was set up as a lounge and a study, and the feature piece was a huge polished wooden desk with an impressive high-backed seat pushed under it.

Where was Sin?

He stepped into the room a moment later dressed in a robe belted loosely, leaving a vast expanse of his chest bare. His hair was pulled back now, making his horns more prominent.

"What the fuck is going on, Sin? Why did you lie to me?"

"Lie?" He arched a dark brow. "I don't recall any lies."

Word games. "Fine, you kept shit from me, like the fact that you're Lucifer? What game are you playing?"

His expression hardened and a warning zing shot through me, a reminder as to what and whom I was dealing with. I kept my back straight and my chin up, though, because despite everything I knew now, this was still Sin.

My Sin. And I knew he would never hurt me. In fact, his electus move had saved my life. I was pissed, yes, but more because he'd kept shit from me.

"I don't owe you any explanations, Nyx. Be grateful you still have your life."

It was all I was going to get from him on this matter but maybe he'd be more forthcoming about other things. "Is it true?" I ignored the catch in my throat. "Have the princes decided to drop one of the trials and only do one more?"

"Yes, *we* have," he said pointedly.

"Of course. You're one of them." I couldn't keep the derision from my tone.

"I'm me, Nyx. Sin. The same Sin you've always known. The only difference is that I'm also a fallen."

"Why did you choose me as your electus? Why didn't you come back sooner. I don't understand any of this."

"You don't need to. All you need to know is that you're under my protection. You belong to me."

"But—"

"No." His tone was a slap.

Anyone else and I'd have fought back, but Sin didn't capitulate. He didn't give unless he wanted to. I knew him well enough to understand that a no from Sin meant no. Period.

He was frustrating as hell but that was part of his charm. "Fine. But if I belong to you, then you belong to me too." Why the fuck had I said that? To make me feel I had some control? Probably. And I was sticking to it.

I lifted my chin and glared at him defiantly.

He arched a brow. "Oh? And what would you do with me *if* I were yours."

I hadn't thought that far, but my attention dropped to his chest, to the gorgeous expanse of skin peeking out from the

V of his robe. Need clamped down on my lungs, making it a little harder to breathe.

We'd fucked before. Been intimate in many ways, but I'd never seen him naked. Never seen the whole of the glorious picture.

This was my chance. "Take the robe off. I want to see all of you."

He slow-blinked, then shucked off his robe.

I forgot how to breathe.

I was familiar with the broad width of his muscle-rounded shoulders, the smooth expanse of chest, and tight abs honed from years of swinging a blacksmith's hammer. Familiar with his solid waist and the V that pointed to the base of his thick, veiny cock. But the rest...the full picture... My mouth went dry, and I licked my lips, dropping my gaze to thighs that could probably crush me.

I needed to see his ass.

He didn't stop me when I walked around him to take in the view. It was an ass to be proud of, one you could probably bounce small rocks off.

Earth and stars, he was beautiful. Every inch built for power. A body perfect for riding. I wanted to taste, nip, and bite. I wanted to straddle his hips and slide onto his cock.

I reached out to touch him, but he gripped my wrist.

"No."

"Why not?" I didn't bother to hide the frustration in my voice. "I want you. You want me. Let's fuck."

His smile was a slow-burn, wicked thing. "You know the rules, Nyx. We play this my way. Always."

What the heck? "We're not trading right now."

He arched a dark brow. "Aren't we?" He leaned in so his lips were inches from mine, his body so close that one step and I'd be rubbing up against him, but I knew better than to disobey Sin.

Disobedience led to frustration and lack of orgasms.

"I saved your life," he whispered. "That debt will take a while to pay."

"Okay, what do I have to do?"

"Do you recall when you walked in on the demon sucking my cock?"

The memory surfaced now, sharp and in detail. "She did a poor job."

He smirked. "Yes, you wanted to take her place."

"How could you know that?"

"I could see it in your eyes."

My pulse quickened. "Yes. I wanted that. I wanted you in my mouth."

He walked over to the bed, picked up a pillow, then dropped it on the floor in front of him. "I want to see your lips wrapped around me now." He curled his fingers around my throat. "Will you get on your knees for me?"

I nodded, reveling in the feel of his fingers against my skin, in this dynamic that had my heart racing so hard that the edges of my vision blurred.

His hand dropped so it bridged my collarbones and lingered there for a moment before falling away.

I dropped to my knees, cushioned by the pillow, and pushed up so I was almost level with his cock.

He was too big, and I'd probably choke on him, but fuck I'd been wanting to do this for too long. Risk assessment complete, I gripped him at the base. His chest rumbled in approval, and my pulse jumped then beat faster.

"Take it slow, Nyx," he said gruffly. "I want to see how deep you can take me."

I licked my lips, then laved him from base to tip. His cock jerked and his abs contracted. Yes, Sin. It's my turn to own you. I licked him again, then licked the slit at the head of his cock. Salty and sweet at the same time.

I raised my gaze to his. "Delicious."

He watched me, jaw tight, chest heaving. I swirled my tongue around him, then took him deep into my mouth before pulling out with a pop to lap and swirl at the sturdy head until he was harder than rock, his abs rigid as he panted.

He fisted my hair. "Take it, Nyx. Take it now."

I locked gazes with him and relaxed my throat, taking him deeper. He groaned, a feral, growly sound. "Beautiful, Nyx. So fucking beautiful."

My pussy contracted, seeping with need. His grip on my hair tightened. I grabbed hold of his hips, closed my eyes, and gave myself to him as he chased pleasure. He stopped before he could come, hauled me to my feet, and crashed his mouth down on mine.

The kiss was a demand for submission, and my knees buckled. He snagged me around the waist and crushed me to him, his body a cage as he bent me back to devour my mouth. Fangs scraped my lips, coppery blood licked at my tongue. He sucked at it, owning me completely.

I was his, completely and utterly in his control. Whimpering, moaning, and gasping into his mouth as he took what he wanted.

He broke the kiss suddenly and released me abruptly to turn away. His shoulders rose and fell with deep breaths.

I stood swaying on my feet, head fuzzy with desire, body buzzing with sensations. "Sin?"

"Take off your clothes."

My hands trembled as I undressed down to my panties, which clung to me with arousal. I peeled them off and stepped out of them.

Sin finally turned to face me. "I'm going to fuck you now, Nyx. Do you want that?"

"Yes." I clenched my hands into fists to keep from

touching myself. My breasts were heavy, nipples pebbled. I wanted to squeeze and pinch.

"Only I get to touch you," he said. "You touch, and the deal is off."

Oh, earth... "Can I touch you?"

"No."

Fuck, I both hated and loved this game. "Okay. Deal."

"Turn around and brace yourself on the desk behind you."

I swallowed the lump in my throat and obliged, placing my palms on the cool wooden surface of the desk.

"Bend over, Nyx."

I did so, heart thundering against my ribs as my breasts made contact with wood. I knew what was coming and I wanted it. Bad.

I sucked in a breath when his hands cupped my hips. Like this, bent over with him looming up behind me, I was hyperaware of how much bigger than me he was. He could break me, and right now, I'd let him.

He kicked my legs wide and cupped my pussy. I throbbed against his palm, aching for him to slide a thick finger into my heat and stroke my clit.

But he didn't; he squeezed gently and released me. "Tell me what you want, Nyx." He stroked his huge palm down my spine, then cupped my ass cheek. "One thing you want from me in this moment."

I wanted him to touch me, stroke and flick my clit, suck on it and eat me out, then fuck me. But he'd said *one* thing.

And if I could only have *one* thing, then, "I want your cock. I need it. Please. Give it to me."

He chuckled deep and raw, then pressed the head of his cock to my entrance. The contact pushed a moan from my lips and my pussy walls contracted, reaching for him. I couldn't breathe with how much I wanted him inside me.

My eyes rolled back as he entered me, and my breath grew shallow and fast as I adjusted to him. A challenge, even though I was soaking wet.

"Relax..." He stroked me again. "You've done this before, remember. Your body knows me." He cupped the back of my neck and massaged, diving deeper until he was in as far as he could go. A sob clawed at my chest because to be this fucking full felt so good. Tingles radiated across my pussy lips and down my thighs as I fought the need to push back and roll my hips against him.

I couldn't lose this game. Couldn't risk him taking this from me. I needed it.

He leaned over me so that his chest brushed my back. His hot breath kissed the delicate shell of my ear, and his earthy aroma enveloped me.

"Will you scream for me?"

Anything. I'd do anything. "Yes." I forced the word past the tightness in my throat. "Please, Sin. Just fuck me."

He dragged his cock all the way out of me, and my chest heaved with a sob at the emptiness. "Damn you."

He drove into me, jolting me across the desk so the lip dug into my hips. The pain was overshadowed by pleasure and a flush rushed up my body to hug my neck, eliciting a strangled sound from me.

He rolled his hips against me as I bit back another sob. My chest was about to crack with the build-up of emotions that made no sense.

"That's not much of a scream," he said. But he sounded breathless too, his tone thicker now.

Yes, I was affecting him just as much as he was affecting me. "More."

He slid one hand down my side and pressed the other to my nape to hold me down. "Only because you've been a very good girl."

He pulled out and slammed into me again and again. My mind shut down, body taking over, sobs and screams of gratification tearing from my throat as he fucked me.

Heat rode up my body in waves, higher and higher. My pussy clamped on his cock, muscles contracting in sharp, starry waves. Oh...Oh, yes. Fuck yes. My vision blurred and blacked out, blood rushing to my head and pounding in a rhythmic pulse.

I came. Hard.

His guttural groan joined mine and heat filled me. His heat. His seed. Mine.

All mine.

FIFTY-THREE

The after-sex glow didn't last for long. Sin pulled on his robe and handed me my clothes. "You can use the bathroom."

I shouldn't have been surprised. This was Sin. We had mind-blowing sex, but we didn't do snuggles.

Still, for some reason, this time it felt...cold. "Seriously?"

He stared at me for several beats. "What is it you expected, Nyx?"

Annoyance sharpened my tone. "I don't know. You make this fuss about me being yours and then you act like sex is a transaction. I thought..." Urgh. What had I thought?

"What did you think?" His eyes narrowed.

"Fuck you. You're an asshole." I grabbed my clothes and headed for the washroom.

"I'm the asshole keeping you alive, Nyx, and don't you forget it."

I slammed the bathroom door harder than necessary, then stood with my back to it. My chest felt tight and achy in that fucked-up way that preceded tears.

I pushed away from the door and glared at myself in the

ornate bathroom mirror. My skin was flushed from the sex, eyes bright with indignation and wet with the threat of tears.

Fuck this.

I blinked them away, biting down on my bottom lip to stop it from trembling. What the heck was wrong with me? I never cried over a male. Sex was sex and...Fuck it. This was Sin, and that bastard had a piece of me I could never get back. But I'd be damned if I showed it, damned if I let him see how much his attitude had hurt me.

I washed and dressed quickly, wanting to get away from this room, from him, from the stupid feelings crowding my mind and body.

My own fault for seeing shit that wasn't there. This was Sin. He dealt in transactions, and interactions were on his terms only. I needed to remember that.

By the time I stepped back into the room, I had my game-face back on.

Sin sat at the desk, writing something on a piece of paper. He looked up as I approached and turned the sheet of paper over so I couldn't read whatever he'd written.

"You can leave now, Nyx. No one will dare harm you."

I tapped the cuff on my wrist. "I can take care of myself if you take these off."

"No."

"Why not?"

"It's been agreed that the cuffs will remain."

"And what if I win the seat?"

"They'll remain but be altered to suppress only your high daimon powers. You'll have access to the seat's power."

I opened my mouth to argue but his expression grew stony, reminding me how dangerous he could be.

"Is that all?" he asked.

"No. Umbrane's managed to secure a betrothal to Veena, one of the spawn. I need you to make him break it."

He arched a brow. "Do I look like your fucking secretary, Nyx?"

I bit back a curse. "No, but this arrangement needs to come with benefits *outside* of an epic shag."

"Or what?"

He sat back in his seat and looked up at me with what I suspected was amusement, and that pissed me off even more.

I placed my hands on the desk and leaned in, narrowing my eyes. "Or you can kiss my pussy goodbye."

His eyes flinched.

Ha. I had him. As much as he maintained the detached, in-control demeanor, there was no hiding the fact that he wanted me just as much as I wanted him.

"Have it your way," he said coolly.

"What? You'll do it? You'll speak to Umbrane?"

"No." He picked his quill back up and dipped it in ink. "Your siblings are not my problem, and I'm sure your pussy will be missing my cock soon enough."

That fucking... "Dream on, Sin. Dream on."

"You better get some rest. You'll need it for the final trial." He looked up, his expression somber, and all the indignation drained out of me. "You all will."

"WHAT DO YOU THINK WILL HAPPEN?" Tristeene asked. "The trial? What do you think it will be?"

"I don't know." I watched the flickering flames dancing in the hearth.

Keelan had built the fire and my siblings had dragged in bedding from their rooms for a sleepover in mine. We hadn't discussed or planned it. But here we were, as if by unspoken agreement. Crammed together.

I sat with my back propped up against the side of the huge bed, legs out in front of me, with Keelan and Tristeene either side of me and Gus and Mallini lying across the floor by our feet. The floor was one huge mattress made of bedding and blankets. A nest for us to snuggle in.

Sev snored softly on the bed. He'd tried valiantly to stay awake, but after a whole night and day of no sleep he was wiped. Chase too.

Ignatius was gone—called to court business. He'd left a message with Sev telling me it had to do with the breach in the Court of Flame.

I knew he wouldn't have left for anything less, and staying here with me wouldn't serve any purpose tonight.

I needed to be with my siblings. Preparing mentally for whatever the princes planned to throw at us in the morning.

"One more trial, then it's over," Mallini said. "One more trial and one of us will have the power to root out the corrupt and fix this place."

"*If* we make it out alive," Gus said softly.

"They can't execute us," Mallini said. "Those contracts were destroyed."

"I know," Gus said. "But that doesn't mean the trial can't kill us."

Silence settled over us.

"Whatever happens tomorrow, we face it together," Keelan said.

I dropped my head to his shoulder. "As a team."

"As a team," they all echoed.

All except Veena. "Umbrane should have sent her back by now."

No one asked who I was referring to. It was obvious. We were all thinking about her.

"I hope she's all right," Gus said in a small voice.

"If anything happens to her, Satan will make Umbrane pay," Keelan said through gritted teeth. "Now, get some rest. We need to be in top fighting form tomorrow."

We settled down under the blankets, but it was a long time before sleep found me, and when it did, I was dragged into nightmares of swords that glowed blue and pits filled with fire.

VEENA

The room is dark and smells odd, like sweet things. Dead things. I don't like it here. I want to go home. But crying might draw attention and remind Umbrane that I'm here, in his manor.

When did he put me in here?

Here...

The last time I was here...

No, don't think about that. Don't remember.

I squeeze my eyes shut and breathe through my nose. It usually helps calm me down. Long seconds pass and my pulse is almost normal when a rustling, scurrying sound sets my heartbeat racing.

What is that?

The sound of breathing.

There's someone...Some*thing* in the room with me.

"Hush, it's all right," a female voice says. "I won't hurt you." Her tone is soothing and my pulse slows.

It's so dark in this room that I can barely make out any shapes. But I sense movement and turn my head in time to see the shadows move.

I press myself to the wall behind me. "Who...who are you? What do you want?"

"I'm a friend. I sensed your fear, and I thought you might want company."

"You...you live here?"

"I suppose you could call it that."

She sounds...nice. "What's your name?"

"Oh my, it's been a long time since someone asked me that." She's silent for a long beat. Has she forgotten her name? "Lilliana," she says finally. "My name is Lilliana."

"I'm Veena."

"And why are you in this place, Veena?"

"Umbrane convinced my mother to give him my hand in mating. He's keeping me here until after..." I have no idea who this female is. Why am I telling her everything. "I don't want to talk about it."

"All right. Then how about a little trip?"

"Wha—"

The dark room melts away and I'm in the sunshine, standing in a field of long grass. I can hear laughter, and the smell of roasting pine nuts rides the wind. Music plays. The tops of colorful canopies are visible in the distance.

This is a safe place. "Where are we?"

"It's called a fair. Would you like to see?"

I look up at the female standing beside me. Her skin is a deep indigo hue, and her eyes and hair are silver. At first it looks like she's wearing a fitted body suit, but she isn't. It's her skin. She is indigo all over, and her skin looks tough.

She holds her hand out to me. "Shall we go and have some fun?"

Part of me knows this can't be true. It can't be happening, but it's better than being afraid. It's better than being alone.

I take her hand.

Fifty-Four

ORINA

Quinn sets two fresh mugs of cider on the table between us and drops into her seat. "You know, this is one of those things about my metabolism that can be both a blessing and a curse. On the one hand, getting drunk is a challenge, but on the other, I can enjoy the crisp, fruity flavor of this cider in abundance and not feel like shit the next day." She grins at me from beneath her freshly dyed pink bangs.

"The bangs suit you." I take a swig of my cider.

"Thanks." She frames her face with her hands and flutters her eyelashes. "I like it."

Her pink and blonde hair and sweet oval face give her the look of an anime character, sweet and naïve, but Quinn is neither of those things. Not any longer.

My childhood friend went through the wringer not so long ago, but she came out stronger for it.

If you look closely, you can see the darkness behind her smile.

I glance at my phone for the umpteenth time. "Micah will call as soon as he has news." I've convinced my mentor to reach out to the Order Mageri contact for me and find out what's going on in Morningstar.

"She'll be fine," Orina says. "I bet she kicks everyone's ass and makes it as Satan."

"Heck, I wouldn't be surprised."

Quinn sips at her cider and a frown mars her forehead. "Who would have thought Nyx was Satan's offspring. Like...he abandoned her in the mortal world. All the shit she went through. Shit she never told us..." Her gaze slips to me. "You know, when we were kids and we talked about our homes and family, you only ever talked about the Order. We asked about your family, and you shut us down."

For some reason her question feels like an intrusion. "The Order *is* my family."

"Yeah, but they weren't *always* your family."

Talking about my past makes my chest ache. The memories are painful and dark.

"It's okay." Quinn covers my hand with hers. "I'm sorry. I'm a nosy bitch."

"No...no, you have every right to ask. You and Nyx have never hidden anything from me...I just...My family is dead. They were killed. Micah saved me. He brought me into the Order. I've been there ever since." I can't help the smile that tugs at my lips. "He taught me to fight. Got me into the apprenticeship program with the Order, and now...Now the Order is my life."

"Is he hot?" Quinn asks.

"What?"

She shrugs. "It's just, your cheeks go red when you talk about him."

What the heck? "He's a mentor, like an older brother."

But the words feel like a lie because the fantasies I've had about Micah are far from brotherly.

"Uh-huh, you totally want to bang him."

"Shut up and drink your cider."

My phone rings and I snatch it up quick. "Micah, any news?"

"I'm sorry, not yet. I'm having some trouble getting hold of our council Mageri contact."

"You never did explain why we need to go through them anyway."

The Mageri make up the council who created the Accords and are the most powerful magic users in the city.

"Morningstar does not liaise directly with the Order," Micah says.

"What? Why?"

"It's not important. I just wanted to give you an update. I'll see you for training at six a.m. sharp."

"But—"

"No buts, Orina." He hangs up.

"He's such an ass sometimes."

"But does he have a cute ass?" Quinn wiggles her eyebrows.

I can't help but crack a smile. "I'm sorry I dragged you all the way here. I thought we'd have news sooner."

"It's fine. I can hang out, and who knows, the guys might decide to leave Hawthorne and venture into the big wide world after me if I'm gone too long."

The thought of any member of the Hawthorne Pack leaving their land for the concrete jungle of the Fringe seems ridiculous. "I can see it now, people running in fear."

She pouts. "Hey, my guys are total sweethearts."

If you call beasts that can tear your head off in one bite sweethearts.

"I'm staying for as long as it takes," she says, eyes flashing stubbornly. "And if those fuckers have hurt Nyx, then fuck the Accords. My pack and I will be paying Morningstar a visit."

I don't doubt that she means it.

FIFTY-FIVE

Nyx

We stood in the courtyard beneath a gray sky flanked by Minorax guards. No special outfits or weapons of any kind had been provided, so we dressed in versatile attire and took our own weapons.

We decided on lightweight, breathable clothes just in case the climate turned out to be warm, but added fur-lined cloaks in case it was colder. Anything in between and we'd be able to compensate.

I took my daggers and put on my sturdy boots.

Tristeene had tied her hair back and had a whip attached to her waist. Gus carried a short sword and some throwing stars, and Keelan had an axe strapped to his back. Malini had opted for her twin blades. I'd seen her in action with those; she and Charod had...

My throat tightened at the thought of the brother whose life had been cut short by these fucked-up trials.

We waited until the air crackled and tore in front of us to reveal a crimson world beyond.

"What the fuck?" Mallini said.

I looked at her in confusion. Why was she so shocked? "It's a portal."

"It's a rift," Gus said. "A direct tear to another place. Portals are networks that can transport you anyplace. They can be adjusted, but this is a direct tear. Only the most powerful conji can create them."

"Court of Flame conji?"

"Or Zepar's mom," Tristeene reminded us.

Ramiel stepped out of the portal followed by Sin, who had to duck to get through.

They were both dressed in black, silver belts at their waist and inky cloaks clipped to their shoulders. Ramiel's hair was tousled as if he'd been standing in a breeze, but Sin's was neatly pulled back, making his horns stand out and sharpening his features.

He didn't look at me.

Not once.

Wanker.

A gust of warm hair whooshed through the portal and hit me in the face, bringing the smell of sulfur with it.

A hot place, then?

Ramiel's gaze skimmed over us. "Where is the zuni?"

"Umbrane has her," Keelan said.

"He hasn't returned her." I aimed this at Sin, but he still didn't look at me.

"We can't go without her," Tristeene said. "You have to do some—"

"Ah, just in time." Umbrane clipped across the courtyard toward us with Veena in tow. "Somebody was being a sleepyhead." He peered down at Veena. "I didn't have the heart to disturb my betrothed's rest." He stroked a knuckle down her cheek, and she flinched. "Off you go then, love," Umbrane crooned. "Win the seat."

I caught the flash of disgust on Ramiel's face before he masked it. Good to know that he saw Umbrane for the smarmy bastard he was.

"You may leave now, Umbrane," Ramiel said.

Umbrane looked at the rift. "I'd be happy to assist."

"No," Sin said. "Go away."

Ha, take that, Umbrane.

Umbrane bowed, then turned on his heel and strode off.

Veena made a beeline for me and wrapped her arms around my waist. I stroked her hair until she stopped trembling.

"Are you okay? Are you hurt? Did he touch you?" I hoped she read the layers in my question.

"I'm all right." She gave me a brave smile. "I'm good."

"Then we shall begin," Ramiel said. "Follow me." He stepped back through the rift and Sin moved aside, ushering us to follow Ramiel.

I couldn't help but look up at him as I passed, and this time he looked back. Our gazes tangled for a hot beat. Long enough for me to imagine conflict in his eyes.

The world beyond the rift was hot and the ground was rocky and barren. The sky churned red and orange above us, as if loaded with battling gases. I unclipped my fur cloak and slung it over my arm. Yep, it was damned hot here.

Six dark pods were lined up on a track to the left of us.

"I know this place," Gus whispered. "It's called Scarlett Canyon. There's a monoport not far from here on the other side of a..." He trailed off, and his face paled.

"What?" Mallini demanded.

"Listen carefully to the conditions of the trial," Ramiel said. "You will be transported to a monoport that leads to Dagan's realm Fertilis. The monoport has been closed for some time. But there is something hidden beyond it that you must retrieve today."

"A key," Sin said. "You will pass through the monoport gate and into the Fertilis and find this key."

"A key?" Mallini stared at him with her what-the-fuck face. "That's like looking for a needle in a haystack."

"Maybe for any other demon, but not for you," Ramiel said. "The key was hidden by Satan himself and enchanted in a way that only he would be able to retrieve it. But Satan is no more, and all that's left of him stands here before me. Your blood will lead you to the key. Whoever finds it and brings it back to us will win the Satan seat."

"The pods will take you to the port," Sin said. "May the best spawn win."

They strode back out through the rift, and it closed behind them, leaving us alone on the rocky terrain.

"That's it?" Mallini sounded disgusted. "Find the key and bring it back."

"We're working together, right?" Veena said.

"As a team," Keelan replied.

"And what about the seat?" Mallini asked. "They said the spawn who brings it back wins the seat."

"It doesn't matter right now," Tristeene said. "We can discuss that once we have the key."

Everyone agreed and we beelined for the pods. The doors slid open as we approached.

Each pod was large enough to carry one person, but Gus and Veena managed to squeeze into one.

The machine beeped in warning and a mechanical voice said, "One passenger only. One passenger only."

"It looks like it's one body to a pod," Tristeene said. "No matter the size of the body."

Keelan folded himself into the first one and the door closed. I helped Veena into the next one, and Gus took the third.

I left Mallini and Tristeene to get settled into theirs

before I climbed into the final pod. The door closed and the air cooled.

The windscreen lit up a soft green, a beep sounded, and we were off, zooming down the track toward the monoport.

A minute or two passed and the landscape remained bland and featureless, but then the track shifted and rose into the air like the beginning of a rollercoaster. Up and up we went into the red sky before leveling out.

Was the air shimmering?

I looked down to find bubbling red lava far below. Was this why Gus had gone pale?

We were crossing a canyon filled with lava, but the pods remained cool.

We were safe, but my pulse kicked up anyway.

The pods hurtled across the canyon in a line. How wide was this thing? The other side came into view. A minute later we dropped into a dive toward the other side. A scream lodged in my throat, dying as we leveled off onto the ground. We continued for several minutes before coming to a smooth halt.

The green light on the window went out, and the door opened with a soft beep. I climbed out on shaky legs to the sound of someone throwing up.

Keelan, shit. I rushed over and patted him on the back as he brought up his breakfast.

"Urgh." He wiped his mouth with the back of his hand. "I don't like heights."

"I feel sick." Tristeene hugged her stomach.

"That was fun," Veena said, bright-eyed.

"You're such a freak." Mallini nudged her good-naturedly.

Where was Gus? I tracked him walking away from us, toward a towering obsidian plinth.

The monoport?

I jogged to catch up with him and the others followed.

"It's huge," Gus said.

"That's what they all say," Keelan said.

I caught the smirk on his face. "Keelan, was that a dirty joke?"

He snorted. "Not a good one if you have to ask."

"How do we get in?" Veena asked, bringing us back to the task at hand.

"They never said," Tristeene replied.

"These were all locked down," Gus replied. "But if they expect us to get through, it means that maybe *this* one was attuned to Satan."

"Attuned to us?" Veena asked.

"That's right." Gus walked up to the base of the plinth and placed his hands on it. The air seemed to vibrate. He looked over his shoulder at us. "I think...I think it senses us. But I think it needs more."

Veena joined him and placed her palms on the plinth too. The vibration intensified.

"Okay, let's do this." I joined them, dragging my fur coat with me, and touched the plinth. Mallini, Keelan, and Tristeene followed suit. The vibration became a hum and the plinth lit up with symbols.

"It's working!" Gus called over the sound. "We're opening it!"

"Now what?" Keelan yelled back.

"Now we—"

Bright light swallowed the world.

FIFTY-SIX

Cold wetness bit into my palm and ice sliced into my lungs. A weight fell over my shoulders, warm and solid.

My fur cloak. "Thanks." I took Keelan's hand and allowed him to help me up.

"Where is the plinth?" Veena asked, panicked. "How do we get back?"

"We can worry about that later," Tristeene soothed. "We'll figure it out."

Veena exhaled and nodded, pulling her cloak tight around her. "Yes, of course."

"So this is Fertilis." Mallini stood hands on hips, cloak draped over her shoulders, hood pulled over her plumes. "Not exactly fertile, is it? Just snow. Not so different from Morningstar."

"Oh, but it is," Gus said. "I remember reading about the indigenous wildlife of this region. These bear-like creatures with six limbs and huge bodies that lived beneath the earth. What were they called? Oh, yes, burras. They'd track prey from below the surface using underground tunnels and snatch them down. Back in the day, when this realm was inhabited, their population was culled by hunters. Their body fat was used for fuel and their hides for fur, but this realm has been uninhabited for so long..."

"It could be filled with nasties." Okay. My breath plumed in front of my face. "So, we be careful. Watch each other's backs."

"But Satan came here," Veena pointed out. "So he must have had a way to navigate it safely."

We needed to find the route he took. A path, a tunnel, whatever, but there was nothing but flatlands and snow around us.

"Look. Over there," Keelan said. "I see a shadow on the horizon."

"Could be a forest, or buildings," Gus said. "But we can't be sure that's the right way."

"Ramiel said we would be able to find it because of our blood," Tristeene said. "So, shouldn't we feel some kind of pull?"

"All I feel is the cold," Mallini drawled.

"Unless..." I pulled my dagger from my boot. "Ramiel was being literal about the blood."

Everyone's attention went to me as I pricked my finger and allowed a drop of blood to fall into the bright white snow.

It sizzled before a pattern bloomed outward from the spot, growing to about five inches in diameter.

"We need more," Gus said. "Prick me." He held out his finger.

I bit back a snort at his use of the word prick.

Mallini rolled her eyes but smiled.

Gus's blood hit the ground next to mine and the pattern grew larger.

"Okay, everyone bleed," Mallini said.

Veena was the last to contribute, and with that final drop the pattern spread to thirty inches in diameter. The ground rumbled and stone plinths shot up out of the earth.

"Smart," Keelan said with a grin.

"And the plinths seem to be leading to the shadow," Veena pointed out.

"Then that's the way we go," Gus replied.

WE HADN'T GONE FAR before I noticed that each rock we passed had a red hand mark on it, and it wasn't much longer before the chill penetrated my cloak.

Veena and Gus were hit the hardest, and Keelan and I ended up carrying them beneath our cloaks. It kept them warm and us too.

The blur on the horizon became a treeline looming closer and closer until we were in its shadow and under canopy.

"No more rocks," Gus said.

"I see something." Mallini rushed ahead. "The tree is marked."

She was right. "Okay, so we look for the trail through the trees."

The wind howled, picking up and whistling eerily through the branches to tear at our cloaks.

We kept trudging.

"Storm's coming!" Keelan called out. "Need to find cover."

But there was no cover. Just the trees and the snow. Nowhere to hide.

The snow rose, swirling around us, and more began to fall until it was impossible to see much.

"Stop!" I grabbed at Mallini. "We need to stop. We'll lose the trail otherwise."

"We have to find cover, or we'll freeze," Mallini fired back.

I couldn't argue with that. The chill here was bone-biting and my lungs ached with each breath. Veena shivered beneath my cloak, holding me tighter.

I hugged her hard.

"I see something!" Tristeene's voice was a reedy wail above the elements.

I turned my body toward the sound, trusting my instincts to guide me.

Keelan put his arm around me to steady me against the elements, and Mallini pressed to my other side.

Tristeene was a dark figure forging ahead, obscured now and then by the blizzard.

"It's a cabin!" Mallini rushed ahead to help Tristeene shove open the door. But it didn't look like they were getting anywhere.

"Go." I pushed Keelan away. "I'm okay. Get that door open."

He jogged ahead, fighting the wind that battered his large frame.

I squinted against the deluge of snow and picked up my pace to get to the cabin just as Keelan shoved open the door with a shoulder slam. We piled into the gloom and Mallini slammed the door, shutting the storm out and plunging us into darkness. I gagged at the awful smell, covering my nose and scanning the gloom as my eyes adjusted.

The scrape of a match was followed by the flare of light.

Tristeene held up a lantern. "Benefits of being a succubus." She grinned and pushed back tendrils of wet hair from her face. "We have excellent night vision."

I lowered Veena to her feet but kept my hands on her shoulders—instinct warning me to keep her close.

Tristeene lit a second lantern, and the room finally came into full focus.

Veena's shoulders stiffened beneath my fingers, and she let out a shrill scream before slapping her hand over her mouth.

I bit back curses as I took in the shredded cushions and splintered furniture, but that wasn't the reason for Veena's scream.

The dismembered carcass hanging from the ceiling was.

FIFTY-SEVEN

SIN

The atrium smells sharply of incense. It's cloying and strong with an undertone that is decidedly...sulfur?

"What if you're wrong?" Ramiel says. "What if the key isn't there?"

I drag my attention from my thoughts. "I'm not wrong."

"What if they die?"

"They won't."

"You can't be so sure."

I'm sick of his doubts. "Do you trust me, or not?"

Ramiel's jaw ticks. "I trust you."

He should. I saved his life enough to have earned his loyalty.

"Well, I don't," Levistus says. "We can't be sure that anything you've told us is true."

He's never liked me much. I was cruel to him in my time as Lucifer, cutting him out of plans with the others and generally being a pompous ass. I can understand his resistance toward me now. But I'm no longer the person he knows, and he needs to understand that.

"I died, Levistus. I died and I paid for my mistakes. I'm here now, changed in a way you couldn't possibly imagine. I'm here to ensure the survival of this world you've created in my absence."

Levistus's expression softens somewhat. "I want to believe you."

"We can't afford to discredit him," Merihem points out. "So accept it."

"We *need* that key," Ramiel says. "And we need *her* to survive."

"Was sending her such a good idea?" Merihem asks.

"Not sending her would have raised too many questions," Levistus points out.

"Fertilis isn't dangerous," Ramiel says. "Satan traversed it without issue. They'll be fine. The key will be with us in no time and then we will place her on the seat in preparation."

My chest grows tight, but I ignore it and focus on the crystal orb in the center of the atrium table. It shows us an image of the monoport the spawn found their way through. We were right about their blood being a key.

The soft chanting of the five conji in the room grates on my senses. It's alien to the part of me that isn't Lucifer. The part that holds its own power. But I grit my teeth and bear it, focusing on the scene in the orb.

"How long do you think it will take them to find it?" Levistus says.

If Nyx has anything to do with it, it won't be long till they pick up the trail. This is her purpose. It was what she was born for.

I just need to ensure I have the strength of will to see my plan through.

FIFTY-EIGHT

V eena stood as far away from the carcass as possible, her eyes wide as saucers.

"It's one of them," Gus said. "A burras. Look, six arms...What's left of them."

"Something more monstrous than it killed it," Veena said.

"Not something...some*one*." I pointed at the beam where a rope was slung and knotted. "A knot takes manual dexterity that not many *somethings* have."

Keelan approached to study the wounds on the body. "Claw marks here, but this looks like a blade was used also."

"What *are* we dealing with," Tristeene asked.

"I...I don't know." Gus's tiny wings twitched in agitation. "But we should hope we don't come across it."

Something clanged and natural light flooded the room.

Mallini had found shutters and a window. The world outside was a blur of swirling white that howled and clawed at the glass.

"As soon as the blizzard clears, we go," she said. "If we stay on the trail, we'll be fine."

We all gravitated toward the window and stood watching the elements.

Waiting.

Were they thinking what I was thinking? Wondering what the fuck had killed the beast behind us and would we be next?

THE BLIZZARD DIED AS SUDDENLY as it had started, leaving the world covered in a fresh, thick layer of snow.

We left the cabin and trudged back into the cold, but it was soon evident that we'd lost the damn trail.

"We came from that way." Tristeene pointed. "I remember."

"No," Mallini said. "It was that way." She pointed in the opposite direction.

Keelan made a sound of exasperation. "If only my wings were ready to take flight." He looked disgusted with himself.

"Hey," Gus said. "You're much farther along than the other Minorax your age. You're doing great, brother."

Keelan snorted, but the harsh line of his mouth softened. "I suppose so."

"We can do this," Veena said. "Let's try each route just a little way and see if we can find the markings."

It was a solid plan. We set off on Tristeene's route first.

"We don't have to go far," Keelan said. "You saw the cabin from the trail, after all."

"That's right," Tristeene said. "I think..." Doubt edged her tone.

But what if we'd already fallen off the trail when she saw the cabin. The blizzard had hit us minutes before. Best to keep this thought to myself. I didn't want to cause panic.

Several minutes passed with no sign of the trail. "This isn't the way."

"I told you," Mallini sing-songed.

Tristeene's dark eyes flashed. "I was so sure. I'm sorry."

"Don't be." I placed a hand on her shoulder. "Let's get back to the cabin and we can take a different route."

We trudged back the way we'd come, at least I thought it was the way we'd come. "Um...guys...Where are our footprints?"

We came to a halt and stared at the blank snow around us. No footprints, not even the ones we'd just left behind us.

"What the actual fuck?" Mallini said.

"The forest is changing," Gus said. "It's shifting. It's alive."

"Please don't say shit like that," Mallini said. "It's creepy and totally unnecessary. Look, you've frightened Veena."

"I'm not frightened," Veena replied.

"Now what?" Tristeene asked.

For the first time in a long time, I had no fucking clue what to do. My mind was as blank as the mystical snow, but they were all looking at me expectantly, waiting for an answer. A plan. A solution. Waiting for me to lead.

An eerie howl saved me from having to tell them that I had nothing.

"What was that?" Veena pressed herself to Keelan.

He scooped her up as another howl, louder this time, drifted toward us.

Keelan turned in a circle, scanning the ground, trying to determine which way to run to get away, as the howls grew closer. The sound echoed all around us and...above us?

Wait, what was that hanging in between the trees, hidden by the canopy?

It looked like a rope bridge.

"Up there!" I pointed. "They're up there." I caught a flash of gray and white amidst the green. "Run!"

I grabbed Gus, swung him onto my shoulders, and broke into a sprint away from the gray things.

My siblings followed, snow crunching, breath puffing in the air as we ran. The howls multiplied behind us and drew closer, the sound becoming frenzied and rabid.

This was a hunt, and we were the prey.

The thought of standing my ground and fighting didn't even cross my mind. I wasn't suicidal.

"A mark!" Tristeene put on a burst of speed. "The trail."

"Where?" I swerved to follow her.

A rock face loomed with a ledge above and more trees hung over it. The mark was slapped onto gray stone where a boulder partially covered an opening.

"In here!" Tristeene ducked inside. "Yes, it's a passage. Come on!"

I lowered Gus in, and then helped Keelan and Veena down.

"Hurry," Mallini said. "Get in." She shoved me.

I scrambled into the passage, which was large enough to stand in. The stone was carved smooth, and a lantern was hooked to the wall, burning bright. It had to be magical. Another red mark was pressed to the wall, confirmation that this was the right way.

I turned, expecting to see Mallini behind me, but the entrance was empty. "Mallini!" I scrambled back and pushed my head out.

She stood with her back to the passage, daggers held loosely in her hands as the howls grew closer.

"Mallini! Come on!"

"I can't," she said. "If I do, they'll follow. They'll kill us all."

"What...What are you talking about?" My scalp pricked as realization dawned.

She looked over her shoulder at me with a smile. "I love you all, you know. So much. But I miss him. I miss him every single day, and it hurts. It's time for me to be with him."

She stepped out of view.

"Wait. Wait. No!" I tried to scramble back out but the boulder partly blocking the entrance rolled, cutting me off. "Mallini, don't do this, please." A sob choked off my words.

"I love you, Nyx. Now go kick ass."

The boulder blocked off the entrance, closing me in and cutting her off.

Bootfalls echoed behind me. "Nyx, what is it?" Keelan hauled me up. "I thought you were right behind us."

"Where's Mallini?" Veena asked in a small voice.

I raised my chin, looking up at them through a blur of tears. "She's gone. Mallini's gone."

My sob broke free and Keelan wrapped his arms around me. Veena began to cry softly, and I pulled her to my hip. Gus hugged my waist and Tristeene held me from behind. I'm not sure how long we stayed like that before Keelan's gruff tone broke through our soft sobs.

"She gave her life to save us. We need to make it worthwhile."

He was right. There would be time to grieve Mallini soon enough, time to celebrate her life too. For now, we needed to make sure that her sacrifice wasn't wasted.

I wiped angrily at my cheeks. "Let's get this fucking key and take control of Morningstar once and for all."

FIFTY-NINE

T his was the end of the line. This door at the end of the passage. The door marked with the red handprint.

There was no handle. No activation panel.

"How do we get in?" Veena asked.

It was obvious to me. "Blood." I made to slice my palm but Keelan gripped my wrist.

"Let me," he said. "Your abilities are muted, which means your hand will take long to heal. You won't be able to use it for a while."

But he would heal fast. I nodded. "Thank you."

Keelan cut his palm and smeared blood all over it before pressing it to the door to make a palm print.

"A red palm print..." Gus said softly.

"He left clues..." Tristeene added. "He knew that we might one day need them to find this place."

Keelan's blood seeped into the door, and it trundled open, admitting us into a small, empty cavern with a stone table in its center. A stone table housing a glass box that contained a dismembered hand.

Nothing shocked me any longer.

"Okay, this just gets weirder and weirder," Tristeene said.

We approached the table together.

"It looks fresh," Gus said.

"It looks alive." Veena shuddered.

"It's holding something," Keelan said.

He was right. "It must be holding the key." Keelan lifted the lid on the glass box and set it aside. He exhaled. "I'm going to touch it now."

He was a warrior, and I had no doubt he'd chopped off a limb or two in his time, but right now he looked downright queasy.

He tried to prise the fingers open. "They won't budge. They're stiff."

"Tug harder," Tristeene said.

"I don't want to...break it." Keelan's lip curled in disgust.

"Hey." I gently gripped his wrist. "Let me."

He backed away, and I reached for the hand. My fingers brushed its cool skin and a tingle passed between us.

"Whoa." I resisted the urge to pull away.

"What is it?" Veena asked.

"Nothing." I gripped the fingers, ready to peel them back, but they opened on their own to reveal a golden key with a gem set into the head. "Got it."

I drew it out of the box and the hand inside closed. Dark veins spread across the surface of its skin. It turned gray and desiccated until it was just a husk.

"Well, that was...ick," Tristeene said.

"We have the key." I held it up.

"Now we can all get out of here," Veena said. "Oh..." I looked down at her to see her eyes brimming. "Not all of us..." She sniffed.

I blinked against the heat behind my eyes. "We'd all be dead without Mallini." I clutched the key tight. "We owe it to her to get back and finish this." We could mourn once we were safe and then we'd put things right, just the way she would have wanted.

Gus was already doing a circuit of the room. He stopped and patted the wall. "This is a portal."

We joined him, and sure enough the wall had a palm-shaped groove etched into it.

"I'll do it," Tristeene said. She drew a small blade from the belt at her waist and sliced open her palm, smeared the blood around like Keelan had, then pressed it to the groove in the wall.

For a moment nothing happened, and my stomach sank. What if this wasn't the way out. What if the only way out was the way in? "Maybe we should—"

Bright light filled my vision.

MALLINI

Die, die, die.

The mantra is a steady beat in my head as I whirl and stab, drop and slice. The long-limbed gray creatures are humanoid and hungry, with wide mouths and black eyes and three-inch claws. A couple even have crude blades made from stone. They attack with vigor but no form or strategy, relying on their numbers to disable their prey.

Not this time.

I stayed behind knowing I'll die, but that doesn't mean I have to make it easy for these fuckers.

Charod and I always fought together, back to back, side by side, a well-oiled machine. Losing him took a part of me that's left me off balance, and as I dodge the swipe of claws and leap back to avoid a stab from a stone dagger, I'm aware of his absence. Of his presence at my back protecting me.

Fire lances through my side.

I whirl and slice the throat of the creature who stabbed me.

Silence.

Absolute silence.

I'm surrounded by red snow and gray bodies.

I've killed them all.

I press a hand to the wound at my side. It's deep. Lethal if not tended to by conji soon.

I won't be able to heal fast enough.

That's all right.

The others are safe. I stagger to the passage that I've covered with the boulder. Can I move it?

I press my palms to it, but it won't budge. Tipping it was easy, but now it's settled...

Instead, I climb up to the ledge and sit staring at the snow-capped view.

Not a bad way to go...bleeding out slowly until the cold turns to heat and the lights go out.

I'm coming, brother.

I'll be there soon enough.

"This is a little extreme, don't you think?" Charod says from beside me.

I stare at his familiar face. At the plumes rising from his forehead and spilling over his shoulders, and into his green eyes so like mine.

He smiles, flashing his dimples. "What's wrong? Imp got your tongue?"

I launch myself at him and hug him tight, not bothering to staunch my tears. "I missed you. I missed you so fucking much."

"I missed you too. More than you can know." He gently pushes me away so he can look at my face. "You look good."

I cup his cheek. "So do you." I glance across at the tops of the snow-capped trees. "I'm ready now. Let's go."

"Go?"

"To wherever the dead go."

He sighs and my stomach drops. "What? I am dead, right?"

He makes a seesaw with his hand.

"What does that mean?"

"It means there's still time." He strokes my cheek, his smile wistful. "Time for you to go back and make a difference."

Go back? Leave him again? "No…It's too hard." My voice chokes off and I have to swallow hard past the lump in my throat. "Too hard without you…"

His eyes darken with empathy. "I know. I know. I miss you too, so very much, and one day we will be whole again. Together again. But not today. Not now."

I grip his arms. "Why not?"

"Because our story isn't done. Not yet."

My breath catches. "Our story?"

He presses his palm to my chest. "I'm here. With you. A part of you. We are two halves of a soul and as long as you live, so do I."

My vision blurs hot. "Charod…"

He touches his forehead to mine. "Get back out there and live a meaningful life, for us, Mallini. For me." He pulls away.

"Wait. No. Charod."

"Now wake up, Mallini. Wake up and find a way!"

My eyes snap open on a gasp and gray skies glare back at me. I'm alive…in pain but alive, and Charod…He was with me. I saw him.

The hollow feeling in my chest is gone.

I sit up. I need to find a way home. Some other way into the passage. Then I see it. A spot heavy with vines where the rest of the ledge is bare.

I scramble over to it and clear it to reveal a passage. Too tight for one of those gray creatures, but I can fit. I know I can.

Hope burns away the pain.

I shove my body into the aperture.

Sixty

SIN

Time passes quickly when you've lived for eons, and it isn't long before there's movement around the monoport. A fissure opens on the other side of the pod tracks and lava bubbles out.

"What is that?" I sit forward. "What's happening?"

The lava sweeps forward and covers all the pods except the final one before it begins to cool and darken.

"What the fuck?" I stare at Ramiel.

He shrugs, helpless. "I...I don't know."

"This has never happened before," Levistus says.

I stare at the single pod. One pod that can carry only one person.

"We need to get to the monoport and—"

The monoport lights up bright and the spawn appear.

"There's one spawn missing," Merihem says.

"There's another fissure!" Ramiel points out. "Can you see it?"

I see it. I see the lava bubbling up out of it.

I'm on my feet in an instant and out of the room in the next.

I cannot save them all, but I do not need them all.

All I need is her.

Sixty-One

NYX

There was only one pod left.

We stared at it, and the cooled lava that had lost momentum before finding it. I shucked off my furs and dropped them. "Only one of us can leave."

"Is this what they planned?" Veena asked.

"I don't think that fissure was planned," Keelan said.

"What do we do?" Gus's wings fluttered manically. "What do we do?"

"If this isn't planned, then someone will be coming to help," Tristeene pointed out. "I doubt they're not watching us." She waved her arms. "Help!"

"No time," Keelan said grimly. "Lava incoming."

I followed his gaze to see a haze of red rushing toward us.

We were out of time.

I pulled the key from my pocket. "Mallini died so we could get this key and one of us could be Satan. We can't all die here." I held it out to my siblings. "One of you take it and go."

"Not me," Veena said. "Umbrane owns me. I...I can't be the one."

"Keelan?"

He raised his chin. "I won't run. I'm no coward."

"Tristeene?"

She smiled softly. "It has to be you, Nyx. You brought us together and you'll carry a piece of us with you on that seat. Go."

"No." I shook my head. "Gus, you're the smartest. If anyone can do it, you can." I shoved the key into his hand. "Go."

Heat flared behind us and Keelan let out a bellow. I turned my head to see the final pod swallowed by a fresh wave of lava we hadn't seen coming.

"It's over," Tristeene said.

The monoport flashed white and a figure stumbled out.

"Mallini!" Gus ran toward her and braced her as she doubled over.

She was hurt but alive.

"The monoport!" Veena said. "We can use it to go back."

Yes! We gathered around it and pressed our palms to it.

Come on, come on.

"It won't open," Gus said. "It's protecting itself."

The heat was so intense now that my eyes sizzled.

Keelan took my hand in his and squeezed. I looked up into his rugged face, seeing my thoughts reflected there.

The fight rushed out of me.

Gus took my other hand. "It won't hurt for long. Barely a split second."

Veena's lips trembled and she clasped Gus's hand, and Tristeene and Mallini joined us.

"This isn't right," Mallini said. "It can't be. We can't be..."

341

About to die? But the wave of lava was almost upon us, and a different kind of wave rose inside me—Indignant fury mingled with fear at these circumstances.

After everything...after all that we'd been through.

This wasn't fair.

To stand here and watch my family die...

I squeezed my eyes closed, blocked out the terror, and focused on my connection to my siblings. "Close your eyes. We're not here. We're at home, back in our quarters, together. Safe. Everything is okay." I needed to take us away from here in our minds. To make this easier. "We're not here." My wrists tingled and burned, and tears squeezed out from the corners of my eyes. "I love you guys. We're together. We'll *always* be together."

Heat singed my brow and stars erupted in my vision.

Sixty-Two

SIN

My wings beat at the hot air as I fly across the chasm of lava. My heart pounds too hard in my chest.

If I fail.

If I'm too late.

The other side of the canyon comes into view, and I dive and pick up speed.

The monoport is surrounded by lava. It rushes toward the spawn who are gathered in a circle, holding hands.

I zero in on Nyx.

She's the only one that matters to me.

I dive, intent on plucking her from their midst, but a flash of light explodes from between them, spreading outward and burning my eyes. A roar tears from my throat as I rear back on instinct, wings beating furiously to gain altitude and stay above the chaos.

The light dies.

No. This can't be...

The lava finally sweeps over the ground and surrounds the monoport, but the spawn who were standing in that very spot a moment ago have vanished.

Where are they?

Where the fuck are the spawn?

Nyx and her family's story continues in *Demon Reign*.

OTHER BOOKS BY DEBBIE CASSIDY

You can find a list of Debbie's books on her website
debbiecassidyauthor.com or on her Amazon Author Page.

There are so many worlds to choose from.

Happy Reading.

About the Author

Debbie Cassidy lives in England, Bedfordshire, with her three kids and very supportive husband. Coffee and chocolate biscuits are her writing fuels of choice, and she is still working on getting that perfect tower of solitude built in her back garden. Obsessed with building new worlds and reading about them, she spends her spare time daydreaming and conversing with the characters in her head – in a totally non-psychotic way of course. She writes Urban Fantasy Romance, Paranormal Reverse Harem Romance and Sci Fi Romance. Follow her on Amazon, Bookbub or Goodreads. Or checkout her website, debbiecassidyauthor.com. Alternatively pop onto Facebook and join her reader group - Debbie Cassidy's Fantasy Realms.